A Little Sugar,
A Lot of Love

A Little Sugar,
A Lot of Love

Linn B. Halton

Where heroes are like chocolate – irresistible!

Previously published as *Sweet Occasions* by the author.

Revised and published 2016 by Choc Lit Limited
Penrose House, Crawley Drive, Camberley, Surrey GU15 2AB, UK
www.choc-lit.com

A CIP catalogue record for this book is available
from the British Library

ISBN 978-1-78189-321-0

Printed and bound by Clays Ltd

To the man who keeps me writing
– my rock – Lawrence.

Acknowledgements

To my wonderful editor, a team-working star –
thank you so much! Mega thanks to the Tasting
Panel readers (Jennifer S, Heidi S, Lizzy D, Alma H,
Sammi S, Heather S, Caro P and Liz R) without whom
I wouldn't be a Choc Lit author and to the wonderful
Choc Lit Team, for making my dream come true!

Hugs to my lovely author-friend
Mandy Baggot for being a listening ear.

Last, but not least, a special acknowledgement for the
lovely reviewers who have supported me every step of
the way on my writing journey – feeling truly blessed!

Sometimes a turning point centres around
one single moment in time; sometimes it takes
two Christmases and three birthdays …

The First Christmas

Katie

The Storm Begins ...

I glance outside and see that the rain is still slanting across in front of the window, the wind driving it at a harsh forty-five degree angle. It's almost five o'clock, time to close up, and I groan inwardly. I'm going to get soaking wet walking to the car and that means frizzy hair by the time I arrive home.

I look up as the last person in the shop steps up to the counter and I have to stop myself from laughing out loud. Everyone else venturing out today has been wearing a thick coat, or waterproof, and has been juggling a soggy umbrella. The guy standing in front of me has no umbrella, no hat, and is wearing a totally inadequate lightweight jacket.

'How can I help you?' I ask, politely.

No response is forthcoming as the seconds slowly tick by. He appears to have lost the power of speech and I struggle to mask the grin that keeps creeping across my face. I watch as a rivulet of water dribbles down from his sodden hair and he raises his sleeve to wipe it away. As I lean forward to wipe random drips off the counter top, I can't stop my eyes from straying to the floor. He's standing in a rather large puddle that is snaking outwards as water continues to drip from his clothes. He observes me checking it out, but says nothing. The seconds continue to pass. I wait patiently, wondering why anyone would venture out on a day like this so totally unprepared to battle the elements.

He shifts from one foot to the other, and then runs his

hand through his hair in an attempt to sweep the wet tendrils off his forehead.

'S-s-sorry, I'm a l-l-l-little wet.'

Well, that's an understatement if ever I heard one. He's embarrassed and I swallow a chuckle, disguising it with a cough.

'Um ... I just need something ... small,' he continues, sounding hesitant.

He's looking directly at me as if that should mean something.

'Small?'

'Yes.'

I'm frowning, so I slide back into smiley-face mode and pick up one of our leaflets. I spread it out on the counter and he leans forward to look at the array of cakes. As he moves his head a few drops of rain flick up into the air, splatting across the front of my blouse and landing on the counter. He looks mortified.

'Um,' he mutters, weakly. He looks up at me, a blank expression on his face.

My eyes stray to the clock on the wall and then I realise he's watching me. This is beginning to feel distinctly uncomfortable.

'Were you looking for a cake you can take away today, or are you thinking of placing an order for a special event?'

As our eyes meet it's obvious that this poor guy is not only soaked to the skin, but his teeth are literally chattering. No wonder he's finding it hard to speak!

'Oh my goodness, you really are wet through, aren't you?' I feel guilty now and point to one of the chairs at our cake-tasting table. 'Take a seat. I'll make you a hot drink. Do you prefer tea, or coffee?'

He looks at me with grateful eyes. 'C-c-coffee would be nice.'

'Why don't you take off your coat and I'll go and find a towel so you can dry off a little.'

Without any further encouragement, he heads across the shop as I disappear into the cloakroom. When I return his coat is draped over a chair and he's standing there, shaking uncontrollably. By now his face looks a worrying shade of grey. I press a button on the coffee machine and then hand him the towel.

'I think you should take off that shirt, too. The radiator is hot, so it will dry quickly. Coffee won't be a moment. I'll go and see if I can find you something to wear.'

Searching around in the back room the only thing I can find is a sweatshirt, which happens to be pink, but at least it's over-sized and warm.

'Here you go. Sorry about the colour.' A part of me was quietly thinking that good-looking guys don't have to worry about what they wear. To be honest, he'd look good in anything. Aside from the haircut, which isn't doing him any favours at the moment, as the top is flopping down over his forehead in wet clumps, he has that effortless quality about him – the proverbial tall, dark, and handsome in a rather understated way. The sort of guy who makes no fuss over his appearance, yet still manages to look good without even knowing it. Even when he's soaking wet.

A trembling hand accepts the item without any sign of hesitation and I'm rewarded with a weak grin. He begins unbuttoning his shirt, very slowly. His frozen hands struggle with each button. It's all I can do to stop myself taking over, but he's not a child and, what's more, he's a total stranger. I'm sure I would have remembered if I'd served him before.

I notice with alarm that his body has a tinge of blue to it as he peels off the wet fabric, which clings to him like a second skin. Then I realise it's probably dye seeping from his shirt. I avert my gaze, but not before he reveals a very fit body. This guy doesn't have an ounce of spare fat anywhere and clearly takes good care of himself. I guess the cake isn't going to be for him, then.

He stands awkwardly, not sure what to do with the ball of fabric in his hands. I step forward to take it from him and wonder what on earth I'm doing. A fleeting moment of panic courses through me and I quickly pull myself together. Spreading his shirt out over the radiator next to the door, I notice that the high street is already deserted. There's no sign of any late shoppers today, as the rain continues to lash against the window. I flick the sign to closed and almost reluctantly turn the key in the lock. When I spin back around he's sitting huddled on the chair and it reassures me he's not a threat. The bright pink of the sweatshirt looks awful against the pallor of his skin.

'Here, drink this and you'll feel a lot better. I think you should put some sugar in there, boost the blood sugar levels ...'

He stares at the steaming mug I've put in front of him and it's obvious this guy isn't in a fit state to jump on anyone at the moment. In fact, I probably need to be more concerned about what I'm going to do if he suddenly keels over and drops to the floor. At least he's upright, albeit hunched over and now with both hands glued to the coffee mug.

'Oh, it's rather hot. I'd hate you to burn your hands.' Come on Katie, he's a grown man. What *are* you doing?

'I c-c-can't feel a th-th-thing,' he admits. Another fifteen seconds and he's feeling it – he almost drops the mug back down onto the table as the life comes back into his frozen fingertips.

'You're right.' He manages an oddly disjointed laugh. At least his voice sounds a little more even. 'It is hot.'

He takes a few sips of his coffee while I make myself a double espresso and then take the seat opposite him.

Looking across at me, I receive a rather sheepish grin from this stranger as he shakes his head. 'An umbrella or a hat might have been a good choice, given the rain,' he admits. He inclines his head towards the front of the shop, as the window flexes from the battering of howling wind and rain.

'Well, I think I can safely say that you are the only customer visiting today that didn't have one ... an umbrella, I mean.'

I find myself blushing as he relaxes a little and his eyes sweep over me. The caffeine is starting to kick in. He takes a deep breath and closes his eyes for a moment. When he begins talking again he sounds more in control and he's no longer shaking.

'You're very kind. That hit the spot, could I trouble you for another? I'll pay, of course, and I do need a cake. I'm afraid it's not going to be a huge sale though as I only need a very small one.'

Now he's talking normally he sounds like a regular guy. My moment of mistrust and panic is over.

'No problem. Are you hungry? Do you prefer sweet or savoury?'

'I'll eat anything; it's been a difficult day. Visibility was awful for most of the drive here and then I had a puncture. I had to change the tyre in the pouring rain. Then I realised I'd forgotten to bring the Christmas present, but it was too late to turn back. That's why I need the cake. It's for

7

my grandmother. I was driving by and saw your sign. Everything seems to have shut already and I thought maybe I could buy a Christmas cake. I bought her a silk scarf, but I'll have to post it now.'

He seems content to chatter away as I make his second coffee. I pop into the kitchen and search through the shopping I bought at lunchtime. We don't sell savoury products, but he looks in need of something filling. Pulling out a mushroom and red wine en croûte, I put it into the staff microwave and zap it for a couple of minutes. Placing the mug and plate in front of him, I walk over to the cupcake display to see what's left.

'Do you like chocolate?'

'Mmm.' He nods his head vigorously, his mouth full. He looks like he hasn't eaten in ages and it's gone in a few bites – he has no idea it was on my dinner menu for tomorrow. I put two chocolate cupcakes on another plate, realising that each one will be little more than a mouthful for him.

'Adam, my name's Adam.' He wipes away the crumbs from around his mouth and gratefully accepts the plate I offer him. 'Sorry, I haven't eaten since breakfast and the cold got to me. I'm not usually such a wimp but it's been the day from hell. I'm very grateful to you.'

He grins and I smile back at him. He has the most fascinating deep-brown eyes that draw you in, and a face that reminds you of your best friend's brother. A guy you quickly begin to feel comfortable around. As the colour returns to his face he's becoming more animated.

'My pleasure. I'm Katie. You're the first case of hypothermia I've had to deal with this winter,' I joke, feeling more relaxed and a little relieved.

'You must think I'm mad. Who would go out on a day like this with no umbrella and wearing a thin jacket? That's a car driver through and through for you. I'm used to dashing from car to door and that's about it.'

'You travel a lot?'

'Yes, I'm an IT consultant. A troubleshooter – I go where the problems are. No two days are the same.'

He finishes the last bite of the second cupcake and proceeds to stack the two plates neatly on top of each other. He gives his mouth one last wipe with the napkin and in one gulp, empties his coffee mug.

'You are a lifesaver. I feel almost human again now.' He flashes a smile that plays around the corners of his mouth. 'Umm ... that cake, as I was saying ... since Pop died Grace is always complaining that the world doesn't cater for people who live on their own. So I was thinking something small. I'll never hear the end of it if I turn up with a family-sized cake. My grandmother is a lovely lady, but she hates waste.'

'Well, I think I have just the thing.'

We walk over to one of the display cabinets and I show him an assortment of small and medium-sized cakes.

'Goodness, these look good. Hmm, I think the tiny one is too small – she's bound to make me eat at least one slice before I head for home tomorrow. Can I take that one? She'll love the decoration. Grace isn't a snowman and plastic robin sort of lady, so that looks perfect. Is the winter scene edible?'

I feel the colour creeping into my cheeks as he inspects the small boy on the toboggan and the miniature forest of trees gracing the top of the cake. I nod and it's clear he's impressed.

'Yes, the decorations are made by hand. Everything is baked on site, too.'

'You ice the cakes?' He looks at me as if he was under the impression I'm just the waitress.

'I do. I bake sometimes too, although I have a full-time baker who is amazing.'

'Oh.' Now he feels awkward. 'Look, I'm sorry to have taken up so much of your time and it's way past five on a Saturday evening. It's probably been a long day for you, too, so if you let me know what I owe you, I'll leave you in peace.'

Suddenly I feel a little flustered as I remember that he has to take off my sweatshirt and put his own shirt back on. I retrieve it from the radiator and it's creased, but relatively dry and warm. Holding it out to him, I immediately spin around and discreetly busy myself boxing up the Christmas cake while he dresses.

Glancing up for a moment, I catch him pulling the sweatshirt up over his head. I can't help noticing he has several tattoos on the side of his arm that I didn't catch before, they look like Chinese symbols. He's fit, I'll give him that. I look away feeling cross with myself and very lucky he didn't catch me looking at him.

'Do you have far to go?' I ask, unable to think of anything else to say to fill the silence. I tie the cake box with a dark green velvet ribbon and top it off with a pretty spray of winter berries, which helps me focus and at least prevents my eyes from wandering again.

'Cheriton Court Mews, it's probably about a ten minute drive, at most. What do I owe you?' He turns back to face me, then pulls his wallet out from the inside pocket of a still-damp jacket. He makes a face and I laugh. He looks bedraggled still, but warmer.

'Nine pounds and fifty pence, please.'

'You haven't charged for the refreshments. Well, it was almost a meal.' He roars with laughter and I join in. He deposits a twenty pound note on the counter and puts his hand up, indicating he doesn't want any change.

10

'Thank you. I hope your grandmother enjoys the cake.'

'She'll be delighted when I tell her that the lady who made that amazing snow scene also saved her beloved grandson from hypothermia.'

We exchange brief smiles and then he walks towards the door.

'You'd better lock up behind me,' he calls over his shoulder. 'There are some funny people about these days. Fortunately for me, you didn't think I was one of them.'

We both laugh a little awkwardly as he turns to look directly at me.

'I'll be back in June for her birthday, maybe cupcakes next time.'

'Great,' I return, sounding rather flustered.

He turns the key in the lock and holds the door ajar until I'm standing next to him, ready to lock up.

Turning to face me for one last, brief moment, he utters a sincere, 'Thank you, Katie,' before disappearing into the wet gloom of a winter's evening.

After I lock up and turn off the lights, I have a broad smile on my face and a warm feeling inside.

'Katie,' I say out loud, 'you have to be more careful in future. He could have been a murderer for all you knew.' A voice inside my head answers me, 'but he wasn't, was he?'

'You're late.' Steve is annoyed and after this morning's argument his patience is wearing thin. 'You know I have to leave by six-thirty at the latest. It's one night a month, Katie, is it too much to ask you to remember that? I seriously doubt you've had a busy day, given the weather.'

'Sorry. I'll make pasta, fifteen minutes and it will be on the table. I had a customer come in at the last minute and I was on my own. As it was pouring with rain ...' The excuse dies on my lips as I see that Steve's head is down and his fingers are flying around the keyboard of his laptop.

I slink into the kitchen, dropping my wet coat and bag in the hallway on the way through. Why does he always make me feel that I have to apologise? He works hard, I know that and he's probably had a bad day himself, by the sound of it. Whatever's gone wrong, I know I'll have to wait until he's ready to share it and a brief moment of anger flashes through me.

As I put on a pan of water and start chopping onions for the sauce I despair of the way he handles his work problems. Maybe the bank rejected the business plan he submitted last week for his latest client and he has to do a quick revision over the weekend. Who knows? Whatever it is, the way he's bashing those keys reflects his annoyance and it's probably the last thing he wanted to have to sort out today.

My mind reflects upon this morning's argument and, again, anger starts to well up. Arriving home late tonight has added fuel to the fire, but it's not as if I did it on purpose. Steve will see it as more ammunition to vindicate his mantra that it's 'all work and no pay, and that's no way to run a business'.

'I spend all day, every day advising small businesses and if you were my client, I'd say it was time to face the facts.' His voice filters through into the kitchen, the words hitting me like a sharp slap. He's probably right, but it's what I enjoy doing and as long as Sweet Occasions is making even a small profit, I'm satisfied. I don't think he realises that I'm not in business to become rich, it's the satisfaction of being my own boss and doing something I love.

He was such a different guy when we first met, carefree and easy-going. Sadly, life has a way of changing people and I know there's no point in dwelling on the past.

We eat in silence, guilt clouding my thoughts as Steve rushes his meal, one eye on the clock. I feel miserable knowing I put a stranger's needs before those of my partner.

'Sorry about tonight and thanks for putting up the new bookcase for me. It's perfect,' I say, trying to placate him and lighten the mood.

'I knew you'd be pleased. You'll fill it with your cookery books before you know it. You should have bought the next size up as I suggested.'

Looking across at it I have to agree he's right, as always, and I nod as he rises from the table. He walks around to my side and his lips brush my temple.

'I didn't mean to be tough on you,' he whispers, 'but you worry me sometimes. I meant what I said this morning. I earn enough to keep us both. You don't need to work and you certainly don't need to work such long hours just to cover the overheads of that shop.'

I look up at him, trying my best not to let him see how his words hurt. Whether it's the harsh appraisal of my 'dream', or the thought of being a kept woman, I'm not sure. What would I do at home all day? Sensing the emotions welling up inside me, Steve wraps his arms around my shoulders and gives me a gentle squeeze.

'Think about it, that's all I'm asking.' He straightens and disappears to finish getting ready.

I thought we had reached an understanding. Since we can't have children, the focus of our lives was going to be on our respective careers. Now, suddenly, Steve's only motivation seems to be money and proving he's successful with a bigger house, a newer car. And now, it seems, having a partner who doesn't have to work. Things that don't matter to me – I'm happy where we are. But asking me to give up on my dream is totally unexpected.

'Why?' had been my first reaction, when he threw it into the conversation this morning.

'Because it would make our lives easier and we could move out of town, maybe buy a property with a large garden. Instead of being rushed off your feet, you would only have one thing to focus on. No more juggling home and work. You wouldn't be as tired and you'd have a really happy guy coming home at the end of each day.'

The way he said it, so coolly as if this was something we'd been working towards, made me feel inadequate.

'Teamworking at its best, Katie. I bring in the money, you keep everything ticking over smoothly at home and you get some time for yourself. No more worrying about deliveries, or staff turning up. Promise me you'll think about it.'

If we'd ended the conversation at that point, the row wouldn't have developed. But when I'd tried to justify what I do and explain how important the shop was to me, it had made him angry.

'I'm working hard for us, Katie, and it seems whatever I do counts for nothing. I want to make our lives easier and yet you'd rather struggle and cause us both a lot of grief by hanging on to your ridiculous dream. You aren't a businesswoman and you never will be.'

I left the house at that point, slamming the door behind me without uttering a single word. If I was in debt, and unable to pay my bills, I could maybe understand why this meant so much to him. So what if I'm not making a big profit, life is about being happy in what you do, isn't it? As I drove to work in the pouring rain, the dark grey sky mirrored my mood. Suddenly I was beginning to feel trapped and the thought terrified me.

Adam
Home Is Where The Heart Is ...

'Grandma, you look lovely as ever. How have you been?'

Grandma Grace stands in front of me, a hint of relief passing over her face. She quickly replaces it with her trademark, playful smile. Her eyes twinkle and I can see she's delighted I'm home again, even though I moved out a long time ago.

'You charmer! I've been very worried, but I'm glad you are finally here and in one piece. What on earth happened? It's been three hours since you rang to say you had a puncture. I was on the verge of phoning the police.'

'Oh, Grandma, I'm all grown up now and I don't think the police would take kindly to a call asking them to find out why your grandson is late. I rang, not to worry you, but to let you know I would be delayed.'

She ushers me into the sitting room as if I need to be fussed over and treated with special care. I can't believe she still worries about me as if I'm six years old and can't look after myself.

'Confession time, I'm afraid.' I throw my jacket on the side of the chair and offer up the cake box with a grimace. 'I left your present at home, so I'm going to have to post it to you when I get back. However, I met this wonderful guardian angel on the way here. She dried my shirt, and thawed me out with coffee and some hot food. She also happens to make the most amazing cakes. This is for you.'

Grandma Grace peers at me with interest over the top of her glasses, taking the box from my hands and placing it on the side. She wraps her arms around as much of me as she can reach, being at least a foot shorter, and gives me a fierce hug.

'Thank you, my dear, but the only present I wanted was to see you standing here in one piece. It's such a long journey and the weather! That rain is relentless, so many places are flooded. To think of you at the side of the road worried me to death and I will admit to saying a few little prayers as one hour turned into two, then three …'

She raises her eyebrow sternly, but it's a brief moment before those twinkly blue eyes are full of love and laughter again.

'My boy is here and that's all that counts.'

'Grandma, I haven't been a boy for many years,' I retort, softly, as she releases me with a tender pat on my back. She might be in her twilight years but her spirit is strong and her mind as sharp as ever. We all thought she'd fade away when Pop died, but the truth is he's the one who would have faded if she had gone first.

'You will always be a boy to me. Now, tell me more about this guardian angel of yours.'

While the tea is brewing and the cake is sliced, I hang around the kitchen as I did when I was growing up. Grandma Grace was always easy to talk to; she seemed to understand even when the words wouldn't come. Her instincts filled in the gaps at times when even I couldn't make sense of what was going on inside my head. After my first failed relationship I began to despair of ever finding someone special.

'You can't hurry love,' she'd told me. 'It takes time to find your soulmate and in the process you change and grow. That's why young love often withers, as Pop would have said. Two people either change and grow together, or they grow apart. Love is about sustaining what comes after that first hormonal rush.'

'But that wasn't the case for the two of you,' I remember pointing out.

'There has to be an exception to every rule,' she'd replied, with a wicked smile. 'We were lucky. Fate was kind to us. But with hindsight, we were too young and naive to understand that until much later in life. Don't fret, Adam, there's a wonderful young woman out there for you when the time is right.'

Sadly, when I reached that point it too turned out to be yet another huge failure. This time the consequences had been more painful than I could ever have imagined. Kelly was everything I thought I wanted in a woman and, after adjusting to the shock of an unplanned pregnancy, she was a fantastic mother. With hindsight I can see now that parenthood came too early in our relationship, we hardly knew each other. Suddenly I was a family man and yet, surprisingly, the role seemed to come naturally to me. I loved Sunday mornings the best. When a little head would appear on the pillow next to me at some unearthly hour and a warm little hand would wind its way around my neck.

Lily Grace is my sanity, my *raison d'être*. Even though Kelly has moved on and has someone new in her life, Lily comes first and being good parents is our top priority. At the time of our split I took it hard. We had this family life that was amazing, but suddenly one day we woke up and things were different. We were merely friends who happened to share the same house. That passionate desire to be a real couple, and to love one another, had silently departed. What held us together was the love we had for our daughter. Kelly and I were devastated, but we knew that it was only a matter of time before things would start to fall apart. We agreed to separate on the understanding that Lily Grace's welfare would always come first, for us both. On alternate weeks Lily comes to stay with me and I organise my working life around 'Lily time'. It means the days I don't have Lily, I'm constantly on the road. It allows me to work from home and do the school-run when she's with me. It's rare I have to call in a babysitter and I hate doing that, as I never want Lily to feel she's inconvenient.

'How's Lily? When are you bringing her down again?' Grandma Grace interrupts my thoughts and hands me the tray to carry through to the sitting room.

'She's great and Kelly sends her love. I told you that Lily is with Kelly this Christmas, but I'll bring her to see you for New Year. Then we'll be down again for your birthday. Kelly's off to France, so I'm taking ten days off to have Lily.'

'Wonderful! What a treat, I can't wait to see her. I bet she's grown.'

It dawns on me that Lily is a gift to us all. I only wish my mother had lived to meet her, but Grandma Grace and Pop were around to give Lily that sense of family. Losing Pop had been tough on us all and it was hard to answer Lily when she asked the question, 'why do people have to die, Daddy?'

'And is there a special lady in your life at the moment?' Sparkling eyes search mine, but I've nothing to hide.

'I've given up on dating. I'm not cut out for commitment it seems, and I'm not sure I want to go through all that emotional stuff again. Besides, I'm not sure Kelly would be too impressed if a new lady suddenly appeared on the scene.'

'Kelly has a new man in her life, so I can't see how she

could possibly be upset. Surely she realises you aren't going to be on your own forever? Forever is a long time, Adam.'

There's a tinge of sadness in her expression, which she quickly hides with a fleeting smile of reassurance. It's obvious what she's thinking.

No one should be alone. Ever.

Katie

Sometimes The Truth Hurts

'You aren't thinking of taking Steve up on his offer, are you?' The look on Hazel's face is one of horror.

'Don't worry, this business is here to stay, so don't go looking for another job. And don't say a word to Francis. He's the best baker we've had and I don't want you unsettling him.'

Hazel is like an open book and you can almost see her mind whirling with 'what ifs'.

'What if Steve delivers an ultimatum?'

You see what I mean!

'Relationships don't grow if one person starts making all the decisions and the other is expected to toe the line,' she adds. 'A relationship is about working together and resolving each little issue as it arises.'

Hazel hands me another tray of purple and silver frosted blueberry cupcakes for the display cabinet. Francis is the best baker I've employed so far and I'm praying he stays. Before him the longest-serving baker we've had lasted eight months and he was enticed away by an offer I simply couldn't match. If Francis moves on then, unless a miracle happens, I'll be back to doing two jobs instead of one. Hazel is brilliant with the customers and she's good with cupcakes, but that's it. I've known her since school and she's my best friend, but in some ways we are very different. She admits she hasn't the patience to develop her skills and the more elaborate cakes can take many hours to decorate and assemble.

'Katie, there's something I need to ask you, but I'm not

sure you're going to appreciate the question. I'll hate myself if I don't put it out there, though.'

I spin around, ready for the next tray and Hazel looks directly at me, her face reflecting friendly concern.

'Okay, if it's something that's bothering you that much you'd better get it out of the way.'

'Why do you stay with Steve when he bullies you?'

I'm a little taken aback by her question. It wasn't quite what I was expecting her to ask. Bullying? Is that really how it appears to people looking in on our relationship?

'Well, Steve has strong opinions but I don't think you can call that bullying. Remember, he has years of experience in starting up new businesses, over-seeing their development and business planning. He has my best interests at—'

'Forcing someone to do something they don't want to do is bullying,' Hazel interrupts, passing me a tray of lemon-frosted ginger cupcakes, then turning away immediately to ready the next tray. She doesn't want to look me in the eye, for some reason. 'Clever bullies get their own way without their victim even knowing it!'

When, at last, she does turn back to look at me, she whispers. 'Sorry, but someone had to say something and I guess that's what friends are for. I'm not trying to hurt you, Katie. I think you are hurting enough already.'

Suddenly my eyes are watering and now I'm the one to turn away.

'It's different between a man and a woman,' I whisper back. I pause to listen out for noises from the kitchen to confirm Francis is out of earshot of this conversation. I'm shocked Hazel regards Steve as a bully.

'Oh, so the fact that I'm gay means my relationship works by a different set of rules? Wake up and smell the coffee, Katie. Steve is a man who likes to have control. It's been like that since day one, surely you *know* that?'

I blink a few times rather than brushing my hand over my eyes, as I don't want Hazel to know I'm tearing up. It's tiredness after a long week, that's all. I wouldn't want her to think she'd upset me and I'm certainly not angry, only extremely surprised she should get it so badly wrong.

'Men have a different way of handling things, that's all I'm saying. When it comes to business, Steve is right in many ways, but Sweet Occasions is about more than money. I love coming to work every morning and that's worth a lot more to me than a bigger profit at the end of the month.'

Hazel shakes her head with concern. 'You're a lost cause, Katie. I only hope that one day you don't wake up having lost your dream and with no idea how it happened. All I'm trying to say – with love and your best interests at heart – is please make sure you know what you're doing.'

She places a hand on my shoulder and squeezes gently. The gesture touches me and I have to walk away before the tears begin to spill over.

June

Grandma Grace's Birthday

Adam

Cake Heaven

'Where are we, Dad?' Lily sticks out her lower lip to blow a waft of air upwards, moving her wayward fringe out of her eyes. It must be the hottest day we've had so far this year.

'We're calling in to collect Grandma's birthday present. I hope she likes it. It's a special one this year as she's eighty years old.'

'That's old. Will Grandma have a cake and candles? It will have to be a big cake.' Her eyes open wide as she pictures a cake covered in candles. 'How will she blow them all out? I had eight on my last birthday and you had to help me.' Her little face frowns as she mulls this over. I can't help chuckling.

'Grandma doesn't like parties, so we're buying her a very special cake just for the three of us. All she wanted for her birthday was a visit from you. You're going to have to help her unwrap some very fun presents.'

Lily swivels her head to look at me with eager anticipation.

'They arrived yesterday at Grandma Grace's house in three enormous boxes. She can't wait to open them and it will make her smile when she discovers what's inside.'

'Oh, okay. I like parties. Why doesn't Grandma like them?'

You can't explain to an eight-year-old that when someone loses their soulmate of over fifty years it's hard to find the will to go on. Each day they wake up is a reminder that the love of their life is no longer by their side. Grandma won't give up, of course, she's from a generation who were brought up during tough times and the spirit remains strong. But her zest for life isn't the same and now she's virtually a recluse. She has locked herself away to spend her days pottering in the garden, or reading if the weather is inclement. If she didn't have the garden ... I can't even contemplate what the future would hold. She's always been there for Lily, and me.

'Grandma doesn't like lots of noise and people, besides she's very happy knowing that you are coming for a special visit.'

'And *you*, Dad. Grandma likes to see you too.'

Lily's face puckers up into an excited smile and her words remind me that she's right. I only wish I lived closer, had more time. Guilt gnaws away at me, pulling me down. I also know that while Grandma loves a visit, she struggles at times to cope with the upheaval. Before I can respond, Lily starts chattering away again.

'I don't think Grandma likes to see Mummy, though. I do miss Pop, Daddy. Do you miss him too?'

At times she takes my breath away. What doesn't she see? Her little mind processes everything and just when you think old memories have been forgotten, they come back as bright and fresh as if they were new.

'I miss Pop, too, honey. We can't see him but I know he's watching over us.' The words sound hollow, but already she's moved on and is flicking between screens on her iPad.

'Here we are.' I manage to find a parking space a few yards away from Sweet Occasions. Lily looks out of the window, excitedly.

'Dad, will Grandma like her cake?'

'I hope so; even I haven't seen it yet. A very clever lady

26

designed it especially for Grandma, so I think it's going to be amazing.'

She smiles at me. A look of pure pleasure flashes across her face, reminding me that a special birthday cake is a big deal.

Walking up to the shop it looks very different seeing it on a bright, summer's day. Somehow the gloom and driving rain on my first visit had hidden the slightly shabby appearance of the exterior paintwork. Inside is still just as cosy as I remembered, though, with a vintage look that screams country living. In my semi-frozen state I was hardly able to take in the loving care with which this not-so-little cake shop has been styled. It is like stepping into a virtual cupcake heaven, but it's the attention to detail that marks it as special. The counters run in an L-shape, beyond which it opens up into an area extending back a little further into the property. Obviously some serious cake selling takes place here, as there are a dozen small tables, all with pristine tablecloths and a vase in the centre with a few fresh flowers. The walls of this room have built-in dressers displaying an array of vintage china. In the middle of the room is a trolley with a range of cake boards, napkins, forks and several of those silver cake slicers. Those, too, look like they are antiques, not just modern stainless steel ones you pick up in the sales. One of the dressers houses a stack of folders, which I presume show off the range of cakes that can be ordered. I hadn't appreciated this wasn't also a cafe, the coffee machine is purely for clients and goodness knows where Katie managed to find something savoury to feed me that day. That's rather embarrassing, as I didn't realise quite how accommodating she was being. Everything here is sweet, sweet, sweet. Lily's eyes are everywhere.

Today it's very busy and there is a long queue of people waiting to be served. Katie, a guy and another woman I haven't seen before are all hurrying back and forth between the kitchen and the shop. They bring out a stunning assortment of cakes and Lily eyes a pink, girlie birthday cake with pure delight.

'Dad, can I have a princess cake like that one for my birthday?' she trills. Her voice rises above the general chatter, attracting a few smiles. Katie's eyes are drawn towards us and she recognises me, giving a welcoming wave.

'Maybe, if we tie it in with a visit to Grandma, Lily.' I smile down at her upturned face. Her eyes sparkle and she reminds me of her mother. I'm such a screw-up. Lily deserves a perfect family life and here we are, her life split in two, with constant hellos and goodbyes. What does that tell her about relationships, I wonder, and how will all this affect her in the future?

'Hi.' Katie's voice is warm and happy. She gives me a brief smile and then looks down at Lily. 'And who are you?'

'I'm Lily,' a shy little voice returns. 'I'm eight.'

Katie laughs and flashes me a broad smile.

'You're a tall girl for eight. Lovely to meet you, Lily. I'm Katie. Have you come to collect your grandma's cake?'

'Yes.' Her shy voice is now merely a squeak.

'Please,' I add, raising an eyebrow at her.

'Please,' Lily repeats, sounding a little more confident.

When Katie returns with the cake Lily claps her hands and does a little skip on the spot.

'Daddeee – it's awesome!' she squeals.

Katie has indeed done a great job. I asked for something that wasn't too big, but I wanted it to be fun. A happy cake, I'd told her and that is exactly what she's made. The simple, eight-inch cake is covered with white icing and a cascade of multicoloured balloons sit on top. They are built up into a tower and how on earth she's managed that I have no idea, but it's perfect.

'My, that's amazing.'

'I aim to please. I do hope your grandma likes it, Lily.' Katie kneels down in front of Lily to let her see the detail on the top.

'She's my great-grandma really and, oh, she will! And I love it too.' Her little voice wavers. What is she thinking now? Please don't let it be that she wishes mummy was here to share this moment. I hope that phase is now done and she can cope with our parallel existence.

'I have to put it into a special box, so that it won't get squashed when you carry it out to the car,' Katie explains. She straightens, balancing the cake expertly on her upturned hand.

'Thank you. Really, you did a great job.'

'You did say eighty, didn't you? I thought you could add this, to finish it off.'

Katie holds out a handmade candle, just the one, with an eight and a zero attached in pale lilac.

'Appropriate, or not?' She looks at me hesitantly.

'Perfect.' Our eyes meet for the briefest of moments and a warm sensation passes over me. That extra touch makes all the difference.

'I'll box it up, then. Come and sit at our tasting table. Maybe Lily would like to try some cake while I finish up.'

Lily eyes the little trays containing cake samples and nods, enthusiastically. She picks up a fork and stabs at a cube of strawberry and vanilla cake, as Katie expertly assembles a sturdy box.

'Business looks good,' I venture, breaking what is fast becoming an awkward silence.

'It is,' Katie replies, biting her lip, 'but not good enough to expand our operation yet. I'm hoping to get a large commercial contract and that will make all the difference.'

'Tough times for small businesses,' I add, wishing I'd picked an easier topic. I'm such an idiot; small talk has never been my thing.

'Well, business rates are high and the overheads seem to mount up. I have a great financial advisor though, and he's helping me grow the business.'

I feel a little embarrassed by her honesty and, I have to admit, a bit surprised.

'Always handy to have someone you trust, I should imagine, giving advice.'

'Well, yes, he's my partner, actually.' The moment the words leave her lips she blushes, and I notice her hands falter as she ties a big ribbon around the box.

'Ah, I hope he's giving you a substantial discount,' I add, amiably.

Our eyes lock for a few seconds and then she glances across at Lily, who is about to devour another cube of chocolate cake.

'Mmm.' Lily turns to face us. 'My favourite. Dad, you must try this one.'

'Thank you, Lily.' Taking the fork I pop it into my mouth and she's right, it almost melts on my tongue.

'Dee-licious.' I roll my eyes, as Katie and Lily chuckle.

We walk across to the counter so that I can pay and Katie hands over the cake box. I take it from her gingerly, hoping the decorations are stuck firmly in place.

'Don't drop it,' she adds, winking at Lily. Then she

hands Lily a little box of her own. 'It's a chocolate and banana cupcake, for later.'

'Ooh, thank you, Katie.' Lily gingerly takes the box into her little hands as if it's made of glass. 'My own little cake,' she adds, softly.

'Thank you so much. I'll be back at Christmas. Good luck with that contract.' I nod briefly as Katie walks briskly around the counter to open the door for us.

'Well done for remembering to say thank you, Lily,' I add, motioning with my head for Lily to walk in front of me.

'She's cute,' Katie says as I pass by, following Lily out of the door. 'Goodbye, Lily. Maybe I'll see you at Christmas.'

Katie turns to face me and her smile almost takes my breath away. I stand there for a few seconds rooted to the spot, before I remember Lily has gone on ahead. I want to say something, but I can't find the words. Instead I throw in a, 'See you at Christmas' and walk out, wanting to kick myself. Hardly parting words guaranteed to make an impression, but then she did mention she has a partner. No ring, I notice, but that's probably because jewellery and baking don't mix.

Katie

Life Isn't Always Fair

'There was a lot of eye contact going on there. Who's the guy?' Hazel sidles up to me as I replace the gaps in the cupcake display.

'A customer.'

'Seems like he knew you,' Hazel adds, expecting a response. When it wasn't forthcoming she added, 'And the little girl had lovely manners.'

'There's nothing to tell. He came in last Christmas and bought a cake for his elderly grandmother. He ordered a birthday cake for her and they're off to deliver it. I don't know anything about him and I had no idea he even had a daughter. He's just a customer, Hazel, it's none of my – our – business.' I give her a look, raising one eyebrow to make the point that there is nothing else to be said.

'Pity. Nice-looking guy, very polite.'

'I already have a partner, Hazel. I'm not shopping around for another guy and I don't steal other people's husbands.'

'I was only saying …'

The unspoken words are too easy to conjure up. I know Hazel cares about me, but she has it all wrong when it comes to my relationship. Steve loves me and he doesn't want to see me fail when it comes to Sweet Occasions. He has reluctantly accepted that I don't want to give it all up and become a lady of leisure and the reason he's now advising me on how to grow the business is because he believes in me, in my dream. Now I sound like I'm trying to convince myself, too.

'Katie ...' Hazel absentmindedly straightens a row of coconut and passion fruit cupcakes. '... what if Steve's plan fails? What if you don't get that contract?'

I lean back against the worktop, sweeping a few strands of hair, which have escaped my French twist, away from my face.

'We'll get it.' My voice sounds confident. In truth I'm not so sure – either that we will win the contract, or that it's the right way to go. If we are successful, I can't even begin to think about the pressure we're going to be under. We aren't geared up for high volume. Even with another staff member, it's going to be hard to cope when it comes to supplying a chain of wedding venues.

'Steve is just doing what he does best, Hazel. Advising businesses about profitability and return on investment *is* his business. He says I should either get serious about it, which means guaranteeing a long-term future for us all, or walk away and find something else to do with my time. His alternative is that I stay home and support him. The consultancy business has really taken off, but it has major peaks and troughs. I think he'd like me to get involved on the admin side when he's under pressure with a new start-up, and then be there to take advantage of the lulls. At the moment there are times he's stuck at home not doing a lot, but I still have to be here.'

It all sounds like such a simple decision. Make it pay, so there's a point to working all these hours, or sell it off and join team Steve. Anxiety begins to grip me like a vice. I've chosen Sweet Occasions, but now it's beginning to feel like a runaway train. It's too late to apply the brakes, so I have to sit tight and see where it takes me. I wonder if Steve is expecting me to fail and waiting for the moment that I have no choice but to acknowledge that fact?

'If you say so,' Hazel adds, grumpily. 'I know you, Katie. Money never was your goal; you're easily contented. But then maybe that's a bad thing at times.'

As Hazel walks away I feel awful for dismissing her concerns. Why is everyone so worried about me? My little dream of spending my days creating cakes to make people happy has turned into an endless struggle to please those around me. Whether it's at work or at home, sometimes I wish they would put their trust in my judgement. Guilt floods through me – I'm being selfish, of course. Hazel isn't only concerned about her own job security; she knows how much this means to me. Steve wants me to be happy and how many men would offer their partner the chance to give up work and have a more leisurely lifestyle? I'm lucky and I should be counting my blessings.

The pain in the back of my head throbs like a relentless drumbeat as I rummage around in my bag for some tablets. Shutting the office door, I settle gratefully into my seat and tilt my head back against the wall. When did my life first start to go wrong? Why are there times when I feel so unhappy I could sit down and weep? That old saying, 'be careful what you wish for, it might just come true', flashes into my mind. But what is the alternative? Turning my back on the passion I've had since I was a young child?

The questions whirl around in my head making the pain worse. Then into it pops the image of a little girl, eyes wide with excitement, as she breathlessly takes a cupcake from my hands. Lily.

'Oh, no.' An involuntary groan escapes my lips and my stomach constricts. Not that, please. I try to shake off the annoying drumbeat pulsing through my body. Is it the pain from this migraine, or is it my body clock going tick-tock like a metronome? Having a baby isn't an option any more and I accepted that a couple of years ago. There isn't room in my life for more anguish, or regret. All of that has to be behind me now.

Grace
Fun and Laughter

'Grandma Grace,' Lily's lilting voice filters into the hallway. It fills the space as this adorable little bundle runs towards me, arms outstretched.

'Steady, Lily. Not too tightly or you'll squash Grandma.' Adam's voice shows concern and I glance up at him. His face crinkles into a smile, but hovering beneath it is the worry I know he feels so acutely.

'She's fine. I love hugs. My, how you've grown, young lady! Stand back and let me look at you.'

Lily dances around in a circle, doing little skips and hops.

'Happy birthday, Grandma Grace. We have a surprise and it's very special.' Lily claps her hands with glee and continues to hop around on the spot.

'Really? Well, Daddy's boxes have arrived and I can't imagine what's inside. I'm going to need some help opening them.'

Adam wraps his arms around me, giving me a loving squeeze.

'And a happy birthday from me. How old is it this year?' he asks, playfully.

'I've stopped counting; the figure is far too obscene to contemplate.' I laugh, and for the first time in a while I feel a sense of happiness, true happiness, flooding through me. Having Adam and Lily here means so much to me; more than celebrating yet another birthday.

'Grandma Grace, we must open your presents. Besides, I'm hungry!'

'Lily, remember, it's a surprise,' Adam says, putting a finger to his lips and turning on his heel. 'I'll bring in the things from the car.'

Lily disappears into the sitting room and I follow her, unable to stop myself from grinning like a Cheshire cat.

'How's school, young lady?'

'It's okay. Mum says I need to try harder because I'm not very good at maths.'

My mouth goes a little dry at the mention of Kelly. It was painful watching them from the sidelines as she tried to change Adam from the moment that ring was on her finger. Whatever he did never seemed to please her and, ironically, the harder he tried the more she seemed to despise him for it. He was simply doing whatever he could to make her happy. He thought the fact that they both doted on their daughter meant they would weather the little storms in their relationship. The truth of the matter was that Adam was in love with Kelly, but I don't think her feelings ever ran as deeply. The person she fell in love with was the version of Adam she had in her head, the man she would turn him into. But one thing I learnt very early on in life is that when it comes to affairs of the heart you can't interfere; love has to run its course, no matter where that leads.

Lily is looking at me, a small frown on her perfect little face. I sigh; I'm just thankful she has two supportive parents. It's times like this I miss my darling daughter, Elizabeth. It's a loss from which Adam has never truly recovered.

'Well, we all have subjects we find difficult. I'm sure there are lots of things you do well. As long as you remember to try your best, that's what counts. It's easy to give up on something if, at first, it's difficult to do. Mummy knows that often, if you keep working away, eventually it all begins to make sense. Remember the time when you were learning to skip?'

'Yes.' Lily beams and she claps her hands over her mouth. 'I could only hop, I was such a baby.' Her voice is high-pitched and excited.

'Eventually you managed to do it, after lots of practice. And now you wonder why you found it so difficult. Lots of things in life are like that.'

'Grandma, can I tell you something?'

Her little upturned face is full of anguish and I know what's coming.

'Anything at all, sweetheart.'

'I wish Daddy still lived with Mummy and me.'

'I know, Lily. But you must never forget that Mummy and Daddy love you so much, as I do. Just because you don't all live together doesn't change that. You don't live with me, but I love you and think of you all the time.'

Lily chews her lip, her little brow furrowed as she considers my words. She nods her head, as if she's drawn a conclusion.

'I'm glad they don't argue any more.'

Out of the mouths of babes ... her words are a sharp reminder of some very unhappy times.

'We want them both to be happy, don't we?'

She smiles up at me, nodding fiercely.

'So our job is to make sure Mummy and Daddy have lots of hugs.'

Adam's footsteps announce his arrival and I turn to see him weighed down with bags, holding yet another box in his hands.

'I did mention I didn't want you spending your money on lots of presents.' I glance at him, eyeing the package he offers up to me.

'This is special, Grandma Grace.' Lily can hardly contain her enthusiasm. She hops up and down on one leg. 'You have to open it now, please!'

Adam deposits the bags in the corner, as we take a seat on the sofa. Lily nestles up next to me and I put my arm around her, giving her a quick squeeze.

'You're the only present I wanted,' I breathe into her hair, softly. 'Can you help me open this?'

Her little hands delicately, and lovingly, undo the bow. As the sides of the box fall away, it reveals the most beautiful birthday cake.

'Do you like it, do you like it?' she squeals, jumping up and throwing her hands in the air. Adam watches, laughing. Behind him, Elizabeth is once more with us. Even more beautiful in the soft light, she gazes at her son and granddaughter with pride. My heart aches, knowing that she longs to be able to hug them and knowing they are totally unaware of her presence. I long to hug you too, my darling daughter. I quickly wipe away a tear, throwing myself back into the happiness of the moment.

'It's the best birthday cake I've ever seen.' I have to admit that the cake is amazing, as lovely as the one Adam brought me at Christmas.

'Now you must open your other boxes.' Lily is already helping Adam to move the three enormous boxes across in front of my chair. I glance momentarily at the seat opposite me. For one brief moment I see Jack sitting there, grinning at me. Another tear forms in the corner of my eye as I toss my head, refusing to dwell on his absence. It's a blessing to know we are all here together, today, and for that I am grateful.

'My, my! Whatever can be inside? I've never seen such enormous boxes before!'

I join in the fun, my spirits lifted high on the wave of excitement and love with which Adam and Lily fill the room. As Adam helps Lily peel away the tape, their voices ring out with laughter and merriment.

I hope Jack is still watching us, sharing this precious moment that is less about a birthday and more about the bond we all share.

'Here, Grandma Grace, here!' Lily indicates for me to step forward. Easing myself up from the chair I walk the few paces. I gingerly lift the lid with mock anticipation that something might jump out at me. Immediately a balloon pops up, then another and another. As the lid comes off they float to the ceiling, a mass of colour and ribbons.

'And this one.' Lily's hands excitedly guide mine to the next box, and the next.

Soon the entire room is filled with balloons and I laugh more than I've laughed for many years. I put my hands to my mouth and peer over at Lily.

'Oh, my goodness!'

She jumps up and down, shouting, 'Happy birthday to you.'

As I glance across at Adam he steps forward to put his arms around me. I have to fight the tears that well up, unbidden. The whole room is like a hug. It's filled with balloons, love and the two people who are the dearest to me in the whole wide world. You are watching, Jack, aren't you? My mind hesitates for one moment, then I dismiss the thought. Of course he is; he's always here.

'How gorgeous, darlings.' My voice is heavy with emotion, the tears I'm holding back taking it up a notch or two. 'Lovely, simply lovely.'

With Lily safely tucked up in bed, Adam and I retire to the

snug. He sits in Jack's old chair, next to me. I reach across and lay my hand over his, giving it a squeeze.

'You shouldn't have, you know,' I admonish. But he can hear the love and gratitude in my voice.

'It was merely a bit of fun. We wanted to make you laugh.'

His grin reminds me of when he was a small boy. I can see him at Lily's age, just eight years old, and sitting in that same chair. He had one of Jack's books on his lap. I think it was all about steam trains.

'Well, fun it was. Laughter is better than any pill, it's a natural tonic. Growing old is a nuisance,' I add, instantly regretting those silly words.

'I know. I wish you would get out more, take up a few of those invitations you receive. It's been—'

I cut him off, there's no point in taking this conversation any further. 'I'll think about it. Oh, and what a stunning cake. Was it from the same baker as that delightful Christmas cake you brought me?'

Subject changed and Adam politely accepts the topic is closed.

'Yes, a shop named Sweet Occasions. When I told her about your present she said, "leave it to me" and she did a great job.'

'Oh, I *see* ...'

Adam smiles in response to my knowing comment and our eyes meet for a brief second, until I'm distracted. My daughter, Elizabeth, appears at his side, her hand lightly touching her son's shoulder. Does she, too, feel that same sense of hope and anticipation that leaps in my heart?

'There's nothing to *see*. Katie is a nice lady, friendly and obviously very kind.'

My eyes sweep over his face. He seems unwilling to say

any more and I might be grasping at straws. However, there's a little sparkle in his eye I've never seen before and he's trying his best to play it down. He wants me to think it's nothing, but could this be *it* at long last?

Elizabeth smiles across at me before turning away and in an instant what appeared to be something quite real fades into nothingness. It might be merely a few moments in time, but it's comforting, my darling daughter, thank you. I live in the hope that one day Adam will bring me the news I so impatiently await. He deserves to find his soulmate. I know, only too well, the emptiness of being alone. It's strange how, often, it's the things that are left unsaid between people that say the most. We each know what we want to say, but hearing the actual spoken words would be too much to bear.

'Well, next time you see her, you can pass on that I think she's one very talented cake designer. That isn't merely a cake; it's a work of art. Her passion shines through.'

'Hint taken, but you'll have to wait and see what you get for Christmas.'

'I love the shawl you gave me, too, for my birthday, but the cake is my favourite,' I add, reinforcing the point.

'It's a pity she isn't single,' Adam retorts, seeing through my ruse.

'Well, that is a great shame. But you never know what the future might hold. One of these days, Adam, you'll be visiting me with a significant other. Mark my words.'

He lets out a sigh. He's not angry with me, it's purely contemplative.

'I'm not sure anyone would put up with me. The week Lily is with me it's all about her routine and working remotely from home. Then the week we're apart, I'm on the road the whole time. When we're together she comes

42

first, above all else. It doesn't exactly make me a good catch, now does it?'

I can see from his sober expression that the question is genuine.

'No one's life is easy or perfect, Adam. Love has a way of making things work when the time is right. Sometimes we have to be patient and wait for Fate to direct us. It always does, even if, occasionally, it feels as if we are going around in circles.'

'Or backwards, as in my case.' His grimace reflects disappointment. I know life hasn't turned out quite the way he'd hoped. He's such a handsome guy, so loving and thoughtful. My heart constricts for the pain he's been through.

I glance across at the photo of Elizabeth, sitting on the shelf next to the photo of Jack. Elizabeth never told us who Adam's father was and we respected her wishes. We were there for her, and Adam, as he grew up. I like to think we helped to make up for the absence of a father figure during those formative years. Jack loved Adam like a son, their bond was strong. When Elizabeth died at such a young age, Adam became the centre of our lives and we all grieved together. It was the same when Adam's relationship fell apart and then, recently, when Jack passed away. We drew close, but I fear that Adam now follows my lead. He finds excuses to enjoy his own company, rather than face the world.

At my age, it's understandable that I want to withdraw into a place where life is more about savouring old memories, rather than creating new ones. Adam has to grab life again and begin living it, rather than letting work and his love of Lily define him. It seems to me that he exists simply to get through each day at the moment. Instead, he should be making wonderful new memories. My heart aches to think about Adam looking back on his life with regret and sadness. Is that why Elizabeth was here today? She rarely visits me these days, but whenever Adam is around she always appears. Maybe it's to reassure me he's never really alone and she's keeping an eye on both him and Lily.

What I hate about growing old is that I'm losing patience with Fate. Adam has had the clouds, now where is his silver lining?

Katie

Running From The Truth

'Katie, you can't be serious! Your business is seasonal and turning away a lucrative contract like this would be sheer madness. The additional profit will allow you to ride the quiet periods. Without that, if the money-making summer and Christmas markets dip at any time, you face turning that bottom-line figure into a net loss.'

I feel myself physically shrinking away from Steve as his words tear into me.

'But I'm not sure we can deliver. What if we can't keep up? I'm sick with worry that this is a step too far, too soon ...' The words die on my lips as I scan Steve's face, which is taut with anger.

He steps forward and I hate myself for being the one to cause him all this stress. It's not good for him and guilt flows through me like ice water in my veins.

'Then get a manager who is up to the job.' He throws the words at me like a snarl. 'If you turn this down, Katie, Sweet Occasions won't last twelve months.' His eyes are cold and angry as he walks away from me.

Once more I've disappointed him, and a feeling of helplessness and rejection overwhelms me. Following him through into the kitchen, I know I have to do something to diffuse the situation. I watch him venting his frustrations as he makes coffee, every movement hard and sharp. I try not to jump as he bangs the coffee mug down.

'You're right.' My voice is soft, hoping the tone will help to calm him. 'I'm sorry. I panicked because I didn't think we'd get the contract and it was a bit of a shock.'

'Why do you do this to me? I only have your best interests at heart and yet you seem to want to fight me at every step of the way. I love you too much to see all your hard work wasted. This contract will secure the future for the next three years. That's a big deal, Katie.'

Steve's anger has evaporated as quickly as it appeared. He walks across to me, leaning his body into mine. Placing one hand either side of me, he lifts me up to sit on the counter top, so that our eyes are level. I can feel the tenseness in his muscles as his arms wrap around me.

'You still love me, don't you?'

My heart skips a beat. I can't answer that at the moment. I'm not sure I can be honest, either with myself, or with Steve.

'I'm sorry I panicked. I know I should feel grateful to have an experienced eye watching over me, and I do appreciate your help.'

He relaxes, his hug becoming gentler, and the question remains unanswered.

'That's my girl. You're my lucky charm, you know that,' he whispers. His mouth lingers against my cheek.

My conscience is screaming, telling me I've lied to him by omission. I care about Steve because of what we've been through together. I'm not sure I'm in love with him any more, but how can I be sure of that? And how can you tell a man whose hand you held through repeated chemotherapy sessions that the gap between you grows with every new argument? The truth is that you can't.

'Katie, it's Adam – you know ... the guy you saved from hypothermia.'

I recognise the voice instantly. My mouth breaks into a smile as a flashback of Adam in a pink sweatshirt floats into my head.

46

'It's only September; I thought your next visit was in December?'

'Yes, well, it's my daughter Lily's birthday on Sunday and she's set her heart on one of those princess birthday cakes. I thought she'd forgotten all about it, but suddenly it's all she's talking about and I had no idea it was such a big deal. To be honest, it's the first birthday party I've had to plan since I split with my ex, hence the panic as I've left it a bit late. By the way, how are things going?'

No doubt he can hear the constant barrage of hammering in the background.

'We're re-designing the layout and making better use of the space. Doubling the size of the kitchen and the storage area is a necessity, or so I'm told.' My voice sounds distinctly lacklustre, even to my own ears.

'Ah, you won the contract. Congratulations. I appreciate that the answer might be no, in this particular case, but I wanted to ask if you deliver? It's a bit of a drive north, I'm afraid. I can do it in just over three hours.'

I start laughing, thinking he must be joking.

'Um … it's a bit further afield than our normal service usually covers.'

'I know, and I apologise about asking for the impossible. It's just that Lily's set her heart on it and I thought I'd ask the question. The problem I have is that she fell at school and broke her arm. She had surgery the day before yesterday and is coming home later today. I need to collect the cake this Saturday and she's not going to be up to the journey. Her mother is away on an important business trip and doesn't fly back until next Tuesday. Whatever it costs is fine. A cake is very important to a nine-year-old, and I'm going to have a dozen of them here on Sunday.'

This is awkward. Even ignoring the cost, I know there's

no way I can tie up the delivery van for such a lengthy journey for one cake. We're going to have our work cut out with the wedding venue deliveries on Saturday as it is, and we don't open on Sundays.

'Look, I can't fit it in on Saturday, but I could get it up to you by eleven o'clock on Sunday morning. Will that do?' Why did I say that? It's a six-hour round trip and I must be mad. Then I remember the look on little Lily's face and it pulls on my heartstrings. I don't have anything better to do and it will be a day out.

'You are a lifesaver! Lily will assume I've had to pick up a cake from the supermarket, so it will be a huge surprise. She's chosen all of her presents herself, or rather her mother did. I admit it's an awkward age and hard to surprise them with anything these days. I'm happy to pay in cash. Let me know the total cost and I'll expect a supplement for a Sunday delivery.'

He sounds happy, relieved even. Clearly he's stressed and it feels like the right thing to do.

'Let me have the delivery address.'

'Katie, I thought you said that the knocking through the wall bit wasn't going to make much mess? Even sealing the kitchen door with polythene and gaffer tape, I'm not sure dust isn't finding its way through. How much longer is this going to take?' Francis folds his arms across his chest, his body language signalling his annoyance.

'I am sorry, Francis. I'll have a word with them. Do what you can and if you prefer to stop for the day, that's fine by me. I'm sure our customers will understand. We're only talking about passing trade, as all of the orders are up to date.'

He turns on his heels, calling over his shoulder, 'I'll soldier on, but it ain't easy.'

I approach Mike Pearce, who is surrounded by three guys. They're all focusing on a small cluster of thick, steel rods running up through a half-demolished wall.

'Problems?' They turn, staring at me as if a mythical creature has suddenly appeared on the scene.

'Well,' Mike says, taking off his hard hat in a welcoming gesture, 'we didn't expect to find reinforcing bars. Pete Morris, our building surveyor, thinks it's a support issue.'

'Yes,' Pete confirms, giving me a serious frown. 'The floor above isn't level; I suspect there was an issue with subsidence, causing a part of this wall to drop. They caught it before it became a major problem, but I don't think the work was done by a professional.'

Alarm bells start ringing in my head, adding to the pain of yet another headache.

'Will this involve extra cost?'

'It's safe enough, but not a standard fix. The floor above has a metal structure to strengthen it, but if we take out these bars we would need to put in some extra support.' Mike looks apologetic. At least they understand the impact of a delay at this point in time.

'Can't you work around it?' The words come out sounding like a plea, which I suppose it is, really. I'm desperate for solutions, not more problems. It's Monday, and everything has to be running properly by lunchtime on Wednesday. Failing that, we won't be able to meet the wedding venue orders for Saturday. Producing three hundred decorated cupcakes takes time. I know the wedding cakes are all ready for icing, but we can't risk the air being contaminated with brick dust for the finishing process. It's going to be tight to get it all done, even if they meet the original deadline. In the work schedule, this final stage of knocking through was supposed to take five days maximum.

49

'The only thing we could do,' Mike rubs his chin, staring at the bars as if he wishes they would disappear, 'is to build a column around them.' The other two guys nod in agreement.

'Is that practical?' Hope leaps in my chest. I could hug him!

'If you can live with it, then it's a quick solution. It will only involve building a wooden frame, erecting a plasterboard outer and a paint job. It would put us back on target if you think having a pillar here won't be in the way.'

I'm exhausted from worry and I answer without hesitation.

'I'm sure it will be fine, at least it's big enough for people to see it. There used to be a wall here, for goodness' sake, so I doubt anyone will end up walking into it.'

The guys laugh but I wasn't trying to be funny. I don't care what they do. I'm way past worrying about what it looks like. I know I should never have agreed to this costly extension in the first place. It's becoming a living nightmare that seems to get worse as each day passes.

'Should we call Steve in to take a look, before we start building the frame?'

I had already turned, and begun walking away when Mike's words spin me around.

'I'll explain to Steve. You can start work on the pillar immediately, Mike.' A look of doubt crosses his face as we lock eyes. Now is not the time to look weak, so I stare him down.

'Okay, it's your call.' He writes something on his clipboard and hands it to the third guy in the group. 'Get that framing in place asap,' he instructs.

My heart pounds in my chest as I walk away, realising that my tone had been sharp. The last thing I need now is the threat of a delay, and while Steve is footing most of the bill for this extension, Sweet Occasions still belongs to me. Owing Steve money and having a contractor hint that I need his approval makes me feel as if this dream isn't mine any more. I'm beginning to feel shackled, where once I felt that the future for Sweet Occasions was like a blank page; a new challenge with endless potential. That anticipation and excitement for where it might lead has been replaced with endless time spent on the computer, typing information into spreadsheets. Everything is about that magical figure at the bottom, worrying about whether it will change from blue to red.

As if some instinct has informed him that there's a problem, my mobile kicks into life. The caller ID alerts me it's Steve.

'Hi, morning. I was about to ring you.' I paste a smile on my face, hoping it reflects in my voice.

'Problems? Do I need to come over?' He sounds his usual, serious self.

'A minor one, but we're back on target. They discovered some steel reinforcing bars in the wall. They're going to plasterboard around them and turn it into a pillar. Thank goodness there's a solution, because things are rather tense here at the moment. Sealing off the kitchen isn't working out as well as we'd hoped. We can't begin icing until they've finished. I can't tell you how relieved I—'

'Are you sure I shouldn't pop in and take a quick look?' Steve cuts in, his voice heavy with concern. 'The simplest solution isn't always the best, you know, Katie. I'm not suggesting the guys would deliberately try to talk you into something because it's convenient ...'

His tone is light, but I know his jaw is clenched. He's upset that I made a decision without consulting him. Then

I realise that this is no coincidence. Mike called him to double-check he agreed with my decision.

'Steve, everything is fine. We're back on target and there's no other option. Please don't turn this into a big deal; the guys have already made a start.'

That's true enough, as I have to walk back through into the office so he can hear me. The noise of hammering reverberates through the building, as two guys set to work in earnest.

'If you're sure it's the right decision then I trust your judgement, of course.' His clipped tone suggests the contrary and guilt sends a rush of heat to my cheeks. He's right; I made the decision without giving it proper consideration. He doesn't realise that I'm long past caring about the minute details of the shop extension. Instead, I'm worrying over whether or not the orders can be filled. It seems there's little joy in my job at the moment, only pressure and anxiety.

'I took the only decision that made sense, Steve, and you have to trust me on that one. Now I have to get back to work. Hazel is rushed off her feet.'

She isn't, in fact there's only one customer in the shop at the moment.

'That's great to hear.' His voice softens, countering the hard edge to my own. He knows that will make me feel guilty, and it does. To my horror, something Hazel said pops into my head. It was about clever bullies getting their own way without their victims realising it. I throw the mobile on the desk and sit, staring at it. How have I gone from wondering whether my feelings for Steve have changed, to tying myself to him financially? My dream is now our dream. Except this is nothing like the dream I had. Each day is draining – emotionally, and physically. Was there more than a grain of truth in what Hazel said?

Adam

Some Days Are Better Than Others

As I replace the handset back onto the receiver, Kelly's voice is still ringing in my ears. Of course she's upset that she's in another country and wasn't here to be with Lily after the accident at school. However, aiming her anger at me isn't fair, and she knows that.

'You told me you'd take good care of our daughter.' Her voice had sounded bitter, and accusatory.

'Yes, I did, but this was simply one of those things that you can't anticipate. Lily is fine and she's healing well. The worst is over. I was at her side the whole time. Well, aside from when she was in surgery. Lily will tell you all about it when you get back, she doesn't want you to worry.'

'You've let me down, Adam.'

I slump back in my seat, feeling like an abject failure. If this had happened on Kelly's watch, then it wouldn't have been such a big deal. I know that and I can't believe I'm even thinking like this. Lily's well-being is all that matters.

Since Kelly's new partner arrived on the scene, things seem to be changing. My heart sinks as I hope Kelly doesn't want to re-think the arrangements. I don't want to end up back in court renegotiating our custody agreement.

'Dad?' Lily's voice reminds me I was on my way to fetch a drink for her, when the phone rang. 'Did Mum give you a hard time?'

Clearly she heard every word and I can only imagine how my side of the conversation sounded.

'Mum wishes she was here, that's all. It's hard for her being away at a time like this. All she wants to do is to see for herself that you really are on the mend.'

I hand Lily her drink and she rolls her eyes.

'Dad, I don't use that one any more. I'm way too old for the Mickey Mouse club.' She sounds indignant and I chuckle, thinking how like her mother she sounds sometimes.

'Sorry, I grabbed the first one left in the cupboard.'

'You need to empty the dishwasher, Dad. I'll do it for you. I'm getting bored sitting here watching videos.'

Before I have a chance to reply, the doorbell interrupts our conversation and Lily rushes off to answer it. I guess the patient is on the mend. As I follow her through into the hallway, I hear the squeal as Lily swings the door open to see her best friend, Emily, standing in front of her.

Behind her is our neighbour, Charlotte, beaming at me over their heads.

'Coffee?' I enquire and she nods, calling after the girls as they race off to Lily's bedroom. 'Careful, Emily. Remember Lily has a poorly arm and you must take care not to bump it.'

We head off to the kitchen and the sound of two girls, giggling and chattering away, seems to fill the entire house. Normality has returned and I breathe a sigh of relief.

'Tough few days?' Charlotte enquires.

She's referring to Kelly, of course. We've been neighbours for more than twelve years and for nearly ten of those Kelly lived here, too. Since Kelly and Lily moved back to be closer to Kelly's family, all contact seems to have stopped between them. The distance is only a couple of miles, but I suspect there were just too many painful memories. It's awkward all round and Charlotte understands that, but it's still a time of adjustment for us all.

'It's a shame it happened while Kelly is away. I feel badly for you. These things happen, Adam, so I hope you aren't letting it get to you. The good news is that the party plans are shaping up nicely.'

Charlotte takes her coffee and I nod, motioning for her to go through to the sitting room.

'Thanks for that and the sympathy. Kelly is understandably anxious and is counting down the days until she flies home. She calls twice a day for an update.' I stop to clear my throat with a meaningful grunt and Charlotte grins, sympathetically. 'As for the party, well, I've ordered the buffet and hopefully the cake will arrive on Sunday morning.'

'Cutting it rather fine, isn't it? I could whip one up for you with some pink icing and a few candles.'

'Thanks for the offer, but I promised Lily a princess cake. Well, it's like a mini wedding cake, would you believe. If it arrives in time it'll make her day. I've explained that it's too far for us to go and collect it. The jostling in the car wouldn't be good for her arm. I feel I owe her at least one surprise. Thanks so much for helping out. Is everything else sorted now?'

Charlotte raises an eyebrow and her mouth twitches at the corners.

'Yes. The entertainment is all set and the house decorations are ready and waiting. I'm assuming Kelly gave you instructions on what presents to buy.'

'Yep, in case I bought the wrong thing.'

'You know, Adam, you can rebel. You don't have to toe the line all the time and settle for a quiet life.' Her eyes are smiling, but there's a hint of exasperation in her tone.

'That's not the reason I give in all the time. It's the guilt.'

'Ah, guilt is a wonderful bargaining tool. I'm not saying Kelly purposely tries to manipulate you, but she enjoys getting her own way. Her new relationship isn't like that, is it?'

It's a fair enough question, but it feels weird talking about it.

'Elliot is a senior partner in a law firm; I seriously doubt anyone could intimidate him. Kelly says it's nice to have someone in her life who can take away the pressure.'

'Ouch, that's a bit of a cutting statement!'

I pull a mock grimace; the words no longer affect me as they did at first.

'She's right. I worshipped her and thought the way to make her happy was to ...' I hesitate, unable to find the right words. I realise that whatever I say here will make me sound like a total wimp.

'... give in?' Charlotte finishes my sentence.

Reluctantly, I nod in agreement.

'It was obvious to everyone that she walked all over you. There were times when I told her straight that she wasn't being fair. You know what she said? Kelly said that she couldn't help herself.'

Somehow, knowing that I was the subject of that conversation hurts more than some of the things Kelly has thrown at me, since our so-called amicable split.

'Hey, I'm sorry. I don't know why I'm telling you all this now. I want you to know that this wasn't all down to you. Kelly is used to getting her own way. And you mustn't let her make you feel guilty about Lily's accident happening while she's out of the country. She's a great mum. It's only natural that she'll feel bad she wasn't here, knowing her daughter has been through surgery. Just don't get hung up over this as it could so easily have happened when Lily was with Kelly. I'm surprised she didn't fly back, though.' Charlotte raises her eyebrow, clearly expecting an answer.

'Elliot convinced her it wasn't necessary.'

'Oh, I didn't realise it wasn't just a work trip. How convenient. Ha! Maybe this is one relationship that has a chance of working. I take my hat off to any man who can handle Kelly.'

If Charlotte called round to cheer me up, she isn't doing a great job so far. My self-esteem begins to plummet. Now there are two women who think I'm a pushover and a bit of a sad case. If I take a stand I'm wrong, and if I give in, I'm spineless.

'Anyway, I hope you're ready for Sunday's onslaught of hyperactive girls. That's quite a group Lily has invited and you are one brave man.'

'Thanks, and I know you're right. To be honest I'm wondering what on earth I was thinking. I should have taken them all to the cinema, or bowling.'

'You're a great dad, Adam. Little girls have a way of talking you into things, you simply have to learn how to steer them a little.'

Charlotte reaches across to place her hand on my arm and give it a reassuring squeeze.

'You'll be fine. Max is away on Sunday, so Emily and I have all the time in the world to help out.'

'You're a good friend, Charlotte. I owe you.'

She leans in to kiss my cheek. 'Hang in there, it will get better.'

'Are you sure you don't want me to come and collect you for Lily's party? I'm sure Charlotte would look after Lily for me.' I'm torn between the thought of leaving Lily so soon after her operation and thinking of Grace, home alone when both Lily and I would love her to be here. I know Lily is missing her mum, though, and still a little tearful at the moment. I'm being pulled in opposite directions and whatever the outcome, I know I'm going to feel I've let down someone I love.

'No, it's fine, don't worry about me. I'm a little tired at the moment and not up to a stay away from home. Too much gardening, I suspect. I've been cutting things back and the leaves have already begun to drop. It's more important that you make sure Lily looks after that arm. She will have a great time and I'm not sure I could put up with all that noise.'

Grace does sound tired. Her voice is bright, trying to reassure me she's not disappointed to be missing out on Lily's celebrations. Maybe this is for the best.

'Is everything sorted for the party?'

'As long as the food and cake arrive, I think we're pretty much all set up. I've been downloading music as directed by Lily and there are two ladies coming in to do "party hair". Braiding, I think is the term. They're also having their nails painted. Can you believe it?'

'She's growing up, Adam. It's a different world to the one even you knew as a child. As long as they have fun, that's all that matters. Do you have anyone helping out?'

'Charlotte has offered to come over. The two party ladies are here for the whole thing, and they more or less run the show. I just had to sort the food, music, and write the cheque.'

'Well, Lily's a lucky girl, that's for sure. How is the arm doing?'

'Aside from wearing the plaster cast, everything seems to be back to normal. Grace, if anything was wrong you

58

would tell me, wouldn't you? If you have any worries I want to share them.'

The pause is followed by a sigh.

'Adam, I'm fine. I'm not as young as I used to be, so you have to accept that. I don't want you worrying about me.' Her voice sounds strong, determined.

It reassures me a little, but I do worry about her now she is on her own. I want to be there for her, as she always was for me when I was growing up. However, I know it's not as simple as that. Grace would never allow me to look after her if she became ill.

Grace is one of life's givers. A lifetime devoted to looking after people you love does not prepare you for being on the receiving end at some point in your own life. I shake my head. It's sad to acknowledge that Jack would probably have been the only person in front of whom Grace would let her guard slip.

'Lily sends her love. She'll ring you after the party is over, to share the details.'

'Tell her I can't wait! It's a shame about the princess cake, though. It's all she's been talking about when she phones me.'

'Oh, I sorted that. They're going to deliver it on Sunday morning. It will be worth every penny to see the look on Lily's face when it arrives.'

'I'll pay for the delivery, and make sure you give the driver a big tip for his trouble.'

Her words come out sounding a little breathless and I suspect she's trying hard to pace the conversation. I can hear the exhaustion creeping into her voice, though. It's not worth arguing and upsetting her, so I agree with a 'thank you'. It's one thing telling someone not to worry, but words mean little when you can feel they are hurting. Maybe I've caught her at a bad time, interrupting a quiet moment of reflection about the old days. Pop's face flashes across my mind and it's like something is squeezing my heart. For a few brief seconds it takes my breath away.

'Love you, Grandma Grace. Don't go over-doing it in the garden and that's an order. We'll call you on Sunday evening.'

The phone rings again almost as soon as I put the receiver down and my old friend Tom's voice booms out.

'Hey, mate, how's it going? Wondered if you were up for a drink tonight and a catch-up?'

'I'm doing fine and it's good to hear from you. Lily's having a sleepover tonight at a neighbour's, so perfect timing.'

'How about eight o'clock at The Belfry? I owe you a drink for sorting out my PC.'

'Hope it taught you a lesson. Pop-ups showing half-naked women are usually hiding something you don't want to catch.' My laughter echoes down the line.

'Point taken, mate. Besides, Wendy went berserk when she found out what caused the virus. I won't be doing that again in a hurry.'

Katie
Business Blues

The income column is growing, but the expenditure column seems to grow faster. After I press the refresh icon, the bottom-line total is still a negative. The red numbers seem to glow on the page with a demonic glare. After I signed the three-year contract with Althorpe Wedding Venues, Steve insisted that I take a loan from him of fifty thousand pounds to extend the shop. Without the extra space in the kitchen we simply couldn't cope with the volume.

I knew it was more or less his entire life's savings, and the fact that he was willing to invest it in my business meant a lot. It was a safe enough investment, Steve had assured me, as the increase to the value of the property was greater than the cost of the work. But a little warning bell had started ringing somewhere deep inside.

He had laid out a detailed business plan in front of me and it would have been churlish to refuse his offer. If I'd approached the bank, I had no idea if they would have entertained increasing the mortgage. One thing was certain, and that's the fact that there would have been a large set-up fee. At least with Steve's investment, I only had interest and capital to repay on a monthly basis. However, the building works have already over-run on cost. Now Steve will, no doubt, point out that I didn't take his advice and factor in a contingency figure. He had suggested fifteen per cent. At the time, I remember thinking he was mad. The likelihood is that it will be at least twelve per cent over budget when I receive the final invoice. Once again, he was right.

The pain over my eyes makes them feel heavy, and my

brain struggles to scan the figures once more. I'm grasping at straws, hoping to find a mistake that will magically turn that little red figure blue. Rather depressingly, as far as I can tell, everything appears to be correct. The only option is to suck it up, and take Steve's advice to look for other potential contracts to boost income. I push the keyboard away with a sigh. It's time to saunter out into the shop.

It's busy and there's a buzz of activity. How can something that looks so successful be teetering on the edge all the time? If I don't get back on track, then Steve has offered to come in and run things for a while. He says I can then spend more time behind the scenes and in the kitchen. He has a point and he means well, but things still aren't right between us. Despite a heart-to-heart and agreeing we should actively listen to what the other has to say, he still does more talking than listening. I saw it as a second chance; Steve seems to have seen it as merely a lesson one of us needed to learn. As in, I need to listen to him more often.

'The difference between success and failure often comes down to the smallest of things, Katie. So many businesses end up closing because they stand still and in this financial climate it's a race for survival. You have to be better than your competition. You have to not only balance the books, but be solvent enough to weather the downturns. Going ten thousand over budget is par for the course, what's important here is that I knew that and you didn't.'

I couldn't argue with that last statement, it was a fact.

'I promise I'll be more receptive in future. I just want you to be proud of me.' Tears had begun to form in the corner of my eyes and instinctively I had pushed my shoulders back, willing myself to be strong. The truth was that if I failed at this I had nothing.

Nothing? I'd still have Steve, and *us*. But would it be enough?

Steve had walked around the dining table and stood with his arms open, looking for a gesture I didn't want to give. I pulled myself up out of my seat and let him wrap himself around me.

'You don't think I'm proud of you? I'm sinking every penny I have, almost, into your dream because I believe in you. But this is going to be a whole lot easier with two heads working on it, rather than one. You said this was what you wanted and you rejected my offer to take you away from it all. I'm selfish, I admit that and I liked the idea of being the provider for both of us. I fully accept that isn't what you want, but a relationship is about compromise. It's time to get serious, Katie, and if that kills off a little bit of your dream then I'm sorry, but that's the price you are going to have to pay. The time for simply drifting along is over and now you have to become that competent businesswoman.'

Wrapped in his arms I'd had a déjà vu moment, reminding me of those early days, shortly after we'd met. He was a glass half-full type of guy then and I loved that about him. I had only just left catering college and had taken up my first appointment as assistant pastry chef in a local manor house hotel. I was nervous but confident, and Steve's career was also taking off, so we fed off each other's enthusiasm.

With hindsight, any relationship is easy when things are going well, but it's how you weather the stormy times that makes all the difference.

This wasn't so much a storm, we'd already weathered enough of those to be able to understand that, so why was I so worried? I suppose it was the fear of losing my dream, of waking up one morning to find that Sweet Occasions was just a job, like any other and that was far too depressing to even contemplate.

A new day dawns and after yesterday's wake-up call, all I want to do is lock myself away in the kitchen and bake, as I come to terms with reality. It's not long though before I'm interrupted as I'm needed out front to serve customers.

'Sam was querying this delivery in the diary for Sunday. You've never asked him to work on Sunday before. He says he doesn't know anything about it.' Hazel looks at me with a puzzled expression on her face.

'Yes, it's ... um ... a friend. I'll make the delivery myself, it's not a problem. Steve is off on a guys' golfing weekend and it will give me something to do.' I can feel the heat rising in my cheeks as Hazel looks at me, slightly bemused.

'But that's a couple of hours' drive away, at least!' She exhales, sharply, implying I'm out of my mind. 'And isn't that the guy, you know, the one with the little girl?'

'It'll be a nice trip out and they're forecasting a sunny weekend. I can stop and have lunch on the way back.' I ignore her comment about the customer, hoping she'll drop the subject. I turn to serve the next person waiting in the queue, as she continues talking to me in a low voice.

'Well, at least business is good. It's great to be so busy, the day simply flies by.'

I shoot Hazel a questioning glance. Is she still happy working here? Has something changed? When she wakes up each morning does her stomach turn over at the thought of the day, stretching out endlessly ahead of her? I think back to the time when I worked in an office. That soul-destroying commute, followed by a day interspersed with meetings, and an inbox that was always over-flowing.

'Is everything all right?' The tentative tone in my voice causes Hazel to frown.

'Yes, of course. What are you worrying about *now*?' Her emphasis was firmly on the *now*, and I acknowledge that I have been a little intense lately. The building work has put pressure on us all.

'Nothing, I'm only checking.'

It's funny how your mind continues to tick over while you perform a series of tasks. I automatically wrap boxes, give change, and thank people for their custom. In my head I'm comparing life as it is now, to then, when it felt like a desk defined who I was. I was an employee in a job from which my dream rescued me. Unease shifts in my stomach. What's that all about? Is it a normal reaction to the new pressures of growing the business, or is this about owing Steve money? Ironically it's added yet one more layer to our already complicated relationship. Yes, we've talked things through as honestly as we can, but it feels like we've merely applied a sticking plaster for a quick fix. What's actually needed is a very large bandage. Instead of bringing us together, it's driving us further apart.

'Can I have six of the purple velvet cupcakes, too?' The young woman I'm serving leans forward to attract my attention. I guess that last thought threw me a little and jarred my autopilot mode.

'Of course, they're one of our best sellers at the moment. I'll pop in a New York vanilla spice for you, on the house. It's this month's new addition to the range.'

The customer grins back at me and adds, 'I haven't tried a Sweet Occasions cake yet that wasn't truly scrumptious.'

As I arrange the cupcakes in the box, my thoughts take over once more. This is still my shop. I began this, and I decide what we sell. I'm in control. Taking a deep breath,

I relax my shoulders. I smile back, grateful to be reminded what this is all about.

'Thank you for the feedback. Always nice to know what our customers think. Can I quote you on that?' We laugh good-naturedly as I take the proffered twenty pound note. Mentally I hear a kerr-ching – one more sale towards paying off Steve's loan.

Grace

Harsh Reality

When the doctor broke the news, I sat there quietly. One half of me was able to accept the inevitable, and the other half wanted to reject it. I shed a few tears, of course, but those were for a future that I wouldn't see. Missing Adam's wedding – the one I was confident would still happen before too long – and, one day, Lily's too.

I'm eighty years old, what did I expect? I would probably be one hundred years old before my great-granddaughter was ready to walk down the aisle. Growing old isn't easy, but I never thought I'd want to give up on life. However, since Jack passed over I'm increasingly weary, tired of fighting and pretending all is well. Now I know that a large part of that is down to my heart problems. Inoperable, the doctor said, and I nodded, thinking that everything wears out eventually.

'I will double the dosage on your medication, but the side effects may increase. I want you to have a Medicare home alarm installed. It comes with a pendant to wear around your neck, which activates an alarm when it's pressed. You are sure about not informing your closest relatives?'

'I've had a long and happy life, Doctor Clarke. I have no regrets and when my time is up, it's up. That, I believe, is down to a much higher authority. If anything happens, I don't want my relatives having to make tough decisions. I think you know what I'm talking about here.' My gaze is direct and he shifts in his seat.

In reality I'm only referring to Adam. I know it's my own fault, as I'm aware that over the years I've pushed people away. Jack and I enjoyed each other's company, and then when Adam came to live with us ... At first it was easier to avoid people, rather than having to deal with their well-meaning sympathy. At that time words didn't help at all. We were a unit of three, and it was easier to manage our grief when the door was shut, and the world remained firmly outside. I realise Doctor Clarke is talking to me.

'Ah, right. Your records will be noted to reflect your wish. No matter what happens, your family will not be informed of your heart condition. Also, that you do not wish to be resuscitated, should the occasion arise. You can change your mind at any time, simply pick up the phone.'

'Thank you, but my mind is made up.'

He nods, briefly, then bends his head over my notes as his pen finalises what's been discussed. Like signing a contract, only this is a contract that will signal the end of my life.

When Jack appeared to me last night, he was standing in the corner of our bedroom. His presence seemed real; he looked across and smiled at me before he began talking.

'You look worried,' he'd said, his voice troubled.

'The usual, my dear. I worry so much about Adam. His job is demanding, and the hours he spends on the road when Lily is with her mother take a toll. He lives out of a suitcase one week out of every two, now. He admits there are times when he's so exhausted he's had to pull over and take a nap before finishing his journey. One day he could be in Cornwall, and the next several hundred miles away on the east coast. It's too much pressure, trying to organise his busy job so that he can be home-based when Lily is with him. He's the expert everyone wants to call in when their IT systems go down, or they get, what is it? Hacked? The more he does, the more they seem to want him to do. It isn't fair, and because he feels beholden to them for giving him flexibility, he ignores the risks he's taking.'

'He's a sensible and sensitive young man. He'll work through the problems and begin to realise that his life has to change.'

'I hope so, Jack, I really do.' My heart felt heavy and it was nothing to do with my health problems.

'Don't forget it's the doctor's tomorrow,' Jack reminded me, in a matter-of-fact fashion. He was wearing his green sweater, the one I bought for him only a couple of weeks before he died. The one I remember taking to the charity shop. 'I'm with you every step of the way. I'm keeping my promise, Gracie, so I don't want you to worry. I'm with you always.'

I wish I could see this life through Jack's eyes, as to me it feels like so many things are up in the air – how can I possibly not be worried about the future for Adam and Lily? Adam gave his heart away once and ended up being badly hurt, so now he's understandably wary. If he meets someone he finds interesting will he hesitate? Because if he does, then he'll only attract the sort of women who, like Kelly, are prepared to make the first move. That's not necessarily a bad thing, unless it indicates a desire to exert control. I just want to see Adam with someone who will be an equal partner, a woman who understands that love is all about the giving, and not the taking. I want him to find *the one* and be sure of that, before I can let go of this life.

I remember closing my eyes with a smile on my face and sinking into a peaceful sleep. I dreamt I was walking through a wood, dappled light from the sun overhead making it feel enchanted. Twigs snapped beneath my feet and the ground was soft and springy. A carpet of leaves, and moss, making my body feel as light as a feather. My mother appeared. She clasped my hand as she walked alongside me, without saying a word. Suddenly I felt as if I was floating, my feet no longer needing to take each step. It was wonderful and comforting, but first there is important work to be done and I know that she's only trying to give me the strength to see it through.

Caring Too Much Can Hurt

I have no idea why I took this order and agreed to deliver the cake in person. Hazel was right to be puzzled by it. Maybe it was the memory of the look on that little girl's face when she saw the princess cake carried through into the shop. As her eyes lit up, she turned to her dad and proclaimed it was the cake she wanted for her birthday. But that was months ago, and I'm amazed either of them remembered. I'm sure Adam could have found something similar locally, and saved himself a rather large delivery charge. Sometimes people are full of surprises though, and I love customers who are loyal, and come back time and time again. In this particular case, it does rather take loyalty to another level but, at the same time, I do feel extremely flattered.

I knew Steve would point out how ridiculous it was, but I have nothing to hide and intended to drop it into the conversation at some point. However, when he informed me he had a golfing getaway planned for the weekend, there didn't seem any point in bringing the matter up. He didn't ask if I had any plans, so it's not as if I lied to him.

He just had the all-clear from his recent battery of tests and, understandably, he's in a mood to celebrate. I assumed he was planning a weekend away for us. If I'm being honest with myself, it was a bit of a surprise when he'd elaborated.

'You don't mind, do you?' He'd sidled up next to me on the sofa and draped his arm around my shoulders. I felt that he was merely trying to avoid an upset. He didn't seem to be concerned about whether I was disappointed he'd chosen the guys over me.

'You go, and have a wonderful time. Let off a bit of steam, and don't think about work, or money, or me. Concentrate on having some fun, but go steady on the beers. And don't get talked into Jägermeister chasers. Remember the last time?'

His eyes sparkled as he tried to look suitably ashamed. For a moment I saw the 'old' Steve, the one I met and fell in love with: boyish, fun and a little unsure of himself.

'Funny how you can forget to pick up my suit from the dry cleaners, but you can't forget one night of excess. In my defence, it wasn't my idea.'

'Yes, I bet they all said that when they rolled home to their partners. But you need to take care of yourself, so everything in moderation. Please.'

He knew I was only thinking about his daily medication, and the fact that his alcohol consumption has to be kept to a minimum. I hoped he wasn't stupid enough to stop taking it, just so he could party. He wouldn't do that, would he?

My eyes scanned his face, wondering what was going on behind that macho façade. Maybe macho was too generic. Maybe the word I was looking for was stern, like a shutter he puts up whenever he wants to hide his real feelings. I began to wonder if he ever truly relaxed any more, or remembered that there was a time when the thought of dying terrified him. We talked openly then, his emotions spilling out of him like a torrent of tears. But he never cried, not once.

Having seen him through the most vulnerable period in his life, I would never have believed that I could look at him now in such a dispassionate way. I felt strangely detached, as if I didn't know him at all and was seeing him for the first time. If someone had asked for my first impression at that exact moment, I would have said *cold*. How very odd, when I'd known his passion and his heartache; held his hand as he cried out in pain. He hadn't been cold then.

'Sometimes,' Steve drew the word out, labouring a point, 'it's like having a partner and a mother rolled into one. I left home a long time ago, Katie.'

One second and his mood had changed completely. He pulled away, and I knew then that I'd succeeded in annoying him again. Would he purposely go out with the intention of making it a drunken weekend, simply to prove he could?

'I didn't mean ...'

'... to nag, I think you were going to say. So don't.'

I watched his back as he rose from his seat and walked away from me. Something deep inside screamed out. What am I doing? What point is there in a relationship where every step taken, every word spoken, has a fifty per cent chance of being misinterpreted?

Regrets

'I can't believe that last round. Luck of the devil.' Simon claps my back. 'Guess I'm buying the drinks. You're certainly on good form, at least tell me you've been practising.'

'No time, mate. If I'm not working, then I'm helping sort out Katie's business venture.'

As our little group walk into the main clubhouse, Simon signals for the barman to line up the drinks.

'Only one for me,' I add, quickly. 'Still taking the medication, so I'm going to be a lightweight.'

'No pressure. I have to say, though, it's great to see you looking so well these days. Is Katie having problems, then?' Gary jumps in, dispelling any awkwardness.

'She's passionate about the business, but she thinks with her heart and not her head. I've had to invest a chunk of money so she can expand. Without it, I doubt she would have lasted another year.'

'Mate, that's bad news. Not what you wanted at this point in your life. After the past couple of years, you deserve to be enjoying some quality time without any worries.' Simon raises his beer glass to begin the toast. 'To good times to come!'

Everyone joins in.

'It's okay, nothing I can't sort out, if she actually listens to me.'

A general grunt of agreement passes around the table.

'That's the problem, though, getting them to listen,' Gary says. 'Charlene keeps on about having another baby.

She tells me her body clock is ticking. No matter what I say, she won't let it go. I mean, man, two kids under three – we hardly get any time to ourselves, as it is. I needed this weekend jolly just to get away from the constant arguments. I mean discussions.' Gary, dejectedly, sinks half his beer in one go.

Simon diplomatically changes the subject, shooting Gary a look. The guys still feel awkward talking about their kids in front of me, knowing that it's no longer an option for Katie and me. I hate the fact that, no matter how much time has elapsed, my illness has changed some things forever. I look at my glass, tempted to sink it in one, but instead I join in the laughter as Simon tells another of his bawdy jokes.

Looking around the table, all I see is our once-young group of lads maturing into worried thirty year olds. All seem to be carrying the cares of the world on their shoulders. It's all about working to pay the mortgage, and the credit cards; juggling complex relationships with partners, or wives, and kids. Where did all the fun times go?

Have I become the man I am because of my illness, and where would I be if it hadn't happened to me? Where would my relationship with Katie be today if our lives hadn't been put on hold? What if I'd listened to her and we'd had a baby before I became sick? Is Katie's cake business a substitute for something I can no longer give her? I stalled over making the decision to have kids because I thought time was on our side. Suddenly it was too late, life events overtook us. It has become a regret that I have to live with, and the bitterness starts to rise as fast as I try to push it back down. It comes in waves, and then the anger follows. I join in with the laughter, although I've no idea at all what Simon has been saying.

No one can understand unless they've been through it themselves. What hurts the most is that I feel like a victim. I also feel that I've let Katie down, in more ways than one.

Gary hangs around until the end and we're the last two in the bar. I've been restricting myself to soft drinks most of the evening and I'm totally sober, but on edge.

'What's up?' The question is too direct to ignore without seeming rude.

'How do I know? Sometimes I feel like my life is one big mess. I can't recall when exactly it all began to go wrong, or why. Katie has stuck with me through all the hard times, and now I'm trying to pay her back by being frank about her business, she's pushing me away.'

'Heck, when it comes to giving advice about women, I'm the last person any sensible guy would ask. What I do know is that Katie is a catch, and without her support it would have been an even rougher journey for you these past few years. Don't take this the wrong way, Steve, but there are times when you can be rather hard-headed. Katie has put her heart into that business, and when she finally opened the shop I think it was a long-overdue boost for her, on several levels. You know, after all the tough times, it was something that she could lose herself in. Try not to rain on her parade, even if you can see the faults.'

Gary's words keep echoing around inside my head. Business is business, and pleasure is pleasure – surely even Katie can understand that? I wouldn't have her best interests at heart if I let her wallow in a false sense of security and ignore the problems Sweet Occasions is facing. If she had just let me take care of her and turned her back on the dream that will become a nightmare if she isn't careful, we wouldn't be going through this now. I had plans for my nest egg and it was a much better proposition than a cake business. But it would have meant a lot of hands-on involvement and spells working away from home. I knew Katie wouldn't be able to cope if she was left on her own for long periods of time. So the choice was easy because it's important to me that I'm there for her. I've already robbed her of one dream and there's no way I'm going to rob her of another. I'll do everything I can to steer her in the right direction and hope that, gradually, she'll let me get more involved. If she doesn't then we both have a lot to lose, and it's not just about the money.

Lily's Birthday

Katie

A Bright New Day

As soon as I draw back the curtains it's evident that it's going to be one of those truly stunning, autumnal days. The sky is that particular shade of blue that seems almost unreal, a colour that no artist's palette could ever do justice. Opening the window to welcome in the early morning breeze, the sound of birdsong is in sharp contrast to the usual sound of queuing traffic. Instead of the drone from idling car engines and tooting horns, the birdsong is deafening, if rather delightful. It does cross my mind that I must be mad driving all that way. I could so easily be in bed relaxing, with a leisurely day ahead of me. Instead I'm up with the lark, and sorting through my wardrobe for something vibrant to wear.

The drive takes longer than I thought, as I'd forgotten I'd be driving the small van. I could have taken my car, but the van is equipped with shelves and strapping to secure the cake boxes. The princess cake consists of three tiers. It's virtually a mini wedding cake and that's why the little girls love it so much. Adam said Lily's favourite colours were pink and white, which worked well for the cascade of intricate icing on the frothy top layer of the princess's gown. The figure stands about eighteen inches high. It's made up of the head and shoulders, upper body, and the skirt of the ball gown. Around the base of the cake are Cinderella-style slippers, an evening bag, and a little white puppy. It's the fairy tale of all cakes.

The van chugs along quite happily at fifty miles per hour, but speeding up makes for a bumpy ride. It's a risk I don't want to take. Driving on uneven road surfaces isn't much fun, but the time goes quickly. Passing abundant fields, trees, and woodland scenery, I do feel happy and rather relaxed. I stop to make a quick call to Adam, alerting him that I'm on my way, just running a little late. It doesn't seem to faze him at all. In fact, given the pounding beat of some rather loud music radiating out from the phone, in contrast his voice sounds rather calm.

The satnav takes me straight to the door, as easily as if I've been here before. The Beeches has a long front garden. It appears to sit on quite a secluded plot, considering there are newer, executive homes either side. The garden is beautifully manicured and the borders are heaving with a whole variety of colourful shrubs. Someone is a keen gardener, that's for sure, as this is a real labour of love. I follow the charming stepping-stone path to the front door and knock twice, then walk back to the van to begin unloading. Adam's voice calls out in the background.

'Lily, your surprise is here.'

An excited Lily shrieks out as soon as she sees the logo on the side of the van. She appears at my elbow, bouncing around and straining to see if she can catch a glimpse inside the van. There's little to see, except for a shelf of boxes.

'You brought me a cake!' she squeals, almost deafening me.

'Sorry.' Adam materialises and diplomatically guides Lily to step aside as I lift the largest box from the shelf. 'Can I help?'

'No, I'm fine, thanks. Just point me in the direction of the table.'

'Thank you so much, Dad.' Lily gives Adam a lopsided hug, her right arm sporting a fluorescent plaster cast. I'm sure she would have flung her good arm around me too, if my arms weren't wrapped around the big cake box.

The house is a surprise. I don't know what exactly I was expecting, but this is olde worlde charm personified. It looks like a former hunting lodge, and it's a couple of hundred years old at least. The windows are new, but sit within the original stone mullions. The front door is solid oak. I have to duck a little as I cross the threshold.

'Oh, I should have warned you about the door.' Adam apologises over his shoulder as he guides me inside. The tiny entrance hall leads through into a cosy sitting room, which has a large, working fireplace. I follow him on through into a good-sized dining room. The pine table has been lovingly waxed and polished; the pungent smell filling my nostrils reminds me of an old country manor I once visited.

'What a beautiful house.' The comment escapes my lips before I can engage my brain and remind myself this is a customer, not some old friend.

'Thank you, we love it here. It was the hunting lodge for Elkcombe Manor. Unfortunately, a lot of the surrounding land was sold off after my mother died, as the property was rented out for nearly ten years. Remarkably, my grandmother seemed to know I would want to come back here and make it my own home one day. There's enough garden wrapped around the lodge, though, to maintain a sense of privacy.'

'Can I show Katie my tree house?' Lily's eyes shine brightly at Adam as she hops from foot to foot, barely able to contain her excitement.

'I think we should let Katie sort out the cake first, don't you?'

'Why is there more than one box?' Lily asks, curiously.

'It comes in sections and I'm going to put the pieces together. I have some very special tubes of coloured icing in the van. Assembling it will take me about ten minutes. Half an hour in situ and the cake will be ready for cutting. You can give me a hand if you like.'

Adam smiles at me over the top of Lily's head. As I look up at him he's suddenly distracted when a rather attractive woman approaches.

'Bad news, I'm afraid.' She chews her lip, obviously concerned about the potential reaction.

Adam spins on his heels to face her. I busy myself putting the box down on the table, and carefully easing off the lid. There's a silver platter in the middle of the table, and I gently slide the lower tier of the cake out of the box, and onto it. Lily watches my every move, with a look of pure concentration on her face.

'What's happened?' Adam sounds concerned. I try my best not to look as if I'm listening. I keep my head bent as I adjust the position of the first tier of the cake.

'Perfectly Pretty have called to say someone has phoned in sick, so they can only send one person. With the best will in the world, she isn't going to be able to attend to all the girls.'

As I look across at Lily her mouth falls open, and her little brow creases. Instinctively she cradles her arm.

'Don't worry, Lily,' Adam jumps in to reassure her, 'we'll sort something out.'

'I'll help out in between arranging the buffet, but I'm useless with nails and I've never braided hair before.' The woman is now standing very close to Adam. She glances across at me for the first time, as if I've suddenly appeared on the scene.

'Sorry, this is Katie, from Sweet Occasions. Katie, this is my neighbour, Charlotte, who knows a heck of a lot more about arranging parties than I do. Her daughter, Emily, is Lily's best friend.'

Charlotte and I shake hands. She gives me a warm smile as her eyes sweep over me. I feel slightly uncomfortable, as if I've interrupted something.

'Dad, what are we going to do?' Lily begins to get visibly upset. Her hands fly upwards, covering her cheeks. The bad arm is forgotten in the midst of this news. Clearly she regards this as a total disaster.

'If you're stuck I can help out.' I wasn't even aware I was speaking until the words are out there. Charlotte peers at me, as if she's assessing my ability to be of use.

'I couldn't possibly ...' Adam begins, but Charlotte jumps in immediately.

'I think that's a great idea,' she says, extending her hand to touch Adam's arm. She gives it a gentle squeeze. 'If Katie wants to help, that's great.'

Adam frowns, his eyes darting back and forth between the two of us, then across at Lily. He looks like a rabbit trapped in the headlights of a car, and he isn't sure what to do.

'Katie's had a long drive and I don't think it would be fair to—'

'Nonsense, Adam. Katie has generously offered, and with a dozen girls turning up in an hour's time, I think it's the perfect solution.'

There's a moment's silence, and Lily appears to be holding her breath. I feel obliged to say something.

'I don't mind, really. I'm in no rush to get back, as I've nothing at all planned for today.'

This is awkward. The silence weighs heavily in the room.

'Please, Dad,' Lily begs.

'If you're sure you don't mind, Katie. It seems like yet another inconvenience, when you've already been good enough to travel all the way here.' Our eyes make contact and a little nervous quiver registers on his face. He makes no attempt to look away and I'm conscious that we're being watched.

'It will be fun,' I hear myself replying.

Fun? A dozen little girls? I must be crazy.

I make a final trip out to the van and then Adam and Charlotte head off into the kitchen, leaving me alone with Lily to assemble the cake. Moments later we are joined by Emily, who has clearly tired of trying to blow up the balloons.

'This is Emily,' Lily informs me. 'She's my best friend.'

'Hello, Emily. You're just in time to help as I have a very important job for you both. As soon as I've finished putting the princess together, there's a small box over there with some little gifts that will need to be placed around the bottom of her gown. It would be great if you can work together, as Lily will need your help, Emily.'

'These?' Lily gently picks up the small box with her good arm. I nod.

'Yes. But they have to be stuck onto the cake board with some very special icing. Emily, if you can grab the other box you can each choose a colour.'

Two heads peer into the box and after much deliberation, Lily chooses a tube of lilac icing and Emily chooses white.

'I need to snip off the end of the nozzles first.' Both girls hold out their respective tubes. As I make the cuts, icing begins to ooze out. They shriek with laughter and Emily instinctively places a finger under the dribble to catch the worm of sugary goo. Lily quickly lays her tube on the desk, so she can follow suit. The small matter of a plaster cast clearly isn't going to stop her joining in the fun.

'Mmm ... yummy.' Lily looks at Emily and rolls her eyes

as they both lick their fingers clean. Two smiling faces wait, hands poised and ready for action.

'Right. Let's see. Okay, here's the princess's cat. Now we don't want him to fall off, so I'm going to put a little bit of icing underneath and then place him here. You need to press down lightly and in a few minutes the icing sugar will dry and glue him safely to the board.'

Two furrowed brows peer up at me.

'Go on, choose something from the box and decide where you want it to go. Lily, you can put your icing sugar directly onto the board first, if that's easier.'

'I want the handbag!' shouts Lily.

'I choose the large box. I love presents. What are you getting for your birthday, Lily?'

I'm fascinated as they chatter away, clearly very comfortable in my company.

'Disco lights and a karaoke machine, I hope. That's if Dad gets it right, of course. Mum is taking me clothes shopping when she gets back. I'm going to ask her if I can get hair extensions. I bet she says no, though.'

Disco lights, hair extensions? I'd better re-think my cake range if at nine years of age their tastes are already changing. It seems there might be a gap between the Disney inspired cakes and the young teens range.

'What's the best present you've ever had?' I ask, tentatively. Both girls look at me and speak in unison.

'My iPad.' Is Lily's answer.

'My Kindle, but Mum is going to get me an iPad for my birthday. Lily has a keyboard with hers,' adds Emily, clearly impressed and maybe a little envious by the sound of it.

The level of confidence and awareness these girls have today is in sharp contrast to when I was their age. I'm pretty sure I was still playing with dolls. They continue to chatter away, while I collapse the boxes and tidy up.

'Mum always makes my cake and it never looks as good as this,' Emily confides, lowering her voice slightly.

'My mum usually makes mine, too. Last year I had a star cake. Don't you remember? All the chocolate buttons slid down the sides because the icing was too wet.'

They both start to giggle.

'Oh, yeah! We had to use spoons to scoop them up.'

Lily looks up at me, smiling. 'Katie, I love your cakes. I hope Dad buys one for me every year.'

'Don't be silly,' Emily jumps in. 'Next year it will be your mum's turn.'

The two girls exchange knowing glances. It's a comment which surprises me and the sad reality is that even at this tender age there's no escaping the harsh reality of life.

Adam

Fun and Games

Charlotte takes charge as soon as the girls begin arriving, and it's a relief. She's a great friend, but when Kelly and I split it could easily have been a very different story. They bonded, not just as neighbours, but their shared experiences of pregnancy and those early baby years forged a closeness that was obviously very special. I wouldn't say they were best friends exactly – the differences in their personalities was very obvious at times – but I wondered if Kelly's resentfulness towards me at the end would affect the way Charlotte felt about our friendship. However, she didn't judge, or take sides, and I guess because we'd been neighbours for a while before Kelly appeared on the scene, she knew enough about me to understand that I was truly devastated by what happened. I have no idea if she's saddened by the fact that Kelly chose not to remain in touch with her, but moved on in all senses of the word.

What I do know, for sure, is that Charlotte's husband, Max, is one lucky guy. I don't think he always appreciates that fact, if I'm being honest. Anyway, it's none of my business and I'm just very grateful that Charlotte and Emily are here for Lily.

I'm consigned to the kitchen to ferry through the platters of food, and the drinks. Katie is amazing; she seamlessly switches from assembling an awesome cake, to plaiting and braiding hair. I feel it's an imposition but she does seem to be enjoying herself, and is chatting away as if it's the most natural thing in the world to be here.

I catch glimpses of her as I walk back and forth. I

sincerely hope that Charlotte will remember Katie's a gracious volunteer, and not one of the Perfectly Pretty employees. As Katie deftly handles the hair, the other lady paints nails. Charlotte is busy showing some of the girls how to make beaded bookmarks.

Lily's face is aglow with happiness. The pain of the accident is no longer at the front of her mind. By the time Kelly flies back home, all will be well and that, too, is a relief. We might have a very good working relationship when it comes to looking after Lily, and parenting, but it isn't the same as being a family under one roof. There's always that pressure, that sense of being judged, whenever anything goes wrong.

Take today, for example. I should be able to run this party without a hitch. Instead I'm in the hands of three, admittedly delightful, ladies who have stepped in to rescue me. It's not that I'm not terribly appreciative, I am, but I feel like a bit of a spare part.

Instinctively my eyes go back to Katie as another peal of laughter makes me turn in her direction. Emily is in the chair and Katie is leaning over her, doing something with her hair that looks very complicated and involves frequent bursts of hair spray. Several girls, including Lily, are shrieking with laughter. Then Katie stands back and it looks like Emily has a cat sitting on her head. Everyone dissolves into laughter once more, but Emily's high-pitched voice rises above it, 'I love it!'

Charlotte looks my way and catches my eye. 'When you've finished, can you give me a hand here?' She holds up a snake of pink and purple beads, indicating for me to take over.

As I take the beads from her, her hand lingers against my arm. 'It's going well,' she whispers. 'Look at their faces, they're having fun.'

She increases the pressure on my arm lightly, indicating for me to lean in closer again, so she can whisper into my ear.

'You are a good father, you know, but kids can be a handful at times. Max would have already found some excuse to disappear, as he can't stand all the squealing and giggling.' She raises her eyebrows and nods slightly, before removing her hand.

'It's just that sometimes I feel a bit out of my depth. I don't want to fail my daughter in any way. It's bad enough her mother left and if it wasn't for the help I'm getting today, this could have been a total disaster of a birthday. You're a star.'

Charlotte's expression is one of sadness. I give her a grateful smile and walk away, feeling rather pathetic and with a string of beads swinging from one hand. As I pass Katie on my way back through to the kitchen, I wonder if it's too early to pour a glass of wine. We exchange tentative smiles and, to my dismay, I sense a hint of something behind those warm, green eyes. Is it disapproval? Does Katie think it's the easy way out to rely upon Charlotte to organise everything? Strangers often see things with a much clearer perspective.

As I push through the door, the cool breeze from the open kitchen window hits my face. It's a welcome relief. After a few minutes I feel calmer and more in control. 'Get a grip, Adam. You can handle this – it's only a birthday party and no one is judging you.' That little voice in my head seems to come out of nowhere.

Looking down at the beads in my hand, I start laughing, but the next thought that jumps into my mind instantly wipes that smile off my face. Is Lily missing out because when she's with me I can only do the best I can? What if it's not good enough? What if I'm not capable of being that naturally competent, single dad? I can already see the subtle differences between Emily and Lily whenever they are together. Lily is more of a worrier and she's always checking up on me, whereas Emily appears to be much more carefree. The trouble is, I don't know if that's normal for a child whose parents have split up, or whether it's because Kelly is better at parenting than I am. I don't want Lily to grow up thinking she has to feel responsible for me and that's something that hadn't crossed my mind before. That nagging little voice inside my head says, 'You need to sort yourself out, Adam, and man up.' It's like a virtual slap and maybe it's the wake-up call I need.

I thought Charlotte would stay until the end of the party, and I'm pretty sure that was her original plan. However, just after four o'clock her mobile rang and she had to leave rather suddenly. Her sister's car had broken down, and Charlotte went to collect her. Lily wanted Emily to stay overnight, so Charlotte said she would call round to collect her in the morning. Before she left, she kissed my cheek, at the precise moment that Katie was walking through with a tray of sandwiches. Katie immediately averted her gaze, clearly uncomfortable and I only hope she didn't read anything into it.

Shortly afterwards, all the girls settle down to watch a film. I leave a heap of beanbags and over-excited females all over the sitting room floor, grateful to be able to escape the noise. Walking into the kitchen, the lady from Perfectly Pretty is thanking Katie for helping out. She is all packed up and waiting to collect the cheque, eager to get on her way.

'Can I help you clear up?' Katie stands watching me as I begin stacking the plates.

'No, honestly, you should be heading back. You've done more than enough, and I need to settle up with you.'

She seems embarrassed, looking up at me and colouring a little. 'Oh, yes, of course. Your invoice is in the van. Look, it won't take long to clear this lot if we get stuck in. Let's sort this while the girls are quietly watching the film.'

'I'm not sure that can be called quiet, exactly.' I incline my head in the direction of the sitting room. Peals of laughter, and chatter, roll in and out like waves. 'Well, if you're sure. They're being collected at five-thirty. Fingers crossed the mums will begin arriving around about the same time as the film/movie finishes. I will admit that wasn't down to my great organisational skills, but pure luck.'

'A little luck can go a long way,' Katie says with a beaming smile. 'It's a great party and Lily is a lovely little girl. You must be so proud.'

'Thanks, I'm biased, of course, but I am. You're great with kids and multi-talented. I'm impressed and very grateful, believe me.'

She tips her head back, giving me a quizzical look. Then she laughs, good-naturedly.

'It's the artist in me.' Those green eyes mesmerise me. A hint of colour starts to work its way up her neck, then into her cheeks.

'Well, it must be nice knowing you have a fall back career as a hairdresser if anything ever goes wrong. Although that cake was pretty impressive, that's quite a skill you have there.' Am I flirting?

'And did you get to try it?'

'No, not yet. What flavour is it?'

I watch Katie carve a slice and expertly cut it into bite-size cubes. She spears one with a fork and passes it to me.

'Strawberry and vanilla.'

The cake literally melts in my mouth. 'Mmm, love it. You did an awesome job. I hope you're charging me a lot of money for this.'

It was an innocuous enough comment, but Katie looks startled. As if she's suddenly wondering what on earth she's doing here. The colour immediately drains from her face.

'Um ... right. I'll go fetch that invoice, then.'

When she returns to the room she's composed. She hands me the invoice and apologises for the fact that the transport cost is more than the cake.

'No, that's fine. I have absolutely no idea what we would have done if you hadn't been here today. You've been a lifesaver. I'd like to pay for your time, as well, if that doesn't offend you in any way?' Suddenly, it seems very important not to wade in and make her feel uncomfortable again.

'That's not necessary, it was my pleasure. Sorry about going blank, but I had this sort of déjà vu moment. Doesn't that feel freaky, you know, when you experience something you could swear has happened to you before?'

'Hmm ... I've had that a couple of times and, yes, it does feel weird. I hope the lodge hasn't spooked you. It might be old, but there aren't any ghosts here – well, none I've discovered. There were a few tenants over the years, but it seems they were mostly professionals, leading relatively quiet lives. I believe someone died here back in the eighteen hundreds, but if they do wander around at night, it doesn't disturb us.'

'Oh, I wasn't implying the lodge had a bad vibe. No, this was a pleasant feeling, like I'd been here before. It's a very warm and welcoming place. Easy to feel at home here.'

And you look good here, Katie. You look like you belong. Unsure of where that thought came from, I say the first thing that comes into my head, just in case my thoughts are reflected in my face.

'As a boy it was paradise. The garden was huge and there was an orchard and a large pond. My mother employed a part-time gardener, and that's where my love of gardening began. I spent hours helping out and in the process I learnt a lot about plants and planting. My mother was a songwriter and although her name wasn't instantly recognisable, many of her songs were instrumental in taking unknowns to their first chart-topping hit. This was a house filled with music and love. Sadly, she died when I was only ten years old and I didn't inherit her incredible talent, but I do play the guitar. She was a wonderful pianist and some would have said, gifted.'

Well, that wasn't exactly a throwaway conversation, was it? What's wrong with me? I can tell by the look on her face she's feeling sorry for me now. Oh, that's so not the way to make an impression on someone you find utterly captivating.

'That must have been heart-breaking for you when she died.' Her words are almost a whisper. I nod my head, sadly. Actually, it feels good to hear the words that have been buried deep inside of me for so many years finally spoken out loud.

'Devastating. Grandma Grace, Pop and I hid from the world for a while. So much fuss over her funeral, but it didn't feel real, as most of the people weren't family, but linked to the celebrity industry she worked in. We understood they wanted to honour her and what she had achieved, but the real loss was in that of her role as a daughter and a mother.'

Surprisingly I feel calm. Katie's eyes seem to reflect empathy, not pity. She's a person who seems to understand that darkness within, the words you can't normally voice.

'The one thing I regretted was that she never told Grace who my father was and for many years I harboured an anger about that. As a teen I went through a phase of feeling bitter, thinking that somewhere out there was a man whom, I guessed, had no idea he had a son. I'd been robbed of my mother and she, in turn, had robbed me of a father.'

She looks directly at me, as if surprised by the matter-of-fact tone in my voice. There is no anger or bitterness in me now.

'What changed your mind?'

'I was going through one of her photograph albums. Most of the photos were of me and even though I never, ever doubted her love, I realised that there was no way she would have kept something from me unless it was for a good reason. Grace, too, was a very loving and understanding mother. If Mum couldn't share it with us, then it meant she'd been rejected. She made a mistake with someone she thought she could love, who broke her heart and turned his back on her. He would have had to be a very hard person to do that to someone as lovely as my mother. She did what she thought was best for the people she loved the most. She was protecting us. You can't miss someone who never wanted to be a part of your life in the first place. When the realisation dawned, it made me love her even more.'

Her eyes are sorrowful. That was too heavy, Adam, she's a guest and you don't want to make her cry over stuff that's way in the past.

'Wow – sort of let it all out a bit there. Sorry, Katie. I don't often talk about her. Guess that's why.' I stop to clear my throat. 'I like to think she's still around, if you know what I mean. Mind you, if I ever saw an actual ghost I don't know what I'd do. Probably run!'

Her laugh is gentle and warm, like an embrace.

'How wonderful that the house was kept in the family and not sold. Grace is one admirable lady, that's for sure.'

And now it's awkward, as it's time for money to exchange hands and I don't want to offend her. For whatever reason, we've just shared a meaningful moment that was totally unexpected. It's hard to let go of that and it seems almost rude to get down to business. I hope she doesn't feel I've taken advantage of her good nature, the fact that she's a good listener.

'Look, thanks for everything today. It means a lot. It wouldn't have been the same without you here and I appreciate that, so does Lily. You came a long way and the cake was the highlight of the party.' As I hand her the cash, I offer her an additional three twenty pound notes for her time, but she declines with a genuine smile. I sense that she understands my dilemma and isn't offended.

'No, it was my pleasure, really. Please tell Lily I enjoyed her party.'

'I'm sure she'd like to thank you for the cake ...'

'Don't interrupt them now. Besides, she already gave me a thank-you hug and it's easier if I just slip away. Will you be down at Christmas?'

I nod.

As we walk to Katie's van we discuss Grace's Christmas cake.

'You're my first order for the festive season.' She turns to face me, and we look at each other, not knowing quite what to say next.

We shake hands, and I have a distinct feeling that I'm mishandling our goodbye. I should give her a thank-you hug, as Lily had done. The slight hesitation that passes between us is about having connected on a much deeper level, as I can sense Katie, too, is holding back. We're two people who have been suddenly thrown together to share the same bizarre day. It was Lily's first party on my watch, without Kelly here to supervise. Whether that explains why I'm feeling this weird mix of emotions today, I'm not sure. I ended up sharing something way beyond personal; something I couldn't even share with Grace or Pop. I guess Katie is one of those rare people in life you meet who just happen to be on the same wavelength. She wasn't shocked by my outpouring, understanding that I wasn't looking for comfort or kind words. It was just a curious moment when it felt right to finally get it all off my chest. What I feel is relief.

As the van disappears out of sight, I find myself picturing those twinkly green eyes.

'What a day,' I murmur out loud. 'Thank you lovely Katie.'

Why is it that the women you'd like to get to know are all in relationships? Doh! Because guys don't hang around when they spot a good one, well, unless their name is Adam, of course. All I know is that after Kelly, I won't be jumping into anything permanent in the near future. But all the same, it's a real shame ...

Katie

The Point of No Return

Driving home from the party it felt like I had stepped outside of my life for a short time and entered a world I hardly recognised. It was full of fun, laughter, a lot of giggling and a bewildering insight into the life of a nine-year-old. When they get together they gossip, get hyper at the mention of their favourite boy band, and talk over each other all the time. It was chaos, pure chaos and yet it was a tonic. So far removed from my day-to-day reality that it was a breath of fresh air. Life through the eyes of a child is very different and I'd forgotten that. Once you become an adult, unless you are around children up close and personal, you forget the innocence and the boundless energy. That naively optimistic way of looking at things without all the worry attached.

I really enjoyed being a part of it, though. There were awkward moments, of course, because essentially I was an interloper and I sort of invited myself to stay. My role wasn't one of supportive friend or neighbour, and Charlotte had that firmly sewn-up. But I also wasn't there in an official capacity, like the lady from Perfectly Pretty. It was interesting, therefore, to see the different reactions I received. At one point the girls were all over me, treating me like a best friend.

'Katie, can we do your hair? Please?' Naomi was the tallest of the girls, although she was still only eight years old.

'I think we should put combs in Katie's hair,' Lily immediately jumped in.

Not to be outdone, Emily, who never moved far from Lily's side, elbowed her way into the circle standing around me.

'I think ribbons would be fun.'

Before I knew it, there were a dozen voices directing Naomi and holding out an eclectic assortment of hair decorations. It was Charlotte who rescued me.

'Girls! Quieten down. Poor Katie, seems like I arrived just in time. I think Adam needs some help making those party bracelets for you to take home. Between you and me, girls, he isn't very good at choosing colours that coordinate. Why don't you go and help him out? Katie and I can then begin clearing the table ready for the cake.'

There was a chorus of squeals and, as the girls headed off, I looked across at Adam as they descended upon him. Poor guy, I think this is the first time he'd been subjected to a whole group of them at once. Every time we passed throughout the afternoon he looked like he needed a reassuring hug. I noticed, too, that Charlotte stepped into that role. Another unhappily married woman, I wondered?

After she 'rescued' me, we spent a few minutes talking while clearing the table.

'Poor Adam, I did warn him and told him a small birthday tea with just a couple of friends would be more manageable. He's doing the *single dad* thing and over-compensating.'

She smiled and I smiled back, but I noticed her eyes were appraising me.

'Well, for me this is an eye-opener. It's my first real exposure to a girls' birthday party and I had no idea they had this much energy. I'm exhausted already.'

'Oh, they'll suddenly tire and then they go from jumping

around to sleepy and grumpy in a heartbeat. You don't have any children of your own, then?'

It was a natural enough question, I suppose, but still it surprised me.

'No. I have too much invested in my business to even think about that sort of thing.' It's not quite the truth, but it will do. Again, her eyes had flicked over my face and I wondered what she was thinking.

'Ah, it's not easy building a business. Being free and single allows you to be focused. The minute you settle down, everything changes.' Her eyes left my own, to seek out Emily and Lily. Or maybe she was taking a moment to check on Adam, I'm not sure.

'You must have arranged quite a few parties, then. Did you say it was Adam's first?'

She immediately spun her head back around to face me. There was a hint of curiosity in her gaze.

'Yes, Kelly was a great organiser and if she wasn't away on a business trip she'd no doubt be organising this – much to Adam's annoyance, I suspect. Splits are never easy. But he's doing well. My husband wouldn't have lasted five minutes before he snuck away to watch football or something on TV. Too much noise for him, but then he has other distractions to keep him occupied at the moment. Sadly, Emily and I aren't top of the list. Adam dotes on Lily, but I expect you've already noticed.'

What is it with married couples these days? Judging by her tone, that's another relationship teetering on the edge. Was she trying to make a point?

'Oh, um, I don't really know Adam, or Lily. We get a lot of lovely people through the doors of Sweet Occasions and because buying a special cake is a happy time, they often share their stories.'

'I guess some are more interesting than others?' She raised an eyebrow and my mouth went dry. Charlotte seemed keen for me to stay when I offered, but perhaps she regretted it with hindsight. I didn't have any hidden motives and I hoped she could see that.

'They're all interesting and diverse. Adam's grandmother, for instance. And then when he brought Lily into the shop her eyes were everywhere. I will admit our displays give you a sugar rush just looking at them!' It was my attempt to lighten the moment and I realised it was nerves talking. I wanted to hand the conversation back. 'This place is so unexpected and tucked away, considering the new builds surrounding it.'

'Yes, our house next door was one of the first to be built when some of the vast garden was sold off. I would have loved to have seen it before the development. It must have been hard for Adam's grandparents, losing their daughter at such a young age. I don't know the full story, of course, he never talks about it. I only know that Adam lived here with his mother until her death. I gather that when he went to live with Grace and Jack it was rented out for quite a number of years. I don't think either of them ever lived here, only Grace's parents. He told me once that the land was sold off because it was too much for them to cope with. That's understandable, given the fact that they suddenly found themselves with a young boy to care for. I don't know why they didn't just sell the property, although I'm not sure what effect that would have had on Adam. He has his heart tied up in this old place. I don't think he'll ever move from here.' She looked directly at me, waiting to see my reaction to her words. It felt wrong to be discussing Adam with Charlotte, as if I knew him on a personal level.

'That's understandable. It's a sad story.' It struck me that letting go of it would probably feel like letting go of his mother all over again. Charlotte seemed to understand that much, which was very clear.

For some reason I can't remember what she said next. I only remember the girls' faces when the candles were lit, shortly before she left. I do remember her kissing Adam on the cheek. It wasn't passionate, but it was still a kiss.

And then it was just Adam and me, alone together while the girls watched a film/movie. He's special. There's something interesting about him that I can't put into words. I could sit and watch him talking for hours, without hearing a word he says. But what I discovered was that when he bares his inner turmoil, those words say so much about the person he is and about his pain. His heart is fragile, covered with so many scars it might be impossible to peel them away so he can be set free. When he talks about Grace, or Lily, he lights up. But what lurks beneath the surface clearly holds him back. You get to glimpse it occasionally, almost as if he forgets to put the mask back in place.

His face has this gentleness, like the boy in him has never gone away. That square jaw and cleft chin of his are fascinating, in a macho, rugged sort of way. His hair is dark, almost black, short on the back and sides, but longer on the top and unruly, which suits him. It seems to frame that smile of his, perfectly. Looking at him you find yourself wanting to take a comb to it, or get out the hair gel. Annoying, but charmingly so. Clearly the only facial feature Lily inherited from Adam is her delightfully dimpled chin. Thankfully it's much softer and rather cute, setting off that heart-shaped face I assume came from her mother. She has the same hair colouring, but her hair is a mass of curls, bouncing around her shoulders every time she turns her head.

I catch myself sighing and decide enough is enough. I've had a lovely day, but now it's time to step back into my own life. I suspect it's a very natural thing to peek into someone else's life and become wistful. What if? If only. Maybe my own inner pain is something Adam can sense. Two people scarred by life and just trying to live one day at a time.

I reach across and press play on the car's CD player, hoping to break a chain of thoughts that I know are just going to end up making me feel sad. I'm not quite ready to let go of the little bubble of happiness that's floating around me after today's experience. It feels like a guilty pleasure, because I know it's not solely about having helped to make a little girl's birthday party a success.

Steve walks through the door about an hour after I get home. He's definitely more relaxed after his guys' weekend away, and immediately things are less tense between us. The fresh air has clearly done him some good and there's a hint of colour to his face from the time spent outdoors. Autumn sunshine is a bonus and it was exactly what he needed.

'Did you have a good time?' I follow Steve as he disappears into the kitchen.

'It was okay.'

I grab two glasses while he selects a rather nice bottle of Chianti Classico from the wine rack.

'Are we celebrating?'

He laughs. 'The wanderer returns. I missed you.'

I feel myself colouring up, hoping he doesn't ask about my day. 'Well, I missed you, too. So how were the guys?'

I feel bad purposely trying to steer the conversation away from talking about what I've been doing, but I sense he's in the mood to chat. He pours the usual small glass for himself and a large one for me.

'My game was on great form, much to the annoyance of everyone else. There were the same old gripes and moans. Charlene wants another baby and Gary isn't keen. That, of course, leads to the usual awkward moments and the subject of my health crops up again. Then someone diplomatically steers the conversation away from talking about kids and Gary goes on a guilt trip. I know the guys mean well, but I'm over it now. I did mention Sweet Occasions and Gary said something that made me stop and think.'

He raises his glass and we chink. I take a cautious sip, wondering what's coming next.

'He said I shouldn't be too hard on you. I think his words were that I could be rather hard-headed when it comes to business. I'm not trying to take the business away from you, quite the reverse. I'm beginning to think that it will bring us even closer together. I've put you through a lot, Katie, and I do know that.'

It isn't easy for Steve to bring this up and the fact that he's been talking to Gary means he wanted a second opinion. Gary has no business acumen, so this is personal. It makes me feel sad to think that he senses unhappiness in me, when even I don't know how I feel at the moment. How can you discuss things you don't understand and can't put into words?

'This isn't about you, Steve. It's about me. Change is scary, it's a journey into the unknown. I'll be honest with you, in that it's taken me a while to get my head straight. But sometimes the dream has to change and I'll get there, really I will.'

'I love you, Katie. I don't want you to change, that's

not what this is all about. I'm here for you and the energy I've been throwing into my career can easily be diverted. Helping you take Sweet Occasions to the next level is an exciting prospect for me, too. How involved I get is up to you, but at the moment I feel you are keeping me at arm's length. Growing businesses is what I do, but usually my involvement is a short-term thing and then I get to walk away. This could be our dream, our future together.'

I can hear the passion in his voice and the genuine concern. His motives aren't purely financial and I've known that for a while. He's reaching out to me because he senses the divide that is opening up between us. He's giving me the power to stop that happening. My heart constricts because I'm just not ready to pick back up where we left off before our life was torn apart. At one point I thought he was going to die, so I locked my feelings away and now I'm afraid to open that door and see what remains.

Sitting down together, we run through the week's sales figures. For the first time ever Steve doesn't explode, or lecture me. When he sees the bottom line he merely shoots me a disappointed look.

'Hey, it's been a good week overall, which is something. When do the builders finish?'

'There are only a few items remaining on the snagging list. That's mostly touching up some paint, and re-laying the threshold strip to take out a lip.'

'That's my girl, health and safety is important. Look, I know you said you didn't need me at the shop, but it's important you have time now to up the pace. What if I take this week off to help out? I'll oversee the last of the snagging, and join Hazel front of house. You can chase up those leads I gave you for the two coffee shops, and the visitor centre over at Hillborough. It's not only about extra sales outlets, but about getting your brand name out there. A lot of your customers are locals, or passing trade, so you need to be pushing further and further afield to increase your visibility. There are three other towns all within a twenty minute drive, and that's a lot of people with easy access.'

When Steve talks to me in this fashion, it's hard not to listen. It's the old him again, and there's no hint of anger, or recrimination in his voice. Instead of making me feel like a failure, it reminds me that he does care.

'Come on.' He places his hand over mine. 'You know it makes sense. And I'm not thinking of my investment, it's simply the next step.'

'I know, and I'm grateful. But I don't want you to get behind on your work; don't you have anything on this week?'

'Nothing that can't wait, and I think this is more important. It's for my girl.'

It's not so much about my concern for his own business, consultancy work often involves evening or weekend meetings with clients, so I know his work pattern isn't nine-to-five. And the peaks and troughs are huge. When he's involved in getting a new project off the ground he shuts himself away for hours on end and sometimes has the odd night away. A part of his job often entails setting up the financial monitoring systems for a new business, but a lot of that goes over my head.

It appears that this week he's at a loose end. A sigh escapes my lips before I can stop it and I tense, wondering if he'll take offence. However, his mood is mellow and instead he grabs my hand and gives it a squeeze. I nod in agreement and am rewarded with a dazzling smile.

*   *   *

That night, lying in bed next to Steve, my mind is whirling. I tell myself it's only natural that my head is all over the place, as the business is demanding every moment of my time. Truthfully though, there is something deeper gnawing away at me. Every now and then Adam's face stares back at me from inside my head.

I keep recalling little gestures. The way his face crinkles when he smiles. His expression when he looks at Lily is one of pure, unconditional love. Is it wrong to lie in bed next to your partner and think about another man? Of course it is; what am I thinking? I'm not free, I've made a commitment. Besides, Steve needs me.

Then I remember the moment I nearly embarrassed myself. I thought Adam said that he loved me! What he actually said was that he loved the cake, and that I'd done a great job. Talk about wishful thinking. The shock registered on my face immediately. I had to pretend I'd had one of those déjà vu experiences in order to explain away my reaction.

None of this is helping to empty my head of thoughts and the moment I relax Adam is back. His eyes are so intense sometimes, as if the words you are speaking aren't enough. He wants to see beyond mere words. For a man, he's very in touch with his emotions, despite the fact I'm pretty sure he'd deny it. I'm inviting trouble by thinking about him, because it's a pointless exercise. It's making me feel disloyal and it's unsettling. I'm not a dreamer, and yet Adam has turned me into one. Daydreams are empty wishes. Even if we do get on well, that in itself doesn't mean a thing.

He's an attractive man, and his neighbour, Charlotte, is a sophisticated woman. There's a sense of glamour and worldliness about her, which makes me feel very dull in comparison. Why would Adam even consider looking at me, when clearly he's used to more captivating company? I suspect Kelly was from the same mould.

I'm doing it again. I can't believe it! Has Adam said one single word that indicates he likes me in any way, shape, or form? No. I feel like a teenager analysing an encounter with a boy she's met. Not only is it ridiculous, but it has a sting to it.

Enough! I will my brain to switch off. Instead of counting sheep, I think about a spreadsheet and how on earth I'm going to solve my financial problems. Sleep comes soon after, and all thoughts of Adam fall to the back of my mind.

Adam

The Games People Play

After the partygoers had all been collected, two over-excited girls had a long chat with Grandma Grace. Each interrupted the other as they filled her in on the details of the party. They fell into bed around nine o'clock, totally exhausted. It was at least another hour before silence reigned.

However, Lily and Emily were awake before six this morning. I had to pull the pillows over my head in order to drown out some of the chatter. At seven o'clock I was desperate for coffee and made my way downstairs.

Wandering out into the garden, the chill of the early morning autumnal air is refreshing. We survived yesterday, and everyone seemed to think the party was a success. I know I couldn't have done it by myself.

'Penny for your thoughts.' Charlotte's voice carries through the air, as she walks up behind me.

'You're an early riser. Coffee?'

'Mm, please. I came to ask you a favour. I guessed the girls would have woken you up already. My sister's car is being recovered at nine o'clock this morning. I'm heading out now to pick her up, so we can meet the truck and hand over the keys. Max is away until tomorrow, and I was wondering if I could drop by to collect Emily when I get back?'

Charlotte follows me into the kitchen and I hand her a mug of coffee.

'Thank you.' Her gaze sweeps over my face. 'You're a nice guy, Adam. That was a lovely thing you did for Lily, yesterday. Most dads would have opted for something a little easier.' Her voice is soft and there's an undercurrent of emotion in her words.

'Next time I'll have a better plan of action. You, and Katie, saved the day. Of course Emily can stay. I'm here all day, so don't feel you have to rush back.'

'You do know, I was always a little bit jealous of Kelly,' Charlotte murmurs the words, wistfully. 'No matter what went wrong between the two of you, at least you were faithful. Pity I can't say the same for Max.'

I gulp down a mouthful of coffee a little too fast and it catches in my throat, sending me into a fit of coughing. To my dismay, Charlotte puts her mug down on the counter top and steps forward. She extends her arm around my shoulders to pat me gently on the back. I feel like the air has been knocked out of me. That's a bombshell I wasn't expecting. I know Charlotte and Max have been going through a rough patch for a little while. I didn't think it was that serious, but then I had no idea Max was having an affair. However, Charlotte is well aware that I'm the last person to come to for any sort of relationship advice. One look at her face tells me she didn't mean to blurt it out. Tears start to glisten in her eyes.

'Oh, don't mind me. I'm just feeling a little sorry for myself at the moment. What I actually wanted to say was, what a lovely person Katie is and how kind of her to help out yesterday.' She swallows hard, maintaining her composure.

'Yes, I kind of underestimated how much supervision was needed, didn't I?'

Charlotte shoots me a glance, her chin quivering a little as she attempts a hollow laugh.

'I did tell you it was rather ambitious for your first solo

party. It went well, though, and you have to stop worrying about every little thing. Maybe it hasn't occurred to you, but when you and Kelly were arguing all the time, that had a really profound effect on Lily. Yes, she was very upset when you decided to call it a day and go your separate ways, but you have to take some of the credit for the way she's adjusted. You underestimate how instrumental you've been in helping her make that transition, Adam. It hasn't been exactly easy for you, either, but you always put Lily's needs first – unlike some other fathers I could mention.'

Charlotte seems to have known a lot more about what was happening in my marriage at the time than I'd realised. I know some things still remain unsaid, but that's for a very good reason. I never wanted her to be the friend in the middle of two very different versions of one truth. The *he said/she said* thing is pointless. No one wins, do they?

'I feel when Lily's with me I have to take on the role of both parents, but I don't know how to do that.' What I can't bring myself to admit is that a lot of the time I'm scared of doing, or saying the wrong thing.

'Don't be so hard on yourself, Adam. You're doing fine and Lily is thriving, that's all that matters. But what about *you*? When Lily is with Kelly you have to start building some sort of life of your own, too. It's something I've been meaning to say for a while, but I know how you hate talking about it. It's just that meeting Katie yesterday set me thinking. She was here to deliver a birthday cake, sure, but I'm sensing there's something a little more to it, am I right?'

Her words stop me in my tracks. If Charlotte picked up on the fact that I find Katie interesting, does that mean Katie can see that, too? Oh no, this is bad, really bad! Should I be honest here, or sidestep this conversation?

'She's easy to talk to and friendly, that's all. I was impressed by the way Katie talks to Lily, not at her, as strangers often tend to do when they are merely trying to make polite conversation. It's important to engage with a child and listen to what they say.'

Charlotte nods, fixing her eyes on me and I shift from foot to foot, literally squirming beneath her enquiring gaze.

'But you're interested enough to want to get to know her a little better?'

My mind goes blank as I search around for something innocuous to say. Then I give in.

'Yes, I'm curious about her. You know me, I've always been rather awkward around new people, but I feel surprisingly relaxed with Katie. I'm not very adept at small talk.'

Charlotte laughs, as she discreetly wipes away a small tear that has formed at the edge of her left eye. I pretend not to notice.

'Well, that's one way to describe your appalling lack of suitable chat-up lines. However, in this case I don't think you have anything at all to worry about. I'd say that Katie is also curious about you and that's a very good start.'

'Thanks for that. I didn't make a fool of myself at all yesterday, did I?' I know Charlotte will give it to me straight.

'Oh, I think I can safely say you impressed her. I only chatted with Katie briefly, but I was intrigued by the fact that she was prepared to come all this way to help out a stranger.' Her eyes twinkle, mischievously.

'Oh no, you didn't grill her?'

'No, just friendly chatter.' Charlotte walks towards the door, then suddenly turns on her heels to face me again. 'And Adam, I'm sorry about just now. Max is just going through one of those awful moments in life when he's begun to question what the future holds. You know, none of us is getting any younger and he's under a lot of pressure at work. I guess we have both became a little complacent, that's all, and this has been our wake-up call. We'll get through it. The grass is rarely greener on the other side and he knows that. The thing is, I love him more than he loves me. Life, eh? It's not always easy.'

I regret my total inability to know what to say in a situation like this, but I'm way out of my depth and I'm better off saying nothing, rather than something that might upset her. Instead, I go up to Charlotte and give her a friendly hug. The look of sorrow on her face is painful to see and I can only hope that Max comes to his senses before it's too late.

Katie

Autumn Chills

Steve's week helping out in the shop didn't quite go as expected. It ended with him hiring a junior assistant to work alongside Hazel to 'free-up' my time. He said I would be better able to manage things without the constant pressure of being behind the counter and I would also be able to do more in the kitchen.

It turned out to be a wise decision. With three new contracts to supply the outlets in Hillborough on a daily basis, we were under a lot of pressure. Fortunately, once everyone had settled into the new routine, it seemed to be working well. I know Hazel felt a little put out at first, but she soon took the new recruit, Marcie, under her wing. The only day I now manage to get out into the shop is on Wednesday, Hazel's day off.

Days are frenetic, and at the moment we're up to our eyes in orders for wedding cakes. Apparently there will be a lull in November, before another rush in December. However, the venues all seem to be indicating that the lull will be very short-lived. I take Steve's advice to book a deep clean of the kitchen for the last Sunday in October.

It's nice to be in work without the usual hubbub of activity going on. I'm there at six in the morning to open up for the cleaning company who get started in the kitchen, while I begin the task of working on the display cabinets. It's a dry day, with a strong wind bringing an icy blast. There's hardly anyone at all in the street as I glance up from my position, crouched in the window. Suddenly, I find myself looking down at a pair of feet.

'Sorry, we're closed,' I call through the glass. My eyes travel upwards and I'm surprised to see Adam grinning back at me.

'Oh, hang on a moment, I'll find the keys.'

As I rush around looking for them, I feel distinctly self-conscious. Adam waits patiently, his shoulders hunched against the cold wind. Eventually finding them in my coat pocket, my hands shake a little as I struggle to insert the key in the lock. Finally the door swings open.

'Hi, this is a surprise. I wasn't expecting to see you for a little while.'

My voice has a slight waver to it, and I groan, inwardly. Why am I always so nervous when he's around? Adam steps inside and I can feel the colour warming in my cheeks.

'Grace isn't very well at the moment and I've come up to spend a few days with her. Look, I don't want to stop you working. It's bad enough you have to come into the shop on a Sunday, let alone put up with interruptions. That was a real surprise, though, spotting you in the window as I was driving past. When I saw you, I jumped on the brakes. It seemed wrong to drive past without popping in to say a quick belated thank you for what you did at the party.'

He doesn't step forward but continues to stand, framed in the doorway. A part of me acknowledges that I should be working and that Adam is giving me an excuse to cut his visit short.

'I was about to stop for coffee. Do you have time to join me? I hope it's nothing serious … with your grandmother.'

While it's good to see him, it saddens me to hear the reason for his visit. His face registers a hint of concern and the smile drops from his lips.

'It's nothing she'll acknowledge openly, or talk to me about. Her neighbour, Marie, rang to say she was a little worried. I've engineered this trip to assess things, driving over on the pretext that there are a few little jobs that need doing in the house. I also want to see for myself how well she's coping at the moment.'

I indicate for him to take a seat in the new cake-tasting area.

'Wow, this looks extremely smart.'

'Thanks. The kitchen is now double the size, plus we have triple the storage capacity. I was worried about losing that back room, but it was a luxury. In reality, reducing the number of tables and moving it into the front of the shop is more practical. We sometimes get a group of people come in if it's a tasting for a wedding cake, but usually it's just mothers and offspring going through the brochures and sampling different flavours.'

'They did a great job. It was a pity to lose the country feel, though, it felt very personal.'

Adam's words remind me of the arguments I had with Steve at the planning stage. I look around at the now crisp, plain walls and the perfectly-lit photographic displays of over-sized cupcakes.

'It's not my style, either, and it felt a bit like selling out, to be honest. Apparently today it's all about swish presentation, while keeping the reference to a handmade product, therefore inferring a higher quality. Albeit the "product" will in the not too distant future be produced in a large industrial unit that has the ambience of a stainless steel cube.'

'Well, I can certainly vouch for the wonderful flavours.' There's sympathy in his smile and in his eyes as they search mine. I shrug; each day it hurts a little less.

I pull two chocolate melting moment cupcakes from the display cabinet and place them on a plate in front of him.

'These look good.'

I have to raise my voice a little to talk over the noise of the coffee machine.

'Left over from yesterday and they will go in the bin tomorrow morning. I'm glad you dropped by, I'll box some up for you. I hate waste. Yesterday was quieter than usual because there was a fete in one of the neighbouring towns. That's why shops which rely on passing trade often struggle, or so my partner, Steve, never tires of telling me.'

Our eyes lock and a strange moment hangs in the air between us. Adam clears his throat, nervously, and there's a sadness in his eyes that touches my heart. He can't hide his anxiety over the reason for this trip.

'You really are concerned about your grandmother, aren't you?' As usual, the words are out before I have time to consider whether or not it's appropriate, or over-familiar.

'Yes, more than I'm letting on. She's often short of breath when I ring her and keeps telling me that's down to some new tablets she's taking. She says it's one of the side effects, but our telephone calls are getting shorter and shorter.'

He looks away, his voice sombre. 'She's my sole surviving grandparent.' He clears his throat in an effort to pull himself together and picks up the cappuccino in front of him. I feel it's the right thing to change the subject, but I don't quite know what to say next.

'Well, it's all go here!' It doesn't come out as breezily as I'd hoped. He shoots me a glance, picking up on the inflection in my tone.

'Problems?'

Stupidly, for no apparent reason whatsoever, tears begin to prick at my eyes. It catches me unawares. I hold my breath, frantically fighting a desire to give in to them.

'Not really.' Oh heck, who am I kidding? We're strangers who pass in the night, well, day. What harm can it do? I shrug my shoulders and move my head to take in everything around me. 'What price, a dream?'

He seems stunned. 'But I thought business was going from strength to strength.'

'It is, but it doesn't feel like my dream any more.'

He places his cup back down on the table and looks at me, soberly.

'I'm so sorry to hear that. I'm a good listener if you need a sympathetic ear. Sometimes it helps to let it all out.'

The moments pass, seconds turning awkwardly into minutes as I struggle to compose myself.

'It's complicated.' I sigh, dejectedly. My fingers toy nervously with the cup in front of me.

'In my experience, life in general is never straightforward. But then I seem to have this aptitude for messing up.' His laughter is comforting. It's like sitting down with an old friend, but I have to remember that isn't the case.

'I wouldn't know where to begin,' I reply, hesitantly. Even if I wanted to, what could I possibly tell him that wouldn't sound like I was being ungrateful?

'Hey, all will probably sort itself out in the end, but I know how hard it can be when you bottle things up. I spend a lot of time trying to make sure Lily doesn't sense my worries, or concerns. I've become an expert at running away from things, rather than confronting the problems head-on. Sorry, I shouldn't have said that. I only meant to pop in ...'

Adam looks mortified and pushes his chair back, ready to stand up.

'No, really, it's fine. Stay and finish your coffee. It will be a shame to throw those cupcakes away tomorrow. You're quite right, though. I've backed myself into a corner and I don't know what to do about it.'

'Well, I can certainly empathise with that. But you know what I've come to realise? When you're in a corner, there's only one way out and that's forwards.'

His words strike at my heart, and for one moment what I want is to be held. Instead I smile as broadly as I can and push the plate towards him.

'Help me out here, while I grab two more coffees.'

I have absolutely no idea why I feel I can chat to someone who is one step removed from being a stranger. I'm not even sure that applies anyway, as he's also a customer.

'Everyone needs someone to whom they can, occasionally, rant and rave. We all need that person who is prepared to listen and not be so caught up in our life that they have their own personal take on what's happening. I had a work colleague who heard some pretty raw stuff when I was splitting up with Lily's mother.'

I look across at him, and he's already halfway through his first cupcake.

'That can't have been easy. Having Lily must have made the decision even harder.'

'Well, it wasn't my decision, if I'm honest. Kelly was the one who decided to call it quits. It was mutual, though, our relationship was only held together by Lily. I guess I was happy to settle for what we had, and that was a mistake. We were arguing more and more. No child should witness a relationship falling apart because it gets ugly at times. At least you don't have that problem to add into the mix.'

Adam's comment is an honest one, but it hurts all the same. He catches the look of sadness on my face as I sit back down, placing the coffees on the table.

'Oh, no, did I say the wrong thing?'

'No, it's fine, really. Steve and I don't have any children, but that's a problem too. You see, I always thought I'd meet someone, get married and have a baby. End of story. Instead, I met someone and didn't progress past the stage of talking about marriage and a baby. He kept postponing the baby decision and I kept postponing the wedding date.' My head has sunk lower and lower, until I'm bent over my coffee. Adam might be a stranger, but I don't feel comfortable sharing my tears of regret with him.

'It's a big decision; maybe he'll change his mind.' His concern is real and it touches my heart.

'It's too late. You see …' I hesitate. Am I being a traitor sharing things I've never been able to voice before?

'I'm good at listening and I don't talk about other people's secrets. If you don't feel comfortable sharing, then maybe you aren't ready. I'm not trying to—'

'He had testicular cancer.'

The words fall out of my mouth like pistol shots, silencing us both. Adam looks at me appalled, the shock written all over his face.

'Life stinks sometimes.'

I nod in response and we stir our coffees in unison. The silence isn't awkward though.

'It came out of the blue. Our lives were on hold while he went through surgery and some pretty vicious treatments. He's only recently had his five-year all-clear, but he still attends a cancer survivors' group meeting once a month. You know the worst thing about it all?' The tears have stopped and for the first time ever I feel it's safe to let it all out. 'When we were over the worst he broke down, saying he bitterly regretted not listening to me. By then I'd moved on and felt grateful that he'd survived, but he was mourning a loss.'

Adam reaches out and touches my hand with no agenda whatsoever. It's merely a friendly squeeze, borne out of sheer compassion.

'A serious illness is a reminder of how precious, and fragile, life is. We take it for granted and assume the people we love will always be there.'

His sadness is tangible. I wonder if he's thinking about the death of his grandfather. The minutes pass as we each face up to the pain we hold buried within. The ache that never goes away is so hard to share and impossible to put into words.

'I'm sorry. I didn't mean the conversation to take such a depressing turn.'

Our eyes meet, and I suspect that the expression on Adam's face is also mirrored on my own. Pain, regret, and something akin to exhaustion, for the way our buried emotions continue to drain our spirits.

'You said your partner was also your business adviser, is that another complication?'

I nod, an involuntary sigh escaping my lips.

'He cares about this, my dream.' I hold out my hands, as if holding Sweet Occasions within them. 'And now he's bought into it. But my feelings have changed. I don't know what I'm going to do.'

The tears come. Not simply spilling over, but accompanied by wracking sobs. Adam places his hand back over mine and sits quietly while I let it all out.

Building a New Dream

The more involved I get with Sweet Occasions, the more I can see that this business can really go somewhere. Working together as a team, Katie and I have a shot at making a very comfortable future for ourselves. My head is so full of ideas I wonder why I didn't get involved much earlier on. It is hard reigning myself in while Katie adjusts to the inevitable changes, but each day represents another step forward.

The reality is that a shop on the High Street was always going to be a small business with a limited turnover. Once the industrial unit is in full production the shop could go, as it will represent only a tiny fraction of future sales. Winning those contracts mean Sweet Occasions is now a brand and our sales outlets will be countrywide virtually overnight. I know Katie's dream was a chain of little bakeries, but in today's market that never was going to be an option. The overheads are too high these days. But I know that letting go of the shop would be a step too far for Katie at this point in time. So to placate her, I laid out a plan to eventually turn it into a place where she can run cake decorating classes. One of the large discount voucher companies is interested in promoting a series of one-day courses that will be easy enough to arrange. It won't make a huge amount of money, but hopefully it will be hands-on enough to keep Katie happy.

They say you should never mix business with pleasure, but it's different for us. There was a point, about six years ago, when we both thought I was going to die. Getting through those dark days was only possible because Katie was at my side. Life was a rollercoaster, no two days were alike and only someone who has experienced it first-hand can even begin to understand how it changes you. But it also changes the person who is beside you throughout the journey and my lovely, carefree and fun-loving girl lost her sparkle for a while. It still hasn't returned as brightly as it was, but I'm hoping that when profits begin to soar, it won't just be merely a sparkle, but pride that I'll see reflected in her eyes.

As I get ready for tonight's cancer survivors' support group meeting, I know everyone is going to be delighted to hear my update, but what I really want to talk about is the underlying issue. And I know it's a subject that is going to be tough to raise.

Katie is on the sofa, feet up and Kindle in hand.

'See you later. Don't feel you have to wait up for me, you look tired tonight.' As I kiss her forehead she instantly smiles, but I can tell she's not her usual self.

'I am a bit, maybe I'll read for an hour or two and then have an early night. Drive carefully.'

'I always do. And stop worrying about me.'

The group meeting is held in a function room behind the Town Hall. There are well over thirty members, but usually only about a dozen or so people make any one meeting. We have a get-together at Christmas and everyone makes the effort to attend. Strong bonds have been forged here, because at some point each and every one of us has broken down in front of the group.

Surviving is one thing, handling the fallout is another. Dealing with infertility and the associated issues is quite a common topic, as is the breaking down of relationships in the aftermath. Also how to cope when the 'C' word is always in the back of your mind. When new people join the group it actually serves to remind us how far we've come on our own, very personal journeys. It's also about payback, recognising that the best way to do that is to help someone else in return. We share our most personal of experiences and there is only one rule – honesty.

Tonight as we go around the circle everyone seems to have something positive and uplifting to report, before moving on to the things that are less easy to talk about. When it's my turn I take a deep breath before I start. Tonight I'm finally going to tackle my personal little *elephant in the room* and it isn't going to be easy putting it into words.

'Well, it's been a great month so far and we've just tied up another contract. Before too long you'll be seeing the Sweet Occasions brand in your local supermarket.'

There's a little ripple of congratulations, as quite a few here have been around long enough to know the whole story. Heck, a couple of them have been clients of mine and I helped sort out financial problems related to time they spent unable to work.

'I'm thrilled, of course. And it's all good, but I need some advice guys. I'd assumed as time goes on that things would get back to normal with Katie, but I still feel that our relationship has no-go areas, with Katie feeling she has to be careful around me. Like I'm made of glass, or something. Does anyone else identify with this?'

Scanning the circle of people, one or two are nodding their heads. Christina answers – she's a two-year post remission breast cancer survivor.

'You're not alone there, Steve. Since the day that the "C" word was first mentioned in our house we haven't had one row. Not even a cross word. We had our ups and downs before, as we've always had a lively relationship. Two strong characters, with very different opinions on some things. But now, suddenly, Jeff agrees with every damn thing I say or do. One of these days I'm just going to explode, I know it. I have tackled him about it and his attitude was that after what we've been through the small things don't matter any more. Well, that might be true, but I don't want a life of *making allowances* for anything.'

Her emotions are strong and her words are heated.

Tom shakes his head, sadly. 'I think you have to step back and see the bigger picture here.'

Tom's usually a rather reserved member and tends to avoid getting pulled into the stronger debates. Clearly this touches a nerve with him, too.

'I have a similar situation going on, but then I'm no longer in remission and feelings are raw at the moment. God willing I'll get through this, but it's been a bitter blow for my family. You have to put yourself in their shoes to understand. They will have read all the guidance about how to support a relative. Ways of reducing day-to-day stresses and the importance of having a positive mindset. We all know how hard, maybe even impossible, that is at times. But it also becomes a way of life. When someone you love is sick, it's only natural you want to protect them in any way you can. Unlike a broken arm that heals, the threat of cancer never really goes away, does it?'

It's a sobering thought and a heaviness begins to hover in the room like a cloud.

'I don't think that should stop someone from pointing out that they would prefer to be treated normally. It's not too much to ask, is it?' Christina's anger seems to be building.

We're probably all looking at her and thinking the same thing. Is this going to be yet another relationship that eventually falls apart? Perhaps I made a mistake dragging this out for discussion tonight.

'What if this is the new normality? I ask myself that question all the time. All I know is that I believe Katie saved me. If she hadn't been at my side I don't think I would have had the strength to deal with the ravages of my treatment. There were times I simply wanted to close my eyes and never open them again. Or maybe Fate is Fate and despite whatever you do, or don't do, the outcome would be the same anyway. What is frightening is the anger that seems to come from nowhere. Katie takes the brunt of that, and sometimes my patience for even trivial things is almost non-existent. The old me wasn't like that and what if she can't live with the person I've become? What if there is no going back for us and to her I'll always be a cancer survivor first and foremost in her thoughts? I don't want a relationship based on pity and I don't want her to stay with me because of guilt.'

Christina appears to have calmed down a little, but now looks tearful. It's time for some words of wisdom from group leader, Doug.

'There is no simple answer and we all know that, but thank you, Steve, for raising this tonight. It seems like the right time to remind everyone that couples' counselling can help, although it won't be right for everyone. The other point is that while we all know anger is an undeniable part of the process, if at any time you feel overwhelmed by it then you must seek professional help. Anger can be a destructive emotion, but there are ways to diffuse and manage it. Help is always a phone call away, but I know it takes a lot of courage to reach out and start dialling.

You have to be prepared to do that for yourself if the need arises and, sometimes, for the person you love.'

On the journey home I try not to dwell on what turned out to be a very emotional meeting. Sometimes a few of us seem to be going through the same thing at the same time, other times it feels more like one person's moment of crisis. Knowing you are not alone is a comfort, but it's also a concern.

Katie

Facing Facts

'The window display is dazzling.' Hazel surveys the results of my hard work yesterday, with approval.

In truth it was a sad turning point for me, the last vestiges of my country-feel bakery theme are now firmly a thing of the past. The new window display is eye-catching, in a sleek and minimalist sort of way. Steve had a specialist company produce a four-foot high cascade of 3D cupcakes made out of fabric. Affixed to the ceiling by a wire, it dangles above the new, glossy white flooring. Yes, it is fun and the detail is awesome, but I miss the country look it replaced. The day the builders ripped out the antique pine floorboards I'd lovingly sourced, and the simple white wrought ironwork table and chairs set up all ready for a tea party, was a sad moment for me. The crisp white cotton cloth laid out with beautiful, rose-inspired hand-painted plates, cups and saucers, reflected the quintessentially English tea party theme. It was distinctive and slightly romantic, in a nostalgic way. Cars often slowed when they drove past our window. Would they slow for this, I wondered?

'You should have said you were coming in to work. I wasn't doing anything special and I could have popped in to help. Although, I suppose I might have interrupted something.'

'Interrupted?'

'I walked by mid-afternoonish, on my way to pick up some milk. I was about to knock on the window, when I saw you were deep in conversation. Was it that guy? He looked familiar, but I didn't like to peer in. I was rather surprised.'

A part of me cringes. Hazel thinks I have a secret. We were only talking.

'He was on his way to visit his grandmother and saw me in the window. He popped in to say thank you.'

'Hey, he's a nice guy; you don't have to explain anything to me. But if I saw you, then someone else might have seen you too.' Hazel is a good friend, and only pointing out the obvious.

'It's not like that and if Steve had decided to turn up, I doubt he would have been upset.'

'Really? Katie, I know Steve, remember? I'm only saying that maybe next time you might want to sit and chat somewhere else.'

This is crazy, it's clear that Hazel genuinely believes something is going on and nothing could be further from the truth. If she'd heard our conversation, she would understand that it was merely two people letting down their guard and sharing their problems. But there are so many things Hazel doesn't know about the last five years of my life.

'Hazel, he's a customer. That's all there is to it. I delivered the cake for his little girl's birthday party because I didn't have anything better to do and I enjoyed the drive. He had his hands full, managing on his own with only a neighbour to help out and a dozen girls to entertain. Lily had also had a fall and her arm was in plaster, so there was a lot going on. Besides, it would have been rude of me not to offer him a coffee, when he was kind enough to pop in to thank me.'

'So he's not with Lily's mother any more. Interesting.'

She turns to face me, leaning back against the counter and lowering her voice.

'He fancies you,' she smirks. 'At least there's some chemistry going on there. I know you and unlike a lot of other people, you don't play around for the fun of it. Sometimes you have to take a brave step and see what's out there.'

'Hazel, I can't believe you said that. I'm not looking to have some fun and nothing improper has happened with Adam, I can assure you. I've nothing to hide from Steve, or anyone.'

She crosses her arms, her body language signalling what exactly, I'm not sure. Discomfort? Or is there something she wants to tell me, and she can't find the words?

'That's a great shame, then. You deserve better.'

'What on earth are you talking about?' I call out as I watch her walking away from me. I need to get to the bottom of whatever it is that's upsetting her. She's been acting very strangely for a while now and it's totally out of character. I know that Steve isn't always very diplomatic when he calls in, which is becoming more and more frequent. Hazel probably feels she has two people to report to these days and that can't be easy. Especially when there are times I know Hazel has overheard Steve and me arguing about the business.

As I absent-mindedly continue stacking the cake trays, ready to take them through to the kitchen, a vague hint of doubt begins to cross my mind. It's obvious I like Adam, who wouldn't? Do I like him in that special way? Given the way we seem to have connected, surely that's simply down to having shared some pretty emotive stuff with a stranger. Would it be enough to make me do something foolhardy? I don't believe that's in my nature, as Hazel said, I'm not the sort to play around for fun. In fact, when she said the words, the thought that jumped into my head was, 'boring'. Boring? Whatever happened to faithful?

I clear my mind of all this trivia and focus on the facts.

It's true what they say about sharing troubles and, if anything, I'm grateful to Adam. I still don't have a solution to my problems, it's true. I'm tied to Steve now in more ways than one, but at least I recognise that my feelings for him have changed. That has absolutely nothing to do with Adam, though, and I can't let Hazel's comments confuse things.

Adam had said he'd been happy to settle for what he had, that his ex-partner hadn't. That was when things started to fall apart. Maybe Steve's feelings for me have changed, too. If that's the case, then we need to seriously look at our future together and agree where we go from here.

My mind reels at the thought of having the conversation with Steve. I'm very aware that for the last five years it's been like treading on eggshells. I've tried hard not to upset him, or cause him any unnecessary stress. Now look at the mess we're in. I owe him the truth and there never is going to be a good time to tell him, is there?

A Waiting Game

'I'm not ready, my dear. Adam isn't strong enough to bear the upset. He's at a crossroad in his life. Now is the time he's going to need someone to listen and not judge him, or steer him into something that isn't right. He'll need someone who understands what's in his heart, when even he isn't sure what that might be. Besides, there's little Lily. How can I let go?'

Jack looks at me with love in his eyes

'It's coming. Your time is nearly done, Gracie. You won't lose them, love is never lost. You can be there for both Adam, and Lily, whenever you want. In the same way that I visit you, it will be up to them to invite you into their lives. If it's not for them, then you'll still be there, walking alongside them. It will simply be unseen.'

'But I won't be able to hug them through the bad times, or the good. Jack, I'm tired, and I do know that you're right. But it feels selfish to give up on life. I want to be here when they need me. I simply have to hang on to every single day, because each is precious and might make a difference.'

We exchange sad smiles, aware that death is the one true constant in life.

'I know, Gracie, my darling. You feel you are letting them down, that old age is merely a weakness. I'll be by your side no matter what happens and, when the time comes, we'll all be there to surround Adam, and Lily, with our love. It does help, my dear – love is a powerful thing both sides of life. They will feel, and take comfort from, the energy around them; even if they never open up their minds enough to accept we are only a thought away. For some people it's easier to let go completely and focus on happy memories.'

It's hard to comprehend the other side of life, but wonderful that Jack visits and chats to me. I long to reach out, knowing full well that he isn't really here at all. Sometimes it feels real, more than simply my imagination.

'There's nothing to fear, Gracie. If there was, I would tell you. Trust me, my love.'

As he fades away, his words are left ringing in my ears and once more I'm alone in the bedroom. He understands my fears; or rather my imagination is playing out those fears, now I know my time is limited.

Adam seems to be so unsettled at the moment, living only half a life. His time with Lily filling the emptiness; his time alone filled with work. It's been quite a while since he ventured out on a date. I suspect the longer it continues, the less inclined he's going to be to begin looking for someone again.

My chest feels tight tonight, the breathlessness oppressive and stifling. A wave of claustrophobia catches me unawares and I reach for my inhaler. My heartbeat slows and the gentle beat turns into a loud thump. It's so loud that I can hear it labouring away. Thump, thump, thump. I hold my breath as the pattern changes. I begin to wonder if this hesitant thud is the last, but it quickly settles down again.

'Not yet, please, not yet,' I whisper to the darkened, empty room. 'Dear God, I want to hang on until I feel Adam is better able to cope.'

Adam

You Can Run But You Can't Hide

I have no idea why this particular visit is bringing back so many childhood memories. It's obvious Grandma is very unwell, she even waved off my questions about the pendant she's now wearing around her neck. Clearly it's an alarm. I've seen them before.

All I can do is to make the place as secure and safe as I can. It's been a busy few days adding grab handles to the shower cubicle and alongside the front and back doors. In the garden I've erected handrails in places where there are steps, or an incline. All little things that Grandma Grace happily accepted and that was the thing that scared me, even more than the silent worries in my head. Grace never accepts help and the fact that she was grateful, and happily agreed with my suggestions, spoke louder than any words.

'You're worrying about me again.' Her hand touches my shoulder as she walks past my chair. 'If you want to make me happy, then I need you to stop worrying and think about your own future instead.'

I lean my cheek against her hand, finding it cold, despite the temperature of the room.

'You're important to me – to us. I know the lodge was never your home, because you were already married and living with Pop when it was purchased. But it was your parents' home for many years and without that legacy to eventually pass on to Mum, it wouldn't have been my family home as a child. When I came here to live it was hard for you, renting out The Beeches, but I'm grateful you did. It meant nothing to Kelly, of course, other than bricks and mortar, but it means a lot to Lily and me. Come and stay with us for a little while. They say a change is as good as a rest.'

My coaxing falls on deaf ears; one look is enough to tell me the answer is no.

'This is my home, Adam. This is where I have wonderful memories of Jack, our beautiful daughter, and you as a boy, visiting with us in the holidays. Then of your life here, through those times that tested us all. This is where I will end my days, God willing.'

Grandma withdraws her hand and as she passes the photos on the wall, she turns and smiles at each of them in turn. Her walk is still graceful, if rather slow, and purposeful. Her demeanour is proud and strong as she lowers herself gently into her favourite chair.

'I hate it when you talk like that. I can't bear the thought of not having you in our lives.'

'My darling, darling Adam. There are things we need to discuss and we can't avoid having this conversation any longer. My will, and papers, are all in the writing desk. You and Lily are the two beneficiaries. My solicitor, Stewart Falcon, is the executor. Stewart also has a copy of the will at his offices.'

I put up my hands, wanting her to stop as the words cut through me.

'You must listen, Adam. Please hear me out, and then it will be done. My wishes are simple. I want to stay here as long as it is feasible. Beyond that, my dear, do whatever you have to do without any regret. As harsh as it sounds, when the end is here I prefer to be alone. I don't want anyone watching for my last breath, or weeping over me.

The very thought of that is abhorrent to me and I love you, and Lily, too much to have that on my conscience. Better to have good memories to cling onto, rather than horrid ones of watching the life seeping out of a loved one. Trust me on this and please honour my request.'

My jaw is rigid and my stomach is in knots. If I speak now, I'll break down. I bow my head, struggling to hold it together. She's strong as iron and I know she wants me to be strong too.

'Pop is with me, so I'm never alone. He often comes to sit with me and his presence is comforting. I know many would say I'm a silly old woman, letting her imagination take over to fill the void of a lost love. Whether it's real, or not, is irrelevant; it's real to me. I simply want you to understand something. I choose to have my memories, and my imagination, as the companions for that final journey. As dear as you are, darling Adam, this isn't going to be something we can share. I want you always to smile when you think of me. Besides, let's not get maudlin, there's life left in me yet. But death comes to us all and when it's my turn, I want it to be as dignified as possible. Celebrate my life by living yours, dearest boy. That is how you will make me both happy, and proud.'

I swallow hard, a guttural sound rising in my throat that's hard to contain. I stifle it with a cough and steel myself to greet her worried eyes, with a strength I'm not sure I have.

'You know that's going to be hard for me.' My voice wavers. My facial muscles are working overtime to keep my tone even, despite the emotion battling to get out. 'I will do my best, but that's all I can promise.'

'That's good enough for me. But, Adam, when the time comes, please let me go without regret. You have to understand that I believe I'm simply passing from one world into another. I'll be with Jack, and my beloved daughter, but I'll always be beside you, too. Now that's enough. It's finally all been said and I feel better for it. No more morbid thoughts, let's have some tea.'

Grandma leaves the room, giving me time to regain my composure. As I listen to her moving around in the kitchen, I look across at Pop's chair. Is he there now? Has he been watching us, and supporting Grandma as she spelt out her last wishes? My only wish is that if he is there, I could be granted the ability to see him too.

Leaving Grandma to head back home to Lily was emotional for us both. Our frank talk had tackled the unthinkable. Although, it still left me uncertain as to whether the problem was with her heart, or her lungs. I didn't mention that I had tried to speak with her doctor, or that he had said he was unable to discuss his patient with me without prior consent. That consent, he informed me, would not be forthcoming. The only outward signs of illness that I witnessed were the bouts of breathlessness and a slight tinge of blue around her lips. With Christmas and my next visit still almost two months away, I know that I will worry about her constantly and vow to phone her every day.

As I pulled away to begin my journey home, my thoughts turned to Katie. For some reason she was suddenly on my mind and ten minutes later I found myself parking up outside the shop.

'Um, is Katie around?'

The young woman behind the counter gave me a smile of recognition, and then shook her head. 'I'm afraid she's at lunch.'

I nodded, thinking it was just my luck, and thanked her. However, as I turned to walk out, she called me back.

'Adam, isn't it?' she enquired. 'I'm Hazel.'

I stepped back, as she indicated for me to move along to the end of the counter. A woman I hadn't seen in the shop before began serving the customer behind me.

'Katie has probably gone to the park at the end of the road. You'll most likely find her sitting on one of the benches eating her sandwiches.'

She gave me a cheerful grin and I smiled back. 'Thank you, Hazel. I um … wanted to talk to her about a Christmas cake.'

'Great, and anyway, Katie would be annoyed to have missed you.'

Her words took me rather by surprise. I nodded and made my way out of the shop in rather a hurry. I jumped back into the car, fully intending to head for home without any further distractions. Two minutes later I found myself pulling into a parking space alongside a grassy area at the end of the road.

The park is a little haven, comprising a large open area surrounded by a row of mature trees. The borders are neatly maintained and it's pristine; there isn't a single piece of litter to be seen anywhere.

Sure enough, as soon as I walk through the gate I spot Katie. She's sitting alone on a bench. She doesn't look up until I'm standing next to her.

'Adam. What a surprise! Are you on your way back home? How was the visit?'

Katie shuffles along the bench, indicating for me to sit down as she gathers together the remnants of her lunch.

'I didn't mean to interrupt, I'm sorry. I called into the shop to say goodbye as I'm heading home. They said you were here.'

She raises her eyebrows, a little surprised. 'Ah, you spoke to Hazel.'

'I hope you're not angry. I said I needed to talk to you about a Christmas cake. Well, I do, of course, but ... it wasn't that.' Words now fail me. I don't know what I'm doing here, or why, and seeing Katie seems to have opened the dam that was holding everything in. Get a grip, Adam, what a wimp!

Katie senses I can't talk at the moment. She sits back, hands resting in her lap, diplomatically gazing around. We sit watching two people out walking their dogs and a young woman with a toddler. A few minutes elapse and eventually I'm calm enough to speak.

'Sorry about that, it's been a tough few days.'

'Worse than you thought?' She sounds hesitant; worried she'll say the wrong thing.

'I think it's her heart. Her doctor says he's unable to discuss the details of her case with me, and worse, she made me promise I'd honour her last wishes. I don't think she knows how long she has left, maybe no one ever knows for sure. But I'm a wreck. I didn't want to leave her here, all alone. I wanted to take her back with me, to Lily.'

'I assume she said no, and I guess she's a lady who knows her own mind. That must have been hard to bear, Adam. Sometimes you have to listen to what people want, rather than blindly assuming what you want for them is what's best. It's tough. Look, if you ever get worried ... you know, can't reach her on the phone, or anything, then please do call me. I can pop round to see if she's okay. It's no trouble at all.'

The offer is a kind and very generous one.

'It's weird. You're probably the only person I can share this with and yet we hardly know each other.'

'Well, after our last little chat, I'd say we know quite a lot about each other. I made a bit of a fool of myself and it was very kind of you to listen. So please, if you are worried at any time, simply give me a call.'

It's a little surreal sitting here, people watching alongside a young woman I met because of a Christmas cake. She stares straight ahead, smiling at the toddler and the young mother anxiously hovering over the little one. Katie lifts her hand as the breeze catches her hair and she shakes her head to disentangle the strands. Something inside me causes my heart to miss a beat. Oh, no, this is bad news, extremely bad news.

She turns her face upwards to look at me as I stand and I begin muttering the first thing that comes into my head.

'Thanks, um, I'd better start heading back. Long drive and all that ...'

At the gate I take one long look back at her and she waves, her hair obscuring most of her face. My heart skips another beat as I walk back to the car. I'm filled with confusion and an adrenalin rush that I haven't felt in a long while. There isn't only a sense of connection, but the associated body chemistry is becoming a little difficult to keep at bay. I suddenly imagine myself scooping her up in my arms, and I actually have to shake my head to clear the vision. Since when did you become the type of man who contemplates stealing another man's woman?

Katie

Sometimes You Have To Let It All Out

'Did Adam manage to find you in the park?' Hazel hits me with the question the moment I step through the door. Thankfully we're alone and she pauses, watching for my reaction as she leans against the display cabinet she's cleaning.

'Yes, thank you and it's not what you think. His grandmother, the one he buys the cakes for, has a heart problem. She lives near here and I've offered to pop in to check on her if there's an emergency. She's eighty years old and lives on her own. End of story.'

Hazel chews her lip.

'He's fit and rather charming. A great catch for some lucky woman.'

'Hazel! Enough, he's a customer.'

'Hmm ... and he's single and free as a bird.'

Now Hazel has overstepped the mark.

'I have absolutely no idea why you find him so utterly fascinating. The subject is now closed and I have nothing further to say on the matter.'

I head for my office before Hazel has time to reply.

Anyway, it's all irrelevant and none of my business. The chance of Adam needing to call on me is slim and he won't be down again until Christmas. By then he could have a girlfriend who will, of course, want to come and meet his grandmother.

Now I have to get my head around a more personal, and

142

pressing, matter. I'm still trying to decide how to approach it, when Hazel calls out that Steve has pulled up outside the shop. I guess my thinking time is over. This is it.

'The after-lunch lull?' He strides into my office as if it's his own and leans over me to plant a kiss on my forehead. 'Why the frown? Problems?'

I'm half-tempted to change my mind and leave this for another time, when I find myself blurting it out.

'I need to talk to you, about us.'

The problem is that I have no idea what to say next. How do I begin?

'All we seem to do these days is talk about us,' he retorts, sounding distinctly annoyed.

'That's not true, Steve. All we do is argue, and that's mainly over Sweet Occasions and the way I run things. I'm talking about the way we feel for each other. The fact we haven't made love in ages. The gap that is growing between us is getting wider as each day passes. Doesn't that concern you?'

It has all come out in a rush and the look on his face tells me he's shocked. I walk across to shut the door, hoping no one was within earshot. He spins his head around to look at me, eyes narrowing as he searches my face for clues.

'What?' He throws the word at me with a vicious tone in his voice. Immediately I find myself preparing for a fight. I pull back my shoulders and, for the first time in years, I don't even consider backing down.

'Let's not play any more games. I hate upsetting you, but I need to know if there's anything left between us on a personal level that is worth salvaging.'

He takes one stride towards me and falters, his arm slightly raised. For one awful moment I wonder if he's going to hit me. Then I see that wasn't his intention, he was going to reach out for me. His mouth is open, only nothing is coming out. Reaching for the chair, Steve drags it away from the desk and slumps down into it.

He lowers his voice, 'I think you'd better say whatever it is that's on your mind. I've given up trying to second-guess what's going on inside that head of yours.'

'I'm glad you're prepared to at least listen to me,' I throw in quickly. I'm trying to buy a few extra seconds of thinking time. He's implying this is a surprise to him, but surely he can see the cracks in our relationship? Is he just burying his head in the sand, rather than facing up to the truth?

I lean against the edge of the desk, grateful that for once he isn't standing over me and I don't feel overpowered by his presence.

'Steve, we're falling apart. We used to be so close and now it's like we're partners in business only. Even when we're together, you're always on the computer and I spend my time trying not to say anything contentious. We don't do fun things together any more. Is there any passion, or desire, left to rekindle?'

'How can you say that? After everything we've been through? I doubt there's an emotion left that we haven't shared. I've put my consultancy business on hold so I could divert everything I have in terms of time, as well as money, into bringing us closer together. Believe me, I had other options but I chose the one that I thought would get us back to where we were. What more do you want from me as proof that I'm committed?'

His tone is clipped. A nerve twitches at the side of his mouth, indicating that either he's nervous, or so angry he's in danger of losing control.

'Look, let's stay calm and be honest with each other. I'm

not talking about the business, or the loan, or commitment. I'm talking about whether there's any love left between us.'

I reach out and touch his face lightly with my fingertips. 'I'm not trying to hurt you, Steve. It's a question I've wanted to ask for a long time, only I've been too scared to go there. You know why.'

He takes my hand in his, holding it gently for a few seconds before letting it go.

'And it all comes down to the big "C". It sucked up five years of my life; it took away any chance we had of having a baby and now it continues to overshadow our relationship. Have I changed? Yes. Have you changed? Hell, yes. You have two expressions, Katie. You either look at me with pity, or with fear. How did that happen? Can you tell me that?' His anger is a little frightening and the look in his eyes is one of pain and regret.

'I live in fear of upsetting you, of adding to your stress levels because I can't seem to gauge your moods any more. The anger you bottled up is close to the surface all the time. Seriously, I think you need to do something about that, to stop it constantly eating away at you. It won't go away on its own; it's a natural reaction after what you've been through and I understand that.' My voice fails me as my throat constricts. I can only hope that my tone demonstrates the sympathy and concern I feel for him.

'And we're back to the pitying look. I'm well now, Katie, so say it as it is and be done with it.'

I hesitate, not even sure what it is I want to say. Then the words are there.

'I don't think I'm in love with you any more.'

'So, what are you saying? That you've found someone else?' His face darkens, as his eyes anxiously search my face looking for the truth.

'No, there's no one else, Steve. Even if you hadn't been ill, this would probably still have happened. Relationships change and sometimes things fall apart because they've run their course. I suppose what I'm asking you to consider is whether, or not, you still love me?'

He sits back in his chair, folding his arms across his body and exhales, sharply.

'Would I be here now if I didn't love you? Life without you wouldn't be worth living, Katie.'

Even as he utters those words, I know it's a lie. Maybe the truth hasn't sunk in yet. Perhaps it remains hidden, deep behind the armour he's worn for so long to shield him from his darkest fears. He's still haunted by the thought of losing his grip on life and of being alone. This is like living in hell and I know it can't continue any longer.

Starting Over Yet Again

As Grandma Grace's words sink in, what gives me hope is seeing Lily's bright, smiling face. Later that evening when she is tucked up safely in bed, I pour myself a stiff drink and settle down to make some sense of the thoughts whirling around inside my head.

With Coldplay's 'Fix You' playing in the background, it takes me back to a time when life with Kelly seemed to be one long argument. Katie pops into my head and my stomach does an unexpected somersault. It's not an option, I tell myself. She's out of bounds and I know it ... but that doesn't stop a warm smile from creeping over my face. Then Grace pops into my head again, along with the sorrow I can't contain.

It was tough when Mum died, worse still losing Pop, because of the devastating effect it had on Grandma. But losing her? I can't imagine it; I don't want to imagine it.

Katie pops back into my head; that shy little smile of hers makes me recall our first meeting. I was a total stranger and yet she didn't hesitate to help me, despite the High Street being deserted. There was no one within earshot to come to her rescue if I'd turned out to be an opportunist robber, or even an attacker!

We've connected, or rather, I've connected with her. There's a definite spark going on and when I'm talking to her, frankly, I find it hard to walk away. Just the thought of her is enough to make me smile, no matter where I am, or what's going on.

What would a woman like Katie be looking for to make

her happy? A guy who treats her well and supports her passion? A guy who can meet that passion, with his own? I'm not thinking about sex at all here, only zest for life. Then that familiar old sensation stirs in the pit of my stomach. I imagine how it would feel to have Katie's hand on my skin, or to be able to run my fingers through her hair.

Damn it! I need to stop adding complications to my life and think about solutions. Katie isn't looking for a new relationship; she's simply trying to work through a few problems. Not once has she indicated she's ready to walk away from her current situation. Clearly she doesn't think of me in quite the same way and I know I can hardly be described as a catch. Too much baggage, I suppose.

Now I have to look to the future. The one thing I can do for Grandma Grace is to be strong. To show her that now is the time she must think only of herself and enjoy what time she has left. Please God, when the end does come, let it be gentle and swift. She deserves that at the very least, for all the goodness she's brought into so many people's lives over the years. My task now is to make her proud and show her that she didn't raise a man who is afraid to live. From here on in, the guilt and self-doubt stops. I'm in pursuit of happiness, and a woman I can love, who will also love Lily as much as I do.

'Sorry, I meant to pop in earlier for a chat. It's been one of those days. Good trip?' Charlotte steps inside as I hold the door open for her.

'Yes, and not really. Coffee?'

'Have you anything stronger?' Charlotte inclines her head towards the half bottle of red wine sitting on the shelf.

'Good idea, I'll grab a couple of glasses. Come on through.'

She follows me into the sitting room, dropping down onto the sofa on the far side of the coffee table.

'I'm shattered.' She slips off her shoes, curling her feet up beneath her. 'Do you mind?'

'Be my guest. And thanks for looking after Lily at such short notice. Kelly couldn't get any time off work and while she is prepared to be a little flexible on the custody arrangements, I don't want to find myself back in court fighting to retain equal rights. It would be just the excuse she was looking for.'

'It wasn't a problem. Emily and I love having Lily to stay and Max was away, again. How is Grace?'

'It wasn't the best of visits, but it was necessary. She's not well at all. This morning I arranged for a domestic assistant to go in every day for two hours. They'll help with cleaning the house and preparing her meals. It's a bit of a relief, if I'm honest.'

'Poor you, it can't be easy sorting this out on your own.'

I hand her a glass and she raises it in a toast.

'To happier days.'

'Funny you should say that, but I'd come to the same conclusion myself. It's time to move on and let go of the past.'

'Have I missed something? You've only been away a few days and you come back a new man. You haven't met someone, have you? Or maybe you just happened to bump into Katie again.' Her eyes sparkle, mischievously.

'Unfortunately for me, she happens to be in a rather complicated, long-term relationship. It's a lost cause, but I admit it was nice having that feeling again. You know; something that reminds you that you're alive and kicking, more than just a dad!'

I raise my glass back at her and she chuckles.

'You're sure there's no hope? That day at the party I'm pretty sure there was a hint of flirtation in the air.'

'Absolutely. She's a lady who is passionate about things – her business and her personal life. She cares enough to get everything back on track.' And thinking about her makes me want to head straight back there, but instead I flash Charlotte a wry smile.

'Shame about that. I thought you two looked really good together and she was brilliant with Lily.' Charlotte lowers her voice in case Lily is still awake. 'However, what do you think about a blind date? I have the perfect someone in mind for you.'

Settling back in the chair, I ease myself into a more relaxed position.

'I'm a bit rusty, but what the heck. She isn't a man-eater, is she?' I add, thinking that most of Charlotte's friends are like Kelly. Women who know what they want and aren't afraid to take it.

'I think you'll be surprised. Pleasantly, I hope. How about Saturday night? I'll babysit Lily, or maybe she can come for a sleepover. That way you'll have a little space, if you want it, that is.'

Charlotte flashes me a look I don't care to interpret and adds a wink.

'I think whatever I do next I'm going to be taking it slowly. As long as that's understood by all parties, that's fine. Now all I need is a little guidance. What on earth do guys talk about on first dates, nowadays?'

'Really? You're nervous about getting yourself out there again?'

The thought of meeting someone in an arranged way fills me with dread. I'm going to make myself go through with this to please Grandma Grace and to prove something to myself.

'I don't exactly lead an exciting life, do I? It's Lily and work, work and Lily; and then there's Grandma Grace. I'm out of touch with just about everything at the moment, except boy bands, of course.'

Charlotte laughs, shaking her head in dismay.

'Don't worry. I'll explain that you're rusty and need to be handled with care. Leonie doesn't come with any baggage, fortunately. She's a career lady, but looking for someone special. It'll be like a job interview, knowing her. She'll check you out before she even considers thinking about any emotional attachment. I think that's exactly what you need at the moment. Two people prepared to be both cautious and realistic, before getting pulled into anything. That's not to say she's averse to a little adult fun, of course.'

That thought is rather intimidating.

'I'm afraid I'm a little rusty in that department, too,' I admit, sadly.

'Well, maybe that's all about to change.' Her glance is loaded and I find myself blushing. This isn't going to be easy. I can only hope it doesn't turn out to be a huge mistake.

Katie

The Cold Light of Day

'What's up?' Hazel stabs her fork into the bowl of pasta in front of her. 'It must be serious for you to suggest coming here.'

I glance around, the pizzeria is half-empty on this grey, wintry evening.

'I've moved out.'

She looks up at me, mouth open. 'You've left Steve?'

'We finally had the talk. It was way overdue. To be honest, he didn't take it quite as badly as I'd feared. At first he said he still loved me and then he admitted things were going from bad to worse. That's why he's been so moody. It was a relief.'

'Where are you staying? Why didn't you come to stay with Jenny and me?' Hazel puts down her fork, her concern pulling forth a host of questions.

'Look, I'm fine. I've rented a furnished house on a short lease. I used the van to move most of my stuff out last night. Once the decision was made I wanted to act quickly.'

She looks dumbstruck.

'Is this to do with Adam?'

I roll my eyes. 'This has nothing at all to do with Adam. I will admit I do like him. There's no point in pretending he finds me the least bit attractive, because I've nothing upon which to base that theory. It would have reared its head by now. No, this is about facing up to the truth. There's a lot you don't know about what Steve went through when he was ill. Things I can't go into, but he isn't a bully. I can appreciate why you might think that, but you have to trust me on this one. You see, a part of it is my fault. I've avoided dealing with the issues because I felt he wasn't strong enough to cope with it. I guess I fell out of love with him a long time ago. I truly believe that a significant part of his anger is due to the fact that he couldn't bring himself to let go.'

Hazel shifts uncomfortably in her chair.

'He knew, all right.' She looks up at me, an anxious expression on her face.

'How do you know that?'

'Because ...' she pauses and I steel myself for something unpleasant. 'Because he slept with someone else. And it was before he knew he was sick.'

Now it's my turn to sit here, mouth open.

'Are you sure? How could I not know this? Why haven't you said anything before?' It doesn't make any sense. She must be wrong.

'I know the woman involved. Steve is aware I saw them together once, but he doesn't realise she's one of Jenny's work colleagues. Shortly afterwards he was diagnosed and everything went haywire. Look, Katie, every time I've tried to have a meaningful chat with you about Steve, you've made it clear it's not a subject for discussion. You couldn't even share the things you were going through when you were supporting him. If I try to raise something about the way he treats you now, all you do is make excuses for him. I sort of thought you knew, to be honest, and had decided it was one of those things.'

I feel like I've been punched in the stomach. Everything we went through, all of that angst he expressed over not being able to have a baby ... when any love he had for me had already been betrayed. He wasn't in love with me; I was merely a crutch, a lifeline.

'So, what happens now?' Hazel looks up sadly.

'Steve will buy my share of the house from me. I'll need the funds to find a permanent base at some point in the near future. Unfortunately, I can't use the money to repay the loan he made for the extension. That's why I wanted to talk to you tonight. Steve is taking over the management side of the business. I'm going back into the kitchen, permanently. I'll be developing new product lines and running cake decorating courses.'

You could cut the silence with a knife.

'I can't believe you're saying this! It will never work.' She slams the table and I cast a glance around the room as a few pairs of eyes turn in our direction.

'I have no choice,' I reply, between gritted teeth. 'Do you think I'm happy about Steve calling the shots? Without a spare fifty thousand pounds in my pocket, I have to suck it up and accept that this is the quickest way of repaying that debt.'

'What happens after that?' Her expression is one of utter disappointment. She's gutted.

'He walks away and I'll be back in full control.'

'Ha,' her tone is full of sarcasm. 'Mr Nice Guy walks away. What's the catch?'

I look down, nervously, not wanting to share the details of the deal I had no choice in accepting.

'In return for converting the money I owe him into a non-interest bearing loan, and to repay him for the time he's going to be putting in, I'm signing over forty per cent of the business to him.'

'He's screwed you, Katie. You're a fool. He's steering the business where he wants it to go and it's already too late. When you try to take back control you'll soon find out you can't run it without him. Mark my words, this is a big mistake.'

Tears of frustration fill my eyes and the look of disappointment on Hazel's face is hard to bear. I have never felt like a bigger failure, but it is what it is and we all have to move on.

'The rat,' Hazel spits out in anger.

'Maybe, but I'm free. I'll be where I'm happiest, in the kitchen. Please, Hazel, be happy for me and accept that at least everyone still has a secure job. Steve has a good business head and he won't let us down on that front. He has big plans for you.'

'Yeah, I bet.'

I have no idea why it's so important to me that I talk Hazel into seeing the positive side of this situation. Maybe it's because I hate the thought of her thinking badly of me. I suppose I'm afraid of being judged and found to be lacking when it comes to having the strength to fight my cause. I did fight, and what she doesn't know is that Steve asked me to marry him as the other option. A loveless marriage of convenience? I know hell when I see it coming.

The Second Christmas

Katie

Is Unhappiness Catching?

Things aren't quite as bad as Hazel predicted. Steve works from home at least a couple of days a week and we quickly settle into the new way of working. Before long he takes on yet another lucrative contract, supplying a chain of wine bars. The bakery has to work flat out to keep up with the orders. There is a great deal of satisfaction all round from the feeling that business is booming.

Steve doesn't even try to become one of the team. However, I'm determined not to let it irk me, when it hits home that he sees himself as the boss. I'm happy doing what I love best and labouring over the design details of some beautiful cake creations. Plus I'm constantly looking for new and exciting flavours for our cupcakes, and that keeps me busy.

All orders go through Steve, so it's a surprise when I log into the system and see Adam's name. He's booked a Christmas cake for collection a week on Saturday. There's a note alongside it, to the effect that the customer isn't sure exactly what time he'll be collecting it. The request is for something imaginative.

It must be my Adam. I laugh. He isn't exactly *my* Adam! A little thrill courses through me, until I realise that Steve has scheduled it as my day off. Hazel will probably be the one to serve him. The thrill is quickly replaced with a sense of sheer disappointment. Life sucks sometimes. Even if Adam was interested, which I doubt, there's no way I can engineer changing my day off without it looking odd. Besides, whenever I see him I seem to find myself blurting out all manner of personal stuff. This latest development is beginning to feel like defeat. I seriously doubt he'd want to get involved with a loser.

Anyway, by now he's probably found some totally gorgeous woman who can't wait to take on the role of step-mum to Lily, and who will worship the ground he walks upon. I find that particular line of thought more than a little depressing. What if he comes into the shop to order an engagement cake, or worse, a wedding cake!

I allow myself a little daydream, as I roll out a large ball of pale blue icing and begin cutting out snowflake shapes. I imagine Adam stepping through the door, flowers in hand, and everyone's eyes are on him. He walks up to me, a nervous look on his face as he begins speaking.

'I give up! If this continues I might have to start looking at guys again!' For a few seconds I'm totally confused. Then I realise Hazel is walking towards me, her voice booming out.

'What's up?' I can see by the expression on her face she's annoyed about something.

'Jenny is having one of her hormonal rants. Of course I can't say that to her face, she'd explode. Seriously, she needs to get a grip on herself, or I'm off. Know any available guys?'

She's purposely trying to inject a bit of humour, but I can see she's totally fed up with the way things are going.

'You don't really mean that. Jenny will calm down and I know you love her to bits. The path of true love is never smooth.' I arch an eyebrow, hoping to reinforce the serious tone in my voice. Hazel's relationship has always been volatile, but it's based on true love.

'Yes, but it's so frustrating at times. I'm a woman, so I

know about the hormonal thing but in Jenny's case it's out of control. Jekyll and Hyde syndrome, if you ask me.'

Hazel leans up against the counter, her arms crossed firmly across her chest.

'Are you sure that's what it is? It's not to do with the fact that you are working extra hours here to help out, is it?'

Hazel looks away, confirming that part of this is to do with being rushed off our feet in the run-up to Christmas. It can't be easy for Jenny when Hazel goes home exhausted every night. I know how I feel at the end of each long day and all I want to do is shower, eat, and jump into bed. Adam's face flashes before my eyes and I stifle a laugh. I think it's time to end my little daydream. Hazel turns back to look at me and I'm mortified to see she's tearful.

'Oh, honey, it will pass.' I step forward to put my arms around her, trying hard not to get icing on her clean overall. She lowers her arms, allowing me to hug her gently for a few moments.

'You two are good together, so please don't do anything rash. If you can't work late it's not the end of the world. It's different for me now; I don't have anyone waiting for me at home, any more. Please, Hazel, don't put your relationship at risk. We'll cope, and if we can't then Steve will have to take on some temporary help for a few weeks.'

A look of relief passes over her face and I can see that conflicting loyalties have weighed heavily on her shoulders. Whatever decision she makes will mean someone she regards as family being let down. I should have considered the effect on Hazel's home life, when Steve asked her to commit to the extra hours.

My temporary home is comfortable and the landlord seems quite easy-going. I have the option of extending my tenancy on a monthly basis, after the initial three month period. Steve has now taken out a bigger mortgage, so that he can pay me my share of the equity in the house. He says he doesn't intend to move, which I find odd. If I was in his position I would want to start again.

With the money sitting in the bank, a thought crosses my mind that I could pay off his loan and then he'd be out of all of our lives. But that would take away my options for the future and I simply can't take the risk. I have no idea what might happen next and now I have to look out for myself, as well as the business. Anyway, at the moment it's all hypothetical, because I simply don't have time to look for somewhere new to live. Renting is fine for a while, until I know what I want to do and the landlord is fully aware of my situation.

Christmas looms and my parents have dropped huge hints about having me home with them for the holidays. I think they're relishing the idea of a Steve-free Christmas.

It's strange how, when you're in a relationship, you automatically assume everyone feels the same way you do about the person you're with. When family and friends feel uncomfortable, then maybe that's a warning to be heeded. I could have saved myself a whole lot of grief, if only I had stepped back for one moment and used my head. The same applies to Sweet Occasions, but admitting that is hard to do. My head now tells me that things are running smoothly since the changeover. I have to thank Steve for that. I rarely see him outside of work and have no idea what's going on in his personal life any more.

It's time for me to pick up the pieces of my own life and begin moving forward. I can't exist on silly daydreams and fancying a guy who pops into my life a couple of times a year. Besides, Adam lives a fair distance away from the part of the world I call home. Hard as it is for me to admit, his only tie here is to his grandmother.

I don't mention anything to Hazel, although when Adam calls in he will, no doubt, ask for me. It's almost the one year anniversary of the day he first walked into the shop. The thought brings a warm glow to my cheeks, as I remember him stripping off his shirt. So much has happened in the last twelve months that it's hard to comprehend where my life is now. I'm still getting used to new freedoms and a real sense of relief that catches me from time to time.

They do say everything happens for a reason. Maybe Adam and I were destined to meet, simply to share our problems. Everyone longs for a listening ear at some point in their lives and it's always easier talking to a stranger. Maybe I need to let go now and step back into that stranger mode. I think I'd rather not know how his life might be moving forward. That hurts a teeny bit, if I'm honest with myself. It also serves to remind me that I need to get out more and start living a real life of my own.

Hazel and Jenny have invited me around for a meal. They want me to make up a foursome with one of their single, male friends. The whole idea is way too contrived for my liking, but a kind gesture that would be rude to refuse. Instead, I try to gain a little time by saying that I'm not ready to rejoin the dating world. Hazel rejects that out of hand. She says that the longer I mope around, the harder it will be to take that first step. I guess I'm lucky that there are people in my life who want me to find happiness. At the moment, that does mean a great deal to me. So, I'm left without a choice and find myself committed to meeting this guy on Friday night.

Adam

Maybe Things Are Moving Along

It's great to be out for an evening, but the venue isn't the best. This noisy wine bar is packed and I hate sitting on these ridiculously high stools.

'How's the love-life going?' Tom knocks back his whisky chaser. He places the empty glass back down, next to the beer in front of him.

'Good. Leonie is a lovely lady. She has a busy and successful career, which she loves. There haven't really been any significant others in her life, so far. She offered to look after Lily tonight. They're organising Lily's bedroom, then I think a chick flick and takeaway was on the agenda.'

Tom grimaces. 'Be careful there. You don't want to end up with a Kelly mark-two. I know the idea of having a female around for Lily must be appealing, but this isn't only about your daughter's future. It has to work on every level.'

I know what he's hinting at. Leonie and I haven't slept together yet, and that's the next step. But it's a big one.

'It's fine.' I put my empty shot glass back down and follow it with a slug of beer. The fire hits my stomach and the cold beer slides down with ease. 'I need a bit of organising. So does Lily. She's growing up fast and it is nice for her to have another female in the house. It's hard to keep up with her social calendar at the moment. There's always a sleepover, a dance class, or a school thing going on and I feel like her personal taxi service at times. Leonie seems content to go with the flow and she's been hanging out with us more and more, recently.'

'That sounds promising. But just wait until Lily's a couple of years older, like my two. I'm glad of an excuse to get out of the house these days. They think all I'm here for is to put my hand in my pocket, or take them somewhere. Kids, eh?'

The pounding beat of the music is incessant and annoying. I indicate that I'm drinking up and heading out. Tom gives me a thumbs-up and downs the rest of his drink.

The night air is refreshing and sobering. A couple of drinks and I'm happy. Long gone are the days of partying into the early hours. The sky above is a strange shade of grey, almost luminescent. It has certainly warmed up a bit after the hard frost we had this morning.

'I think they're right, we're going to get some snow – look at that sky.' Tom turns up his collar as we walk towards the taxi rank.

'How's Wendy?'

'Good. I don't know how she manages to juggle everything, but she does. The girls don't always make her life easy, but she's firm when she needs to be. I pretty much do as I'm told and try to stay out of trouble.'

I laugh; Tom's life would fall apart without Wendy. She's another Grace, her family come first in everything she does.

'You're lucky there. I don't know what she sees in you.'

'Hey, what can I say? I know how to keep a good woman happy.'

As we walk I think about Leonie. Is she from the same mould as Wendy? The last six weeks have flown. She has stepped into our lives without any fuss and she doesn't seem to be demanding. When she offered to look after Lily tonight, she said it would be fun. I was pleased, of course, and if our relationship is going to move forward it's important they bond. However, I'm holding back and I don't know why. Maybe Leonie is trying a little too hard. It's a concern, but I can't wrap Lily up in cotton wool and keep Leonie away from her, on the off chance that something goes wrong. I suppose I should be grateful my girlfriend wants to spend time with my daughter. What more can a single dad ask for?

'It is good to see you dating again. The way things are going, it looks like it could be the start of something more permanent. Make sure you're really happy before taking that next step, Adam. Don't rush things if you have any doubts.'

Tom's a good friend. I know he's worried I'm going to get burnt again. As the first snowflakes begin to fall, I glance up into the still greyness above.

'It's only just beginning and I don't know where it's going. Leonie is staying over for the first time tonight and I'll be sleeping on the sofa. I want to take it slowly and I've told her that. It doesn't seem fair on Lily to rush into something that affects her, too. I don't want her witnessing yet another break-up if it doesn't work out. I hope that Lily thinks of Leonie as a new friend, rather than as my girlfriend.'

'Wise move. Leonie likes kids, then?'

'I know what you're thinking. Yes, I'm sure a part of the attraction is that we are a ready-made family and that's something Leonie admits she's missed out on, so far.'

'Does she want kids of her own? It's one thing taking on someone else's child, but another to have your own.'

It's a fair enough question and it has been on my mind too.

'To be honest, I have no idea. If we move on to the next level, that's going to be the big question. Do I see myself with more than one kid? Not at the moment. It would have to be the perfect relationship for me to even contemplate that. I know how hard it is making things work after a split when a child is involved. Any woman coming into my life on a permanent basis will have to love Lily as much as I do.'

Tom's right to point out the pitfalls, but I've already gone through all of this in my head. At the moment, I have to worry about whether what I have is actually a commitment problem. Charlotte has hinted that Leonie is very keen to become more involved. However, the week I don't have Lily, I'm away most of the time. So far, there hasn't been a chance for me to ask Leonie if she'd like to stay the night. I wonder if I'm actually making excuses here and I'm simply too scared to admit that to myself. Is it stalling tactics? Am I trying to postpone moving forward, because it all starts to get really intense if everything between us does begin to gel?

I'm thinking of asking Leonie if she'd like to come with me when I go to visit Grandma Grace. Kelly is taking Lily to Disneyland Paris for four days and I thought I'd use that as an excuse to pop down to check on her. I've ordered one of Sweet Occasions' Christmas cakes.

The plan this Christmas is for Grace to spend three days with Lily and me. If she's up to it, I'll drive down to collect her on Christmas Eve. It will be the first time that I've had Lily over the holiday period. I must admit, I'm excited at the prospect. Christmas isn't the same since the split with Kelly. Even spending time with friends, or Grandma Grace, is hollow because Lily is constantly on my mind.

It's quite a step for me to introduce a new girlfriend to Grace, but a part of me knows that it will also make her happy. If it goes well and things continue, then Leonie may well be spending Christmas day with us all, too.

Katie

Mr Wrong Is All Right

I can't decide what to wear. After changing my outfit at least a dozen times, I'm feeling extremely stressed. Isn't dating supposed to be fun? This sure feels more like purgatory. I settle on jeans and a comfortable black and white top, wondering whether it even matters in the grand scheme of things. I don't know anything at all about this guy. Only that Hazel and Jenny think it's a good idea. Really?

When I eventually find myself knocking on their door, I'm already twenty minutes late. Talk about making an entrance! Hazel leads me straight into the sitting room so that I can make my apologies.

'I'm very sorry I'm late. The phone rang just as I was about to leave.' It didn't, I was sitting in a chair next to the phone, trying to get up the courage to ring and say I wasn't feeling well. Only the fact that I hate lying to anyone stopped me from doing it. I figure at least this lie has less impact.

'Well, you're here now. This is Chris. Chris, this is Katie.' Jenny does the introduction and I step forward to shake Chris's hand. It's a firm handshake, which is a good start, I suppose. He's tall, about six-foot, and he looks friendly. He flashes me a big smile and I'm dazzled by his ultra-white teeth. He's a pretty boy, so what's the catch?

'It's great to meet you, Katie. What do you think of these girls, hey? Aren't they the best?'

'Yes, great.' Am I being unfair, or does he sound distinctly cheesy? Maybe he's nervous. I know I am, so I'll give him the benefit of the doubt.

'Go through to the conservatory. I don't know about you, but I could murder a glass of wine.' Hazel, bless her, ushers us through. I catch her giving Jenny a strange look behind Chris's back.

As we settle down, wine is dispensed and nibbles are circulated. It's an awkward case of juggling glasses and plates. I put my plate and glass down on the coffee table, in case I drop something.

There's a little banter between Hazel and Jenny, before Hazel brings Chris into the conversation.

'Chris, why don't you tell Katie what you do for a living?'

This feels like wading upstream against a current. No one feels comfortable and I wish I'd made that phone call.

'I sell drugs,' he smirks. Hazel and Jenny fall about laughing, watching intently for my reaction.

I start laughing. It's forced and there are a few too many, 'Ha! Has' in there. However, Chris seems content to have made me laugh.

'All prescription drugs, I assure you. I'm a Business Development Manager for a pharmaceutical and biotech company. I attend trade shows, as well as managing the regional sales team. If you ever take a headache tablet, it's probably one of ours.'

He looks like he enjoys his job; I wouldn't say he's smug exactly, but he's confidence personified.

'Sounds interesting.' I pick up my glass and take a large gulp of wine. This is not the best start.

'It keeps me busy and I get to travel to some great places. The prospects are good, but it has a downside.' He mimics a sad face.

'No time to date,' Jenny throws in.

'Oh.' How tragic.

I can see Hazel is concerned that I've already lost interest.

'Come on, guys, let's cut to the chase. Chris, you go first. Three sentences that sum you up and remember, you're out to impress.'

I groan inwardly, but then when I think about it, it's actually a very clever idea. Not much time to think, so honesty will hopefully rule. Chris looks a bit hesitant and thinks for a moment, then he's off and running.

'I make in excess of fifty thousand pounds a year and my career is very important to me. I love the sea, whether that's sailing, surfing, or scuba diving, and I hate football and rugby. I'm a black belt in Taekwondo, love reading biographies and have only had one semi-serious relationship with a trainee doctor.'

I almost start laughing again, but for real this time. That tells me that money and status are important to him. He enjoys outdoor pursuits that are way above what most working-class people can afford. The fact that the last thing he mentioned was his relationship indicates where it comes on his scale of important things in his life.

'You're next, Katie.' Jenny looks at me eagerly, clearly quite impressed by Chris's offering.

'Umm ... I've only had one serious, long-term relationship and I'm finding it hard to adjust to life as a singleton. My cake shop isn't doing too well, because I run it with my heart and not my head. I'm renting a small house while I sort out the mess I'm in and decide what's next.'

Obviously my little summary hasn't gone down quite so well. All three faces looking back at me appear to be rather appalled.

'It's not quite as bad as that,' Hazel jumps in.

'Oh, I think it's a pretty fair assessment of my situation, Hazel. No point in pretending I have everything figured out. After all, who in their right mind would walk out of a failing relationship and walk straight into a business partnership with their ex?'

Chris looks shocked. Whether that's because of my honesty, or the fact that my life is in such a mess, I'm not sure.

'Rather chaotic, I should imagine,' he replies. I think he's trying to sound upbeat, but his voice sounds distinctly unimpressed. I catch Hazel shooting a glance at Jenny, who rolls her eyes.

'Do you have any hobbies?' Chris asks, clearly floundering for some sort of common ground.

'Well, if you count poring over financial spreadsheets to get the red figure at the bottom to turn blue, then I suppose that's my main hobby at the moment. I love reading, I'm a great Jane Austen fan,' I add. I'm hoping he'll be impressed, but I might as well have said I love reading about zombies. It's his turn to take a large gulp of wine and he absentmindedly rearranges some of the nibbles on his plate.

Thankfully, Jenny breaks the silence. 'I bet scuba diving is fun, Chris.'

'I love it. I try to schedule at least four trips each year and I've been to some really awesome places. My job is quite pressured at times, so holidays are very important to me.'

This is beginning to feel like an extremely painful interview and I know I'm next in line for a question.

I can see Jenny looking quite pointedly at Hazel, who is floundering to think of something to ask me. The seconds stretch into minutes and I decide I might as well throw something out there.

'I used to enjoy gardening, but the house I'm in at the moment only has a tiny triangle of lawn. It also has two small flowerbeds. I do consider myself to have green fingers, though, and I haven't killed off a plant, yet.'

For an off-the-top-of-my-head comment I thought it was pretty safe, but Hazel and Jenny look exasperated.

'Katie is a very talented cake designer, Chris. You wouldn't believe the range of cupcakes that Sweet Occasions has on offer. People come from all over and now it has a business manager it's doing really well. Katie is being very modest. It's all down to her vision and talent. This time next year Sweet Occasions cupcakes will probably be in every supermarket around the country.'

I sit there dumbstruck. Chris seems to have perked up a bit and gives me a nod and a smile.

Jenny passes around the canapés again and Chris refills his plate. I politely decline, looking at the clock on the shelf and wondering how soon I can excuse myself and leave.

In fairness, the conversation does get a little more interesting. After an hour and a half it's very clear there isn't really much left to talk about that hasn't already been covered. To my horror, when I announce I have to go, Chris stands up and says he'll walk me to my car.

I'm not sure who's more relieved – Chris and I, as we make our escape, or Hazel and Jenny to be waving us off.

Within twenty paces Chris and I exchange a look and, in unison, begin laughing.

'Was that ghastly, or am I being overly critical?' He breaks the ice, for which I'm grateful.

'I'm so sorry. This was such a bad idea and I'm not normally so pathetic. Or maybe I am and tonight is the first time I've realised that.' I'm feeling acutely embarrassed and I think he feels the same way.

'Well, I sounded like a pompous twit, so I think we're quits.' He sounds both amused and relieved, at the same time. 'I don't suppose you'd like to go for a drink?'

Now I have a real dilemma. I don't want to be rude, especially after such an appalling experience. Maybe he isn't as bad as I thought at first, and I probably came across as overtly trying to put him off. As I'm considering how to get out of this, he steps in to put me out of my misery.

'No, sorry, scrap that as a bad idea. To be honest, I'm not looking to start up a new relationship at the moment and clearly you're not ready. Friends mean well sometimes, but I'd say we don't really have anything much in common. Am I reading this right?'

Ironically, he's impressed me more in the last few minutes than he has all evening. It's bold of him to admit that tonight was a big mistake.

'Well, I can't swim and I'm afraid of water. I didn't like to throw that into the conversation as I think Hazel and Jenny would have been mortified. I agree with you, they meant well. This is my car here, thanks for walking with me. It has been nice meeting you, Chris, and I'm envious of the scuba diving. If I ever get up enough courage to conquer my fear, it's something I've always longed to experience.'

He holds out his hand and gives a friendly shake.

'Well, if that day ever comes be sure to look me up. I'd be happy to give you a lesson, or two.'

As I drive off I'm chuckling to myself. I've been scared of the water since I was a tot. Although I'd love to see what lives on the bottom of the ocean, it's a dream I know will never happen. Guess this really is 'the one that got away', in more ways than one.

Adam

What a Difference a Year Makes

'Hi, I've come to collect my order. The name is Adam Harper.' My eyes sweep around the shop. I can't see Katie anywhere and I don't recognise the woman serving. This time last year it was pouring with rain and blowing a gale. I was standing here bedraggled, soaked to the skin and half-frozen. I have to stop myself from laughing out loud and looking like a lunatic. Although I wish she *was* here maybe it's for the best. Today we couldn't have had a meaningful chat, anyway.

What does strike me is that every time I call in the place seems to feel a little less welcoming. The loss of that wonderful, cosy atmosphere is a real shame, in my opinion. Gone are the personalised touches and now everything, including the displays, is what you would expect from a corporate chain.

I'm relieved to see Hazel walking towards the counter. She smiles, recognition instantly flashes across her face.

'Hi, there. One very special cake coming up!'

As she disappears to find the cake, I turn and smile at Leonie. She slips her hand into mine and squeezes it.

'What a fabulous cake shop. I can feel myself putting on weight just looking at those cupcakes.'

'Wait until you check out the Christmas cake. Lily had a princess cake from here for her last birthday and it was amazing. Katie, the owner, is one talented lady.'

'You know her?' Leonie looks surprised.

'Only as a customer, I've purchased a few cakes. You know, Grandma's birthday and, of course, the festive cake.'

I can see that Leonie is impressed when she glances at the cake that is placed in front of us.

'Wow, the detail is amazing. It's so cute. Shall we take some cupcakes as well?' She looks at me with a broad smile on her face.

'Oh, so the diet goes out the window.' I laugh and Leonie leans into me, giggling.

'I think we'll take four of those as well, please.' She points at a tray in the display cabinet.

As the cakes are being boxed up, I'm surprised there's still no sign of Katie. I feel too awkward to ask after her. The last time we talked she indicated she was at a bit of a turning point and I hope she's now moved on. Certainly the shop is busy today and everything is running efficiently. I'm pleased for her. She deserves to have her dream and make a huge success of it.

But it seems wrong to leave without saying anything. As I hang around waiting to pay, I start up a conversation with Hazel.

'Another great cake. I love the village scene. Will you thank Katie for me?' I glance across at Leonie, standing next to the counter with two boxes in her hands. She looks back at me and smiles warmly.

'I will. I'm sure she'll be very sorry to have missed you, but it's her day off.'

'Ah, right. I hope she's doing something nice. Business seems brisk.' I look around at the queue and at the two other people busy serving.

'It is, we can't keep up with it at the moment,' she replies, amiably. 'How's that lovely daughter of yours? Lily, wasn't it?'

'Great, thanks. She's off with her mother on a trip to Disneyland.'

'Fab, bet she's having a marvellous time. I hope you, and your girlfriend, have a nice visit.'

'Thanks so much. Tell Katie I'm here again next week, so I might pop in. Are you open on Christmas Eve?'

'Yes, we're open until four o'clock and Katie should be here. Merry Christmas and I hope your grandmother enjoys the cake.'

It's funny, but I can't recall having mentioned Grace to Hazel. I don't suppose … no, I'm sure Katie wouldn't have any reason to discuss our little talks. There's no time to puzzle over it as I step forward to hold open the door for Leonie. I'm conscious we're running a bit late and Grandma will be worried.

Assessing Grandma with a quick glance I notice that she's beginning to look rather frail and there are dark smudges beneath her eyes. As we hug, it hits home how much weight she's lost. She appears to be shrinking. I could almost wrap my arms around her twice over and I feel as if I tower above her diminutive frame.

'Grandma, this is Leonie.'

Grandma Grace's face breaks into a welcoming grin. It's wonderful to see her light up when she looks at Leonie.

'It's so lovely to meet you, my dear. Come in and sit down. Adam, the kettle has boiled and there's a tray already prepared in the kitchen. Can you do the honours?'

I nod, knowing that what she's asking for is simply some time alone with Leonie. I guess she's looking out for me, in case I lose my head and grab the first available woman. I'm pretty sure that Leonie will pass the test, though – she's smart, kind and looking for a steady relationship. Job done. What can go wrong?

176

Katie flashes into my mind and I deliberately push all thoughts of her away.

I linger in the kitchen as long as I can, washing up a few dishes while the tea brews. Then, with a manly cough, I walk back into the sitting room.

Leonie is sitting in Pop's chair, chatting away to Grandma with apparent ease.

'No,' she shakes her head in response to an unknown question. 'I never wanted children. When my friends were pregnant their experiences were enough to put me off the whole thing. Cooing over babies isn't something I do and I'd be bored stiff being at home with a small child all day. At Lily's age, at least you can hold a proper conversation with them. Plus, they don't need watching every single second of the day.'

I don't know what they've talked about so far, but the last question is obvious. Grandma is giving her the third degree. I decide not to interrupt and take a seat on the spare sofa.

Grandma looks a little put out by Leonie's response.

'It was always a concern to me that Adam was an only child. It would have been such a comfort if he'd had a sibling, someone he could turn to in troubled times.'

'I'm an only child too, so I don't know if that's how it works. I have a friend who hasn't spoken to her brother for eight years, so I guess nothing is guaranteed. Anyway,' continues Leonie, 'the benefit of having only one child is that you get time to have a life of your own. They demand a lot of attention, don't they?'

Grandma raises an eyebrow and I jump in to change the subject.

'Tea, ladies?'

'Leonie's been telling me all about her job. I often

wondered what exactly happens in those laboratories, when they say they're testing food. Nice to know someone is keeping an eye on all those additives.'

Jeez. They've only been alone together for ten minutes tops and Grandma has worked her way down the list of essential information. The next question would have undoubtedly been about me. I can picture it, 'Do you love my grandson?' My unwittingly sharp intake of breath attracts their attention. I say the first thing that comes into my head, as both pairs of eyes settle on me.

'Um … did Leonie tell you her parents live in the States?' It begins a long exchange as Leonie talks about the fabulous lifestyle they have, living in Palm Springs. I feel a little more comfortable with the topic of conversation, until Grandma responds.

'You must feel very lonely at times, Leonie, with no family close to hand. But maybe that works for you. I've always felt that maintaining the family home was important. Adam's roots are here. It's somewhere he can return, where memories are a comfort. Life isn't always easy, so it's important to have something to hang onto.'

The conversation ends abruptly and I'm surprised by Grandma's words. I fill the void with polite chatter about the garden and the atmosphere becomes more relaxed. My mind is working overtime – Grandma doesn't seem to have taken to Leonie as easily as I'd hoped.

I marvel over the thought that, even after all these years, she can still surprise me. I know our relationship is a lot closer than most, because of the sorrows we've shared. Tragedy has a way of making people cling together. What I hadn't stopped to consider was how much work went into making that happen. Grandma was always the cornerstone, the tower of strength for Pop and me. In return we loved her for the kindness, support and selfless love she gave us. We took that for granted, but where would we have been if she had been a different type of woman? What if she'd insisted on having her own life and her own space, rather than always putting her family first?

I glance across at Leonie. What attracted me to her from the start was her determination. That sense of wanting to succeed at whatever she decides to do. Is she another Kelly? Am I simply drawn to the sort of women who will inevitably have their own agenda, because it counters something lacking within me? What do I want out of life, aside from Lily's happiness?

Unease stirs in the pit of my stomach. I think Grandma was trying to make a point; highlighting what she feels is important to me. Things so inherent in my makeup that I hardly notice them, but without which, everything would fall apart, as it did with Kelly.

The afternoon flies by and with one last hug it's time to say goodbye. Leonie politely excuses herself to touch up her make-up, giving me a few minutes alone with Grandma.

'Thank you for a lovely day.'

'My dear, I hope I didn't say anything out of order. I have to say what's in my heart. I mean well, but naturally, I'm anxious for you. I don't want to see you hurt again.'

It's an awkward moment and she hugs me with a fierceness that belies that look of frailty.

'Hey, I'm fine and there's nothing at all to worry about. I do need you to take good care of yourself, though. We're counting down the days until Christmas Eve and our trip to come and collect you.'

She eases away from me, those sparkling eyes looking up into mine, reflecting love, and pride.

'Oh, I nearly forgot to thank you for the beautiful cake. I would also like you to give this to Katie, at Sweet Occasions. It's only a little something. She has talent and a passion. I admire that and I hope she knows that the personal touch means a lot. Every time you bring me one of those little boxes I can't wait to see what's inside. I love you more than words can possibly say, Adam.'

Her eyes mist over. I take the small parcel she picks up from the table in the hallway to hand to me.

'It's breakable,' she warns.

'Hmm, right, well, I'm sure she'll be delighted. I'm not sure when I'll have a chance to drop it in though ...'

'I was rather hoping you could pop it in on your way back today,' Grandma says, pointedly.

'Okay, although it's her day off and I'll have to leave it with one of her colleagues.' I know a command when I hear one and I'm not about to argue. Normally, I'd be delighted to have an excuse to pop into the shop. Knowing Katie won't be there, and with Leonie in tow, it isn't quite the same.

'Drive safely, Adam, and don't forget to ring me as soon as you get home. Give Lily a big hug from me.'

When Leonie reappears she stoops to give Grandma a kiss on the cheek, which I think is a nice thought. Maybe it wasn't quite the grilling it appeared to be and Leonie was expecting a thousand and one questions. As Grandma admitted, it's only natural she should be protective of me.

However, as soon as the car door is shut, Leonie lets out an exaggerated sigh.

'Wow, you should have given me some advance warning about that.' She exhales, loudly. 'I thought I was a strong woman, but your grandmother is one tough cookie. Has she ever approved of any of your girlfriends?'

There's an air of sarcasm in her voice. I change the subject, feeling it's an unfair question and I'm disappointed in her more than I care to admit. I acknowledge that Leonie didn't find today's visit an easy introduction. Maybe she genuinely can't understand the natural sense of wanting to protect one's child, or grandchild. I will admit it probably wasn't very fair of Grandma to question and judge Leonie's opinion on things she hasn't personally experienced. So far Leonie's been great with Lily and I can't fault her in that respect. Perhaps the Christmas visit will be easier, as everyone will be relaxed, and happy. Today felt more like an interview than a visit and I was equally as uncomfortable witnessing it. But if you can't be a little forgiving to an elderly lady when it comes to her grandson, what does it say about you?

Jingle bells, here we come. I can only hope the season is full of festive merriment – for us all.

Life Is Full of Surprises

'Oh no, you missed him. He was in this morning and called in again about ten minutes ago with this, for you.'

If only I'd left home a little earlier, I would have caught him. I can't believe the bad timing. I was secretly hoping he would call in at the end of the day, when it's quieter. Just like last year. I popped in, hoping to use the excuse that Hazel has a party tonight and she might want to leave early. Guilt floods through me as I realise I can't even be honest with myself about how I feel about him. It's quickly replaced by a heart-stopping sense of disappointment.

'Who? Steve?' I paste a cheery smile on my face.

'Don't pretend you don't know I'm talking about Adam,' Hazel declares, hands on hips. '*Your* Adam. And he came back, I'd say on the off chance you'd be here. He obviously wanted to see you. Were you expecting a package?'

She hands me the small parcel which is wrapped in brown paper and has, 'Katie, Sweet Occasions' handwritten on the front.

'No, I wasn't expecting a parcel. Was Lily with him?' I ask, rather too casually.

Hazel hesitates.

'No, he was with his girlfriend.'

I pretend not to be flustered, or devastated, to hear those words. Of course I'm very pleased for him and I try hard to push the negative feelings away.

'Great!' The word comes out sounding rather odd. Hazel shoots me a glance, pointing at the parcel.

'Are you going to open it, then?'

It seems silly to make a big deal out of it. Especially given that his girlfriend accompanied him on his visit. That, in itself, is meaningful and I have no choice but to wish him well. I place the package on the counter top and tear away the wrapping paper. Inside there's a pretty box. Lifting the lid, there's a polystyrene case which I lever out to expose an exquisite little snow globe. I lift it carefully from the casing and hold it up.

'How fab!' Hazel exclaims. I shake it gently and a cloud of snow descends over the little village scene. 'It reminds me of one of your Christmas cakes.'

I was thinking exactly the same thing. As I pull off the brown paper wrapping to throw it away, something falls to the floor. It's a pale yellow sheet of handmade paper, the sort that has an interesting grain. Unfolding it reveals a short note, written in the most exquisite handwriting.

Dear Katie

I simply had to let you know how much I enjoy the wonderful cakes that Adam brings, when he comes to visit me.

They are such a perfect gift and you are a very talented lady. You pour your heart and soul into your creations, and clearly love what you do.

I have a favour to ask and wondered if you wouldn't mind giving me a call in the next day or two.

Warmest wishes

Mrs Grace Harper

Homelands, Cheriton Court Mews
05894 516933

'How very odd,' I say out loud, looking up at Hazel to gauge her reaction.

'Perhaps she wants to leave you something in her will,' Hazel says in a conspiratorial tone.

'Hazel! I said she wasn't very well, not that she was on her deathbed. I suspect she wants to place an order for something. It's no big deal.'

'What? The grandmother of the man who makes your heart leap, but are too scared to tell, asks you to call her? No big deal, huh?'

My jaw drops open.

'He's a nice guy who happens to be easy to talk to, that's all. I offered to be his emergency contact if he had trouble getting in touch with her by phone. She lives about a ten minute drive away from the shop. Besides, despite living so far away, he is a regular customer. There's no hidden agenda here, as I've told you before.'

Hazel smirks. 'No need to give me a lecture. I believe you,' she protests. Then mutters under her breath, 'Though thousands wouldn't,' as she walks away.

I am very surprised by it, though, and more than a little bit intrigued. Walking home I feel a warm glow. Holding this personal little gift feels like a connection to Adam and his family. It's silly, I know. It's merely a very sweet gesture from an appreciative, and rather lonely, old lady. Someone who purchases expensive writing paper and a pen that uses old-fashioned, bottled ink. Old values that stem from an upbringing that is full of sweet gestures and little kindnesses. She's a lady who is appreciative of detail and notices when time, and effort, have been put into something.

I wonder if Adam felt awkward dropping this into the shop. We're ships that pass in the night, brief acquaintances who happened to cross each other's path. I doubt he ever thinks about me, except for when he's placing an order. How I wish I could say the same. He's become the person who fills my dreams. He has become my guilty pleasure.

For some women it's chocolate, for me it's imagining I'm at the lodge with Adam and Lily. Sitting in the garden and relaxing as if that's where I was always meant to be.

The word *tragic* pops into my head, although I suspect *pathetic* is probably more appropriate. The warm glow continues and I savour every little moment of it.

'Hi, this is Katie ...'

'... from Sweet Occasions. My dear, thank you for getting in touch.'

The voice on the other end of the line is vibrant and she sounds much younger than her years. I thank her for the note and the snow globe. Grace asks if she can place an order for Christmas cakes for her two closest neighbours. She would like them gift-wrapped and hand-delivered to her home, the day before Christmas Eve.

As soon as she makes the request, I know I will be delivering them personally. Of course, I'm grasping at straws and all of this would be rather touching if it wasn't so utterly ridiculous. I feel a connection with Grace, but it's only through Adam, and what he's told me. I need to get a life of my own and not attach myself to a family who have nothing whatsoever to do with me. I'm determined to meet her, this wonderful woman who means so much to her very special grandson. I imagine myself knocking on the door and the person who opens it isn't Grace, but Adam ... Oh, Katie! Get a grip.

I put the order on the system and mark it down for collection. That way no one will ask any questions about why I'm making an out-of-hours, special delivery. Everyone will assume someone called in for it. The last thing I want is twenty questions from Hazel, or Steve. Not that it's any business of his, either, but I know it will look odd. The only time I've ever delivered a cake was for Lily. Heck, what is it with this family, I chuckle to myself. They must really like cake.

'Mrs Harper?'

The old lady who answers the door is rather fragile looking and beautifully dressed. Lively, bright eyes shine out a beaming smile as soon as she spots the two boxes stacked in my arms.

'Call me Grace, my dear. You must be Katie. Wonderful, my special delivery! Mind the step; we don't want you tripping up.'

Her voice is soft and genteel, the sort of voice that instantly makes you feel welcome.

She leans heavily on her walking stick to turn, leading me back inside as she excitedly chatters away. I feel a little concerned that she might stumble.

'Take care, I'm just behind you,' I call out.

Grace leads me into a charming sitting room, with family photos lining the walls. It's light, airy and very warm, despite the bitter temperatures outside.

'How lovely to have an open log fire,' I exclaim. It crackles, and the smell of the wood burning is even more festive than the lovely Christmas tree standing in the corner.

'Well, I wouldn't be without the central heating, but there's something so cosy about sitting in front of a real fire. Do sit down and slip off your coat. Would you like tea, or coffee?'

It would be rude of me to cut and run, when obviously

having someone new to talk to is probably the highlight of her day.

'Coffee would be lovely, thank you.'

I place the two boxes on a small side table and pull the phone out of my pocket. I took photos of both cakes before I gift wrapped them.

'Here's your order, take a look.' I walk over to Grace, holding up the screen for her to see. The first one is a snow scene, with a small boy in a red bobble hat sitting on a toboggan. The second one is a snowman, with two small children standing back to admire their creation.

'Such fun!'

Her smile is like a hug, so warm and genuine. She looks into my eyes as if she's searching for something, or maybe I remind her of someone. Whatever it is, it's a strange moment. Maybe it's because of what Adam has mentioned in our little chats and I'm making a subconscious link that doesn't really exist. I know at least a little bit about her and so I don't feel that she is a complete stranger to me.

'Incredible to believe it's all made out of icing sugar. The detail is truly amazing. It's almost an art form.'

I smile. 'Well, I hope that all of my cakes get eaten very quickly. I do take lots of photos. It's very satisfying to look back at previous designs. I'm a bit of a perfectionist.'

'And it shows, my dear,' Grace says, kindly. 'People with a passion are to be admired. Creativity is such a wonderful gene to have running through your family.'

I notice her breathing is laboured, as if each breath is purposeful and doesn't come easily. A wave of sadness touches my heart. No wonder Adam is worried.

'I have the coffee tray all set up, if you'd be so kind as to carry it into the sitting room, my dear.'

'Of course, lead the way.'

An elegant, white china coffee pot and two matching cups and saucers sit on a tray. It's covered with a hand-embroidered, white lace cloth. Grace flicks on the kettle, which boils in seconds. She's a lady who cares about the small details in life. Welcoming her visitors, and being prepared to make them feel comfortable, is important to her. I find the fact that she's been patiently awaiting my arrival rather touching.

'Right, you go first and I'll follow with the tray.'

'It's so lovely to meet you at last,' Grace calls over her shoulder, as we walk through into the sitting room.

Her words are a bit of a puzzle. At last?

'The same here. Your great-granddaughter is such a pretty, lively little girl. You must be very proud.'

I don't feel comfortable mentioning Adam, a paying customer, as if I know him personally. I feel on safer ground talking about Lily.

'She's a stunner, isn't she – that little heart-shaped face and such a lovely disposition. She's as happy as the day is long.'

I offer my arm to Grace, as she takes her seat. Her hold is light and she smiles up at me, gratefully.

'Thank you, my dear. One of my bad days today, I'm afraid. The cold weather seems to affect my chest and I find that I get tired very easily when I'm moving around. Old age doesn't come alone.'

Despite her words, she sounds accepting and feisty, as if it's merely a temporary inconvenience. I'm rather at a loss for what to say, so instead I move the small table closer to her, so she can reach the tray more easily.

'Thank you. Well, this is so lovely. Adam has talked about you and his admiration is plain to see. He's such a special young man, don't you think? Of course, I'm rather biased, because I adore my grandson and he's given me Lily. He has a heart of gold.'

Pride gleams in her eyes and she looks at me expectantly. It's a difficult moment. I wrack my brains for some suitable, but safe, comment.

'He's always very particular about his orders. He told me you love traditional Christmas scenes and he wanted your balloon birthday cake to be fun.'

'And don't forget Lily's princess cake! I saw the photos and she was thrilled with it.'

Grace pours the coffee, handing me a cup.

'Do help yourself to cream and sugar. Now, how do we make my grandson realise he's in danger of making yet another big mistake?'

I almost drop the scalding coffee into my lap. What on earth … I'm sitting opposite this little old lady, with my jaw hanging down and a look of total shock on my face. I close my mouth and swallow hard, wondering what exactly she means.

'I'm not sure … um, a mistake?'

I replay her words in my head. He's already picked up the cake he's ordered and probably delivered it to Grace the same day. Did I give him the wrong cake? I remember Hazel said he was coming up again on Christmas Eve, that's tomorrow. Now I'm really confused. Grace simply chuckles.

'I may be an old woman who probably doesn't have very long left on this earth, but I know my grandson better than he knows himself. When he was telling me all about Sweet Occasions, and the guardian angel who saved him from hypothermia, there was a gleam in his eye. Something I've never seen before. A connection like that is very special. It happens for a reason, and that reason is Fate.'

'But ... he never said anything, I mean ...'

'He kept coming back, didn't he? He's a very private young man, and yet he found himself wanting to sit down and talk to you. I have a feeling he's shared more with you than he's ever done with anyone else in his life before. Well, aside from his grandma. Oh, don't worry, he actually says very little, but I see a lot. I recognise the strength of feeling, and emotion, behind the words he chooses to share with me. He believes you're in a relationship and Adam isn't the sort of man who would come between two people. Sadly, and unlike myself, he has no faith in Fate. But I know better. I knew we'd meet, my dear, and I knew we'd have this conversation. What I need you to share with me is what Adam can't tell me. Are you happy? If I'm reading this all wrong, then my excuse is that I'm a silly old woman, desperate to see her grandson happy before her journey comes to an end.'

I've been sitting on the edge of my seat the entire time, holding my breath in total disbelief at what I'm hearing. I'm speechless, to the extent that all I can do is collapse back into the chair in silence.

The sounds of the old-fashioned clock ticking and the hissing of the logs in the fire grate dominate the room.

Several times I begin to say something, but before I can even open my mouth the words drain away.

'Oh, forgive me.' Grace puts down her cup with a shaky hand; her voice is uneven, reflecting the tears in her eyes. 'I was so sure—'

'No, please, don't get upset. The truth is that my relationship began to fall apart a long time ago. The circumstances were difficult. Sometimes it's hard to make the break. Life has a habit of throwing things in your way which complicate it. I am worried that you're reading more into this than exists, though. I'm rather taken aback to be honest. Adam is a lovely guy, but aside from delivering Lily's birthday cake, when admittedly I did stay to help out for a couple of hours, we've never spent any time together. It's just been the odd chat here and there at the shop. All of that is down to his visits to you, actually. He hasn't said anything specific, has he?'

'It's not so much what he chooses to tell me, my dear, it's what I can see in his eyes whenever he's mentioned you. It's a look I haven't seen before, either with Kelly, or Leonie.' Grace continues sipping her coffee, peering at me over the edge of her cup. I can't hide the puzzled look on my face.

'Hazel, my assistant, did mention … I mean, when he called into the shop last Saturday, apparently he was with his girlfriend.'

There's no point in pretending I don't know and as this conversation gets more surreal by the minute, I might as well be honest about what I'm thinking.

'He's been seeing Leonie for a little while. It began with a blind date, I think that's what they call it. She is a friend of his neighbour, Charlotte. She looks out for Adam. I think she feels sorry for what he's been through with Kelly.'

So that day at the party I think I might have misread Charlotte's questions. She probably thought I wasn't interested, when I was only trying to tread carefully. What a disaster!

'Opposites attract, I've heard that, but Leonie is merely ticking the boxes of what she feels she needs in her life, to make up the perfect picture. Somehow her feelings have become disconnected. Trust me; she'll soon tire of having to accommodate the needs of a little girl and a doting father.'

I sip my coffee, thinking this was the last thing I was expecting to hear today. Common sense tells me I need to conjure up an excuse, so I can make a quick exit before this gets out of hand.

'You think I'm losing my grasp on reality,' she challenges. Grace sounds more like a young girl than an old lady. 'There's nothing wrong with my mind, my dear. The problem I have is one of time. My heart is failing. If I wait for Adam's new relationship to fall apart, I may not be around to help pick up the pieces. Who will steer him in the right direction? I'm simply trying to hurry things along.'

When someone chooses to tell you they aren't deluded, it doesn't mean to say they aren't.

'I'm very flattered, but you don't know the real me. I have some awful habits. My ex-boyfriend will tell you I'm a dreamer and I have no head for business. I hate to disillusion you, but I don't think I'm the best option, if you're looking for a happy-ever-after tale for Adam.' I'm babbling and Grace shakes her head, putting up a hand to interrupt my flow.

'You can't choose the person you are going to fall in love with, my dear. It's one of those things that simply happen. Look inside your heart. If you can sit there and tell me in all honesty that you don't have feelings for my grandson, then we'll say no more.'

I start laughing to hide my true feelings, but within moments the laughter dies in the wake of an onslaught of tears.

'How stupid of me, I'm sorry.' I swipe at the tears with my sleeve.

'You came to see me today because you felt a connection to Adam, and to me. He's spent time talking to you and, in the process, getting to know you. You understand more about him than Leonie ever will, because they aren't on the same wavelength. I'm not being judgemental, dear Katie, I'm being crushingly honest. This has to be sorted before anything happens to me. I have to know Adam, and Lily, are in safe hands. He might not have faced up to his feelings for you quite yet, but they are there. I knew that from the first moment he mentioned your name. Then, when he ordered Lily's cake, I could hardly contain my excitement. Even Lily's accident was Fate taking a hand; everything happens for a reason and it allowed you to have a glimpse into his world, his and Lily's life. Bakeries don't deliver long-distance, but he gambled on the fact that you wouldn't let Lily down. Stranger or not, you care, my dear, and that's priceless. It's one of the things you both have in common, which is a very good place to begin.'

The tears are still streaming down my face as her words wrap themselves around me like a virtual hug.

'I don't know what to say.'

'What we need is a plan. Lily and Adam are coming to collect me tomorrow, to take me back with them for a few days. Now what if, when they arrive, I don't feel like travelling immediately and need an hour or two's rest? You happen to drop by with a surprise delivery for me, from one of my neighbours …'

This lady is unbelievable.

'It feels like entrapment,' I reply with a chuckle, wiping away the last of the tears. 'I'm not at all sure Adam thinks of me in that way. It could all go horribly wrong.'

'Trust me, my dear. I'm a bit of a psychic, always have been. I talk to people who have passed over, and while I keep it to myself, I know what's in people's hearts from the moment I first meet them.'

I frown, how honest can I be with this gentle, but surprisingly enterprising, lady?

'I don't mean to be rude, but why didn't your gift help when it came to Adam's ex-partner? A lot of hurt could have been avoided. Is it possible that sometimes your instincts aren't, well, accurate?'

Grace looks at me intently and replies without a moment's hesitation.

'Everything happens for a reason, and the reason was Lily.'

Point taken. I stand corrected, this lady isn't only enterprising, she's on a mission.

'What about Leonie?'

'Goodness, Katie, you're rather slow catching up! Leonie is here to stir you into action. Adam is being a gentleman and his principles won't allow him to acknowledge his feelings for you. Clearly, he doesn't realise your relationship has ended.'

'Ah, now I understand. Goodness, can you solve any problem, or are relationships your speciality?'

Our laughter fills the room and suddenly I know that this is the right thing to do. Yes, there's an element of risk here, but nothing ventured, nothing gained.

Before I leave, Grace asks me to write down my mobile number on a piece of paper and leave it next to the phone.

'I'll ring you in the morning, as soon as Adam's been in touch to say he's on his way.'

At the door Grace gives me a hug, lingering for a moment or two before releasing me.

'My prayers have been answered, dear Katie. You are everything I knew you'd be and more. We're doing the right thing, just bringing it forward. Without intervention it would still happen, but I can't afford to wait around for Fate to take its natural course.'

'But you don't know me, not really, Grace,' I reply. I feel the need to add a caution.

'I can see what's within and you have a good heart, Katie. That's all I need to know, and that's all I want for my grandson.'

To say that my feet don't touch the pavement as I make my way to the car is obviously not true, but I feel like I'm floating on air. Did that really just happen? Is a fairy tale about to unfold?

I Refuse To Let Go

'Oh, Jack, we've raised a very sensitive and genteel young man, which is quite a thing in this day and age. It's just that Adam is so very... black and white. There are no greys when he assesses a situation and I know his gut instinct will be to let his head rule his heart. It will, no doubt, be telling him to think of Lily and Katie, first. If he does nothing about how he feels for Katie, then there's no chance of a disappointment for Lily, or himself, if things don't work out. He'll justify his lack of action by telling himself that Katie's relationship can probably still be saved, as long as he doesn't interfere. He wouldn't stand in the way of anyone's happiness and we both know that's the truth.'

Jack looks across at me and smiles, giving me a wink and I love that he still has that sparkle in his eye.

'You worry too much, my dear. There are greater forces at work here. You can't put an old head on young shoulders; but you also shouldn't underestimate our boy. When the time is right he will be strong and he'll fight for what he wants.'

I study Jack's face, which often seems so real I feel I could reach out and touch it. Then at other times it's merely a shadow, as if his energy wanes.

'Do you know the answer? Can you see the future?'

He sighs and begins walking towards me, except when I glance down at his feet there's nothing there.

'When you dressed this morning you forgot to put on your shoes,' I admonish, and he begins laughing.

'Give me a break, Gracie. It takes a lot of energy to show

myself to you, my love, but it's worth the effort.' As if to confirm that he fades slightly, making the fact that he's only visible from his head to his knees less obvious.

'You haven't answered my question.' I fix him with a stare and he shrugs his shoulders.

'It's not me you should be asking.' Suddenly his expression is one of deep sadness and I wonder if he's going to cry. Can a spirit shed tears? 'I'm here for one reason only, my love, and that's to be here for you when you begin your journey.'

'I am tired, but I don't want to let go. I have to hang on to see this through and no one is going to tell me otherwise. Some people fight for what they want out of life, and if other people get hurt in the process they accept that as a natural part of the process. Katie and Adam are two of life's more sensitive individuals, who tend to accept their lot without question. They feel they have a responsibility to the people they care for that requires them to put their own needs last. With that, unfortunately, comes a vulnerability because it's easy to manipulate someone who will put others before themselves. I can't, and won't, let them miss this opportunity to grab the happiness I can so clearly see ahead for them.'

Jack hovers behind me and I can feel the weight of his hand on my shoulder, although it's no longer visible. His image is fading fast.

'And aren't you doing the exact same thing, Gracie? Putting those you love before yourself? I've been sent to help you to let go of that sense of responsibility you feel, which is such an enormous weight upon you it's obscuring the path you are about to follow. It's time for you to step back and put your trust in Adam and Katie.'

A tear trickles down my cheek, but I continue to hold

my head aloft. The room almost hums with the heaviness of the silence, but inside my head a voice is shouting out with anger. 'I won't let go until I know they are together.'

Before Jack's image fades away into nothingness there's one last smile, but I hear his words clearly.

'Prepare yourself, my dear, and know that I'm never more than an arm's length away. I'm asking you to put your trust in me for the last time.'

Katie
This Can't Be Happening

A sleepless night is followed by an anxious start to the day. Hazel isn't in work and one of the Saturday girls is helping out. Only a dozen orders are due for collection and after about eleven o'clock it's very quiet.

I'm watching the clock, and wondering why Grace hasn't called. Has Adam been delayed, or has something gone wrong with the plan? I can't believe I'm seriously intending to be a part of this. It feels wrong, even though at the same time it also feels very right.

I walk through into my office, on the excuse of taking a coffee break. Instead I pace back and forth for a few minutes, trying to make some sense out of a situation that feels like sheer madness. What was I thinking?

I reach for the phone and dial Grace's number, assuming she'll pick up within a few rings. I imagine her hovering next to it, waiting for Adam's call. It rings a dozen times and there's no answer. Now I have a dilemma. I wait five minutes and ring again. Twelve rings, and still there's no reply.

Unlike Grace, I have no psychic ability at all, but I do have a gut feeling that is telling me something is very wrong. Of course, Grace could be answering the door, or in the bathroom. My head tries to rationalise the situation, but fear keeps creeping in, like a cold hand reaching out to grab me.

'I'm heading out to do a special delivery. I'll be back in an hour.' I throw the words over my shoulder, without as much as a backwards glance. Now is not the time to stop and explain. I have to know what's happening.

I run to my car, a bead of sweat beginning to form on my upper lip, despite the icy cold wind whipping around me. I fumble with my keys, having to press the key fob repeatedly to get the mechanism to release.

'Damn it, not now!' I shout at the car, as if it's doing this to me on purpose. My heart is racing, pumping adrenalin around my body.

When I arrive at the house it's hard to tell from the outside whether or not Grace is at home. I ring the bell several times and bend to look through the letterbox. There's no response, but nothing appears to be out of place, as far as I can tell. I simply know that an old lady is unlikely to have ventured out on her own in this weather. She must be inside the house. I step over the shrubbery in front of the sitting room window and cup my hands around my eyes as I peer inside.

I can't see Grace, but the fire is lit and everything looks very normal. Something moves to the right-hand side of me and I notice the neighbour's curtain being pulled back. A face appears.

I wave out and a woman opens the window to hear what I'm saying.

'Is everything all right?'

'I'm … um … making a delivery, but can't get a reply. I'm a little worried as the fire is lit and I know Grace is waiting for her grandson. I'm not sure what to do.'

The look on my face is enough to communicate my concern and the woman indicates for me to wait. She closes the window and within a few minutes is standing next to me.

'I have a key, for emergencies.' She waves it in front of me. 'I don't think Grace will mind, she's probably resting upstairs. She might have fallen asleep.'

'Thank you so much,' I add as she inserts the key and the door swings open.

'Hellooo, Grace, its Marie – from next door. You have a delivery.'

When there's no reply, Marie gives me a nervous glance and then steps inside. In silence I follow her in, as she checks the kitchen, and then the sitting room.

'Grace, are you upstairs?' she calls, a little tremor catching in her voice.

'I'll go.' I indicate for her to stay downstairs.

Even before my foot is on the first tread, I know what's happened. My eyes fill with tears that start to track down my face.

'Grace,' my voice is barely a whisper, 'it's only Katie.'

She's on the bed, fully dressed, and lying there peacefully as if she's merely resting. Without having to check, I know it's too late. Her skin is rosy pink. She looks content and there is a faint smile on her face. The end was not a struggle, it was a release, and for that I whisper a little prayer of thanks.

It's Over and I Can't Believe It

'But, she can't be dead.' Adam's voice doesn't break, it remains steady and he's insistent. 'I tried to ring to let Grandma know we were leaving, but she was asleep.'

Grace's neighbour, Marie, gently takes Lily by the hand to lead her out of the room. The house is full of people and I hope Lily doesn't understand what's happened. Adam isn't in a fit state to comfort her. Marie, at least, is calm and will no doubt take Lily back to her own home.

'Adam, please sit down. I'm so very sorry.' My voice is reduced to a faint plea. I mop at my eyes once again with the soggy tissue in my hand.

'She can't be dead.' He repeats the words, his voice emotionless. His face is now ashen and his hands begin to tremble. 'She … can't … be gone …' His words fall apart as the tears stream down his face. His body is wracked with sobs.

What can I do? What can I say? I throw my arms around him as if I have every right to be the one to provide comfort. He clings to me, our tears mingling. I'm not even sure he knows who I am. His confusion and distress tears at my heart. He begins to rock back and forth ever so lightly on his feet, but he doesn't loosen his grip for several minutes.

Gradually he stills, and then pulls back, gently. The pallor on his skin is such that I wonder if he's going to faint, but he remains upright.

'Sorry, sorry … it's just … the shock.' He rubs his face roughly with his hands, raking them across his eyes in an attempt to compose himself. Taking a deep breath, he turns to look at me, our eyes lock and recognition sets in. 'Katie ... it's you ... what? What are you doing here?'

He shakes his head in an attempt to clear his mind. He's clearly confused and finding it too much to take in.

'I was making a delivery. I'm so sorry this should happen now. Your grandmother is upstairs. I think her passing was peaceful. She was all ready for your visit, but it seems she simply went to lie down for a while. It's a lovely way to go, Adam, as she looks at rest.'

He's struggling to take in what I'm trying to tell him. His head keeps turning towards the hallway and then back to me, questioningly, as if he doesn't understand.

'Lily ...'

'Lily's fine. Marie has taken her next door. Adam, the doctor is with Grace, and she's upstairs. You need to see her. Do you want me to come with you?'

I speak slowly, letting him digest my words. He nods his head, but doesn't make any attempt to move. Touching his arm lightly, I guide him out into the hallway and past two policemen, who immediately step back out of our way. His legs don't seem to be working properly, and we climb the stairs slowly, one at a time. I have to apply pressure to his arm, to encourage him to take each step.

The doctor appears on the landing and can see that Adam is in a state of complete shock. He gives a curt nod of acknowledgement and moves to one side. He leans into me and whispers, 'An ambulance is on the way. I think she passed about two hours ago.'

Adam takes a step forward, turning around to look at me for approval.

'Go ahead,' I say, gently, increasing the pressure on his arm.

He enters the room, barely glancing at the bed, and walks straight over to the window. He places both hands palm down on the sill. His silhouette trembles with wracking, dry sobs. I can't control my tears once more and I lean against the wall, overwhelmed by the scene I'm witnessing.

Minutes pass and my head begins to pound. I can't take my eyes away from Adam's back; it's the saddest thing I've ever witnessed. Then he turns, walking on unsteady feet across to the bed, and drops down onto his knees.

'Oh my love, my love,' he cries out in anguish. He very gently takes her hand in his. 'You can't leave us. I'm not ready to let you go.'

After a few moments, he moves his other hand up, to gently touch her cheek.

'She looks like she's sleeping. Maybe the doctor is wrong.' His voice is begging, his eyes wild with torment.

'I wish that, too, Adam. But in your heart, you know it's a blessed release for her.'

'Is it true what they say?'

I look at him, my mind a blank. I have no idea what he's talking about.

'That when the soul leaves the body it stays close for a while, before it finally departs.'

The look of desperation on his face is too much to bear. I drag my sleeve across my eyes, so that I can see him more clearly. I kneel down, facing him across the bed.

'I don't know, Adam, I wish I did. Shall we stay here for a little while, so Grace isn't alone?'

'I'd like that. Katie, will you do something for me? Will you hold her other hand?'

I nod, unable to speak, and gently take her right hand in mine.

'You're not alone, Grandma,' he whispers. 'We're here

with you. I don't want to let you go, but I have no choice. It will be all right. I promise.'

How much times passes, I have no idea, but the doctor reappears and hovers. He wants to say something, but is hesitant to disturb the vigil.

I look up at him, and he clears his throat, going on to explain that the ambulance has arrived. He tells Adam to take as long as he needs and leaves the room.

After a while, Adam looks across at me. I think he's ready, but a part of him also doesn't want to let her go. I think he wants someone else to make the decision. What right do I have to be the one to say it's time for her to be taken away? The reality of the situation is that there is no one else and maybe this is something I can do for them both. The words *everything happens for a reason* flash through my head.

I gently lay Grace's hand back down on the bed and walk around to Adam. Kneeling next to him, I place my hand alongside his own.

'It's time, isn't it?' His words sound fearful. 'I can't seem to let go.'

'Hold my hand, Adam.' I take my hand off the bed and hold it out to him. He stares at it without moving. After a few moments, he shifts his position and raises himself up onto one knee, his hand still covering Grace's. Gradually, inch-by-inch, his hand withdraws from hers. He grabs mine with an intensity that almost makes me cry out.

Hand in hand we leave the room and he doesn't look back. He follows me as I lead him downstairs and into the kitchen. When I let go of his hand, he stands there seemingly unable to move. I steer him in front of a chair and press him down into it.

Discreetly I shut the kitchen door, I don't want Adam

to see the ambulance men when they enter, or exit. Then I begin searching through the cupboards, until I find a bottle of something alcoholic and a couple of glasses. Sitting down next to Adam, I pour two fingers of brandy into each and slide one glass in front of him.

He stares down into it, blankly.

'I don't drink brandy,' he states, with a puzzled look on his face.

'Neither do I.'

I touch his hand and smile at him, pointedly. He acknowledges with a grunt and lifts the glass to his lips.

Summer

Adam

A Battle of Wills

'Lily, Leonie's here.'

Lily waves, but doesn't seem to be making any attempt at all to move, content to remain in the tree house. 'We need to leave very shortly,' I add, in case she's forgotten.

Why is it that kids have absolutely no sense of time, or urgency? Lily knows full well that Leonie and I have a dinner date tonight. When I agreed she could go and sit in the tree house to read, she promised me faithfully she'd pack up the instant Leonie arrived.

'Ten minutes and we have to go, darling. Being late is so rude. Everyone else will be on time.'

Leonie is looking very chic tonight. Her little black dress is perfectly accompanied by the delicate gold chain she chose for her birthday.

I quickly run the clothes brush over my jacket and then pop my head out to hurry Lily along.

'Lily, it's time. Your bag is ready. Charlotte and Emily will be waiting.'

Lily looks back at me sulkily and very reluctantly begins climbing down. I wander out to meet her, hoping to avoid any hint of a tantrum.

'What's up?' I kneel down in front of her and her bottom lip trembles.

'Do you have to go out tonight, Dad? I don't feel well.'

'Where does it hurt?'

She hangs her head to one side, considering her answer.

'I'm itchy, on my arms.'

'Well, maybe we didn't apply enough sunscreen. They

209

are a little pink and I suspect that's making them feel a bit sensitive. I'll grab some moisturiser and after you've had your shower, you can ask Charlotte to help you apply it.' I plant a kiss on her forehead. 'That's my girl. Now, go and grab your bag and I'll walk you next door.'

Back in the kitchen Leonie looks up and then taps her watch.

'We're ready.' I'm annoyed at the reminder. 'Two minutes and I'll be back. I'll meet you at the car.'

Lily saunters past Leonie and there's no eye contact whatsoever between them. I sigh, wishing one, or the other, would make an effort to lighten the tension.

Leonie utters, 'Good night, Lily,' but I know she's only saying it for my benefit. Lily knows that too, so it's a wasted gesture.

Lily's response is hardly audible, but fortunately Leonie is in no mood to pick up on it.

'Two minutes,' I mouth as I follow Lily out of the door. I throw the house keys across to Leonie. 'Just the front door, everything else is locked up.'

I explain to Charlotte we're running late, give Lily a kiss and a hug, then make my way to the car.

After Leonie convinced me that my old job was too demanding, it was a big step backwards accepting the IT support job they offered me. My boss thought so too, but it was good of him to accommodate my request. I thought it would solve all of my problems, although I appreciated that my new working day was going to be rather mundane from that point onwards. The switch from troubleshooting major problems to carrying out routine maintenance was the price for keeping Leonie happy.

Leonie used to dread the week I was travelling because I was rarely at home. Now I'm working from home permanently, it's the week Lily is with me that causes all of the problems between us. By necessity it has to revolve around school-runs, after-school activities, father/daughter time with Lily, and running the house. It seems I can't win, no matter what I do. I understand that sometimes Leonie feels like an outsider when Lily's around. She doesn't seem to appreciate that kids have to be the centre of your world while they are growing up and that's the sacrifice every parent has to make. Except, of course, Leonie isn't a parent, and I am. She's already tired of constantly having to make an effort with Lily. The novelty of being around a nine-year-old waned very quickly and now it's like a war zone around here at times. The divide between Leonie and Lily grows with each passing day. I'm caught in the middle, trying to keep them both happy.

I'm tired of Leonie's complaints. 'You spoil her,' she accuses and, 'You don't have to jump every time Lily snaps her fingers.' If she could only hear herself, some of her comments are unnecessary and untrue. I don't spoil Lily, I often lay down the law and Lily knows where the line is drawn. She's growing up, and yes, they can all be a little difficult at times, but trying to push the boundaries is a part of the learning curve. Leonie can only ever see things from her own perspective. If something inconveniences her, then all hell is let loose.

I've tried to explain that Lily won't be a child forever. As each year passes, she will become more, and more, independent. Leonie's response to that was to rant on about how awful teenagers can be. She then proceeded to tell me that I was an over-protective father, whose actions were guilt-driven. Of course, that wasn't just upsetting, I then had to go away and think about whether she had a point.

I know the situation isn't easy, but Leonie refuses to have any sympathy, or empathy, for a little girl growing up under difficult circumstances. I know it happens to so many families these days, but that fact doesn't change anything, or make it any easier. We all want the very best for our kids and maybe Leonie will only ever understand that if she has a child of her own. The worrying thought that crosses my mind is whether some women simply don't have that natural mothering instinct within them. As a loving father, I know how difficult I find it taking on both roles when Lily is with me. As much as I dote on my daughter, there was so much I didn't understand until I found myself having to cope on my own, twenty-four hours a day.

I'm trying to be fair and see things through Leonie's eyes. I will admit that Lily can be demanding at times, but she isn't some spoiled kid who makes ridiculous demands and always insists on getting her own way. Admittedly, there are times Lily forgets that as three, we now have another person's preferences to consider. However, on the whole, I think she's handling it well, given the circumstances. As for Leonie, it appears she's digging in her heels and picking up on anything and everything she can, simply to prove a point. What she can't see is that if she doesn't start trying to build bridges, this isn't ever going to work. It's not about winners, or losers – or scoring points.

'Going through probate is such a chore, bet you're glad that's all behind you now. Does that mean the house is up for sale?' Alan looks across at Leonie and then turns his head in my direction.

'Yes, everything is sorted, and no, the house isn't on the market.'

I feel I'm being set up here. Has Leonie been talking to Alan about it and primed him to raise the subject?

'What are you going to do with it?'

'Yes, Adam, what are you going to do with it?' Leonie repeats, with a slight edge to her voice.

I lay down my knife and fork, rest my elbows on the table, and take a deep breath.

'The answer is that I don't know.'

'You'll never live there, your home is here. It has to go, unless you want to rent it out.' Clearly Alan can't understand why I'm holding off, and I'm well aware of Leonie's view on this. Alan continues, seemingly unaware that this is still a very sensitive issue between the two of us.

'The money could be invested and earning you interest, Adam. You can't be sentimental about bricks and mortar. It's an asset, pure and simple. Your grandmother wouldn't have wanted it to remain empty forever.'

'I agree,' Leonie softens her voice and gives me a reassuring smile.

'I need a little more time, that's all. I'll do the right thing in the end. Maybe I will rent it out for a while.'

The thought of some stranger living in Grace's house is more than I can bear, but I'm not going to admit that. Lily, too, has asked about it once or twice. She misses our little trips and we haven't been back since the funeral. A removal company went in to pack everything up and put it all into storage until I can face sorting out the contents. I pay one of the neighbours to call in once a week to check over the house and to keep the outside tidy. Marie, from next door, has a key and she keeps a general eye on things.

I wish someone would change the subject and I flash

Amanda a look of sheer desperation. She rises to the occasion, as I knew she would, and launches into a conversation about hot tubs.

Maybe it is time Lily and I did the trip once more. Maybe if we said our goodbyes to the house, we could move on. I accept that it's a house designed for a family and Grace would be sad to think of it standing empty. Knowing that doesn't make it any easier, though, and I keep putting off making a decision.

Suddenly, I feel very tired and I want to check on Lily.

'I won't be long,' I say, rising from my chair. 'I'm going to give Charlotte a call to see if Lily's okay. She wasn't feeling well earlier.'

All heads turn my way as I walk towards the bar and Leonie doesn't look pleased. I don't know why, because I've hardly contributed to the conversation this evening.

'Charlotte, it's me. How's Lily? She said her skin was itchy when she was in the garden.'

'She's fine. We put on some moisturiser and now they're tucked up in bed, both of them are sound asleep.'

She seems relaxed, I'm worrying over nothing.

'Great. Thanks.' I feel like I'm being over-protective and I'm sure that's how Leonie looks at it.

'It's only natural she's still a bit clingy, Adam. There are bound to be times when she thinks about her great-grandma and wishes she was still here. She probably doesn't mention it because she knows how upset it would make you. Today might have been a sad day for her, but she's been absolutely fine all evening.'

'Thanks. If she wakes up and she wants to come home early you will call me, won't you? No matter what time of the night it is.'

'I thought Leonie was staying over?'

'She is, but she'll understand. You know – if it's important.'

As I walk back to the table and take my seat, a wave of laughter erupts.

'What?' I ask, looking at them all blankly.

'We were taking bets,' Alan admits, winking at Leonie.

'On?'

'On how long it would take you to check in with the babysitter.'

I stand up and as I push back my chair, I shoot Leonie a look of complete and utter distaste.

'You don't get it, do you? I don't care about possessions and money, or what people think. Having a child means you put them first, every time. My daughter's missing her great-grandmother and if she wakes up feeling upset, I want to be there for her. I'll call you tomorrow, Leonie.'

Most of the people in the restaurant are staring at me now as I make a quick exit. Outside I grit my teeth, willing the anger to subside before I get behind the wheel of the car. I need to calm myself down and think about why, once again, my life is beginning to feel like one big mess.

Katie

Picking Up the Pieces

I feel like a plane that's flying in autopilot mode – nothing that happens seems to invoke any reaction in me, as if I'm a robot devoid of feelings. I get up, go to work and come home. Then it happens all over again – Groundhog Day without the desire to change anything, because I can't even figure out what I could do to make it all right.

The truth is that I simply can't allow myself to feel any more and I know that if I do, I will sink into a depression. After Grace's death I felt like I'd just stepped off a rollercoaster that had taken me from dizzying heights down to sub-zero level in mere seconds. When my body finally equalised there was nothing left to distract me. I decided that it was easier to live in freefall, detaching myself from any emotion whatsoever, than it was to face up to those deep, dark feelings. If I wasn't going to find true happiness, what was the point of getting up every day to face the world? That's a question I'm still trying to keep at bay, hoping that one day I'll wake up to find it no longer applies.

Looking back it feels rather like a dream, if I'm honest. As time passes those mixed feelings of grief, disappointment and heartache are receding and I refuse to let them slip back into my day to day life. When I find myself thinking about Adam, or Lily, it's with fondness. I suppose it's only natural that I should feel for their loss and wonder how they are doing, because it touched my heart. But from now on in it's all about survival and when I feel ready, I have to begin thinking about the future again. But I'm not ready, not just yet.

* * *

'I do wish you'd snap out of this funk you've been in, lately.' Hazel ignores the shrug I give her in response. 'It's not like you to wallow in self-pity. Isn't it about time you told me what's going on in that head of yours? It's like someone has turned a switch off, or something. I'm worried about you and I have been for quite a while.' She ends on a softer note and I know it's not the first time she's tried to get me talking.

'Stop worrying about me all the time. I'm doing fine.'

'Fine, you say. Well, life's too short to live it in a mediocre way and from where I'm standing that's exactly what you've settled for. It doesn't suit you, Katie.' She leans back against the counter, her eyes flashing over my face looking for a reaction.

'Life can't be all fireworks and parties. Sometimes it's about hard work and keeping your head down.'

She laughs, but there's more than a hint of sarcasm in her voice.

'So this is it? This is how it's going to be from here on in?'

In exasperation I place the last cupcake inside the glass cabinet and then turn back to face her.

'It won't be forever, Hazel. It's time to stop dreaming about the unobtainable and make the most of what I have.'

The look on her face is one of shock, as if she's been slapped. She steps forward, placing her hands on my shoulders and leans in, lowering her voice.

'I knew you were devastated, but I didn't realise you'd given up all hope. I mean ... you know where he lives, you could go and see him.'

Her eyes reflect such depth of concern, I find myself holding my breath for a moment. Hazel knows me too well. Did I really think I could fool her?

'That's not an option for so many reasons I couldn't even begin to explain. We all dream, Hazel, but how often do dreams come true? Just be a true friend and accept that it is what it is, and I'm moving on. When I'm good and ready I'll know what to do next, but at the moment I'm content just to get through each day.'

She shakes her head, miserably.

'In my opinion, and as a true friend, I want to tell you that you're making a big mistake. I thought you just needed some time ... but now ... Look, promise me one thing, just ONE thing. If Adam comes back to see you, you'll tell him everything. Just promise me that you won't let him go until he knows the full story.'

'I don't think that would be right. It wouldn't be fair to drag him—'

'You owe it to Grace, even if you don't think you owe it to yourself.'

'It's unlikely I'll ever see him again, anyway.'

'Then it's no big deal to make a promise, is it?'

I nod my head and, at last, Hazel seems satisfied. I don't allow myself the indulgence of fantasy conversations with Adam any more. It's called self-preservation.

Adam

It's Time

'You don't have to go in if you don't want to.' I'm kneeling next to Lily, with my arm around her shoulders. We're standing in front of Grandma Grace's house. 'We can do this another time. It doesn't have to be now.'

Lily chews her lip, glancing anxiously from the house to me and back again.

'When people die, Daddy, are they gone forever?' She looks at me expectantly because, of course, I have all the answers.

'Well, let me think about that one.' I have no idea what to say. 'Hmm ... how can I explain it? We can't see them, but they are always with us, in here.' I pat my chest, hoping Lily realises I mean in our hearts.

'I know that, Dad. I mean, some people see ghosts. Is Grandma Grace a ghost?' She looks at me with hopeful eyes, awaiting a revelation.

'Ghosts aren't real, Lily. Sometimes people want to believe that because it's hard saying goodbye. But it doesn't have to be so hard. You keep on talking to the people you love, as if they are always by your side. We might not be able to see them, but they know what we're feeling.'

I'm not sure what I said even makes sense. How do you explain the unexplainable to a child?

'We can go in now,' Lily replies. 'I'm glad the furniture is gone. It's not Grandma's house any more, is it?'

Lily never fails to astound me. Despite the sadness and the feelings that are still so raw, she's a strong little thing. Her mind is coping with this in the only way it can. I think she was disappointed when I said Grandma Grace isn't a ghost, whereas I thought she might have been frightened by that thought. It hadn't occurred to me she saw it as a potentially positive thing.

Inside the house it feels very strange walking around the empty rooms. Even with the old carpets still on the floor and the familiar curtains hanging at the windows, there's a strange hollowness now it's devoid of furniture and personal effects.

'It feels lonely,' Lily comments. She seems touched by the thought and yet completely unfazed by it.

The irony is not lost on me that I was thinking exactly the same thing.

'Dad?'

'Yes?'

'Can we buy some cupcakes?'

Her eyes follow me as I walk across to peer out of the window. When there's only emptiness inside, the only option is to find something, anything, to focus upon.

'I don't know, Lily. Maybe not today.'

She pulls a face. 'Please.' Her voice raises a pitch or two, as it does when she's trying to talk me into something.

'We don't want to upset Katie, now do we?'

Lily thinks about it for a moment. We haven't seen Katie since the funeral. I can't imagine how awful it must have been for her, being the one to discover Grace. We didn't have a chance to really talk about it. I remember she was very kind, but most of it is a blur.

'Grandma Grace says we need to let Katie know how we are. She's worried about us and we shouldn't go home until we've seen her.'

A chill runs through me, wondering what on earth is going through Lily's head. She makes the statement, as if it's a simple fact that I've overlooked.

'It's lovely that you think about Katie, she has been a good friend. Yes, we can go to see her if it's important to you. Grandma can't talk to you now she's in heaven, Lily, it's simply the thoughts going around in your head.'

'Does Grandma talk to you, Dad?'

'Well, no.'

'Then how would you know?'

How can you argue with the logic of a child's mind? You can't. So we head off to Sweet Occasions and I admit that my stomach is doing somersaults. Is it because it's the first time since Grace's passing? Or is it the prospect of seeing Katie again?

As usual, there are no free parking spaces outside the shop. We have to park up and walk back to it. As we approach I notice something looks different and it registers that the sign above the shop is sporting a new logo.

Inside there's the usual Saturday lunchtime queue and two people are busy serving. One of them is Hazel, who acknowledges us with a cheerful wave when our eyes make contact. As usual, while we are waiting in the queue Lily deliberates over which cupcake she's going to have. Every time we come in there are new and exciting flavours. Business must be good.

'What can I do for you today?' Hazel beams at us, when finally we're at the head of the queue.

'I'm going to have one of those, please. Lily, have you made up your mind?'

Lily curls up her hand, resting it beneath her chin in thinking mode.

'Hmm, not quite decided ...'

Hazel smiles. 'It's been a while. How are you both?'

'We're good, thanks. The new sign is eye-catching.'

'Yes. Steve's a partner in the business now. We've won a contract with a supermarket chain and Sweet Occasions' cupcakes will be going into mass production. The bakery is being moved to a big new unit up on the industrial estate. The kitchen here will be used to run cake decorating courses, eventually. Steve says it will then justify keeping the shop open.' Hazel sounds excited at the prospect. 'I'll give Katie a shout; she'll be pleased to see you both.'

Hazel disappears before I have time to stop her. It's not quite the news I was expecting and while I'm glad things are going well, for some weird reason I feel … disappointed. People's lives move on. Katie and Steve have obviously overcome whatever problems they had. Besides, I have Leonie. What on earth is wrong with me?

The moment I spot Katie, I know precisely what's wrong with me. Oh, no, this is bad, very bad. Katie walks around the counter and kneels down next to Lily.

'This is a rather nice surprise. That's a very pretty dress, Lily. And you've had your hair cut. You look very grown-up.'

I watch with dismay as instead of returning Katie's smile, Lily's bottom lip begins to quiver and suddenly, without any warning whatsoever, she throws her arms around Katie. It isn't a gentle hug, she appears to be clinging on as if she has no intention of letting go. Katie is clearly taken by surprise and looks up at me, her eyes reflecting concern. She makes no attempt to draw away, but instead talks softly into Lily's ear.

'We have some very special cupcakes today with icing the same colour as your dress. Would you like to try one of those, or how about the fondant sparkle – it's covered in glitter and has a little wand.'

With Lily's arms still firmly clasped around her, Katie

turns slightly to point to the display case. Lily's eyes follow her hand, but she makes no attempt to reply.

'Can't decide? Go and sit down at one of the tables and I'll bring you over a little selection to try.' Lily rather reluctantly lets go to make her way to a table. Katie stands and looks at me, searching my face with her eyes.

'It breaks my heart to think of how much Lily misses Grace. How are you doing?' she asks, softly.

It takes a moment for me to reply. The feeling that grips me isn't one of sadness linked to Grandma Grace's death, as I'd feared, but much worse. It's a feeling of longing. I want everyone to disappear, so that it's just the two of us. I want to sit down and pour out my heart to her. Instead, I say the first thing that comes into my head.

'Some days are better than others. I see you have a new sign.'

She frowns, what was she expecting me to say?

'Yes, lots of things happening at the moment. Time to move on. But it's all good. Coffee?'

I nod and, as she walks over to prepare the drinks, I can't take my eyes off her. She looks different in some way. Happier, I suppose and, stupidly, it feels like a blow to my stomach. I don't want her to be unhappy, ever.

'Dad, I love coming here,' Lily's sing-song pitch touches my heart as I sit down next to her.

I smile, ruffling her hair. 'Spoken like a true lover of cake. What's not to like here? And don't go getting any more ideas about birthday cakes. We can't expect Katie to make another trip this year.'

Lily fakes a trembling lip, but ends up giggling.

'Aw, Dad. The princess cake was such fun. Of course, I'm too grown-up for that now.'

Katie overhears Lily's response as she places a tray down

on the table. There's a large plate with several cupcakes sliced into quarters, two cups of coffee and a milk shake.

'Well, I can't believe how much you've grown since I last saw you.'

As soon as Katie finishes speaking she flashes me a worried glance. No doubt remembering that the last time was, in fact, at the funeral. Lily, though, seems unaware and is already sampling one of the cupcakes.

'Thank you, Katie, this is delicious,' she mumbles, her mouth full of cake.

Katie seems genuinely pleased to see us. It's clear she wants to say something, but is hesitant because Lily is watching us both intently.

'Lily, why don't you go and take a look through one of Katie's cake catalogues? I'm not promising, but if we're this way maybe we would be able to pick one up for this year's birthday party.' Almost before I've finished speaking, Lily is up and racing over to begin looking.

'She's growing up so fast,' I automatically comment as I watch her.

Katie nods.

'She's a lovely girl, Adam. How is she taking it? This must be your first trip back. I'm assuming that's what the hug was all about. It really brought a lump to my throat.'

I place my coffee cup back down on the table and turn to face Katie. Our eyes meet and I know we're both thinking about that awful day.

'It's been tough, I'll admit. She was fine at the house today, though. A little disappointed, I fear, when I had to explain that Grandma Grace wasn't a ghost. I think she hoped that when we went inside she'd still be there. It rather took me by surprise, but it reminded me how resilient kids are.'

Katie's eyes look sad. She leans in, lowering her voice.

'And how are you doing – really?' Katie looks up into my face and something tangible passes between us. Whether it's sympathy, empathy, or sorrow, I don't know, but it's powerful, and we both feel it. I have to look away, as I'm scared I'm going to say something I shouldn't. Instead, I take a deep breath and make light of it.

'I'm doing fine. Besides, I have to stay strong for Lily.'

I can see that Katie has something on her mind, but whatever it is she doesn't share it. Instead, she picks up the plate and smiles, a little sparkle in her eyes.

'Sample the latest flavours. Lavender cream dream and very berry sparkle. Watch out for the glitter, though, if you get it on your fingers you'll end up with sparkly bits everywhere.'

We start laughing and I take the largest piece on the plate.

'It's worth the risk! Things are going well, I hope?' I have to ask the question, despite kicking myself for being such a fool. Katie takes a deep breath, as if she's going to make an announcement, but she doesn't get a chance to reply as Lily comes bounding back with an open catalogue in her hands.

'Dad, can I have a guitar cake? Please, please, pretty please?'

I roll my eyes. 'I said maybe, young lady. I can't promise, but we'll have to come back to Grandma's again soon. I'll try my best to arrange it so that it's around your birthday. We can place an order as soon as we know for sure.'

'Oh, Katie! My friends would think this cake was so cool! Dad, I'll be super-good and I promise I'll be on my best behaviour with Leonie.'

As soon as Lily mentions the name, Katie looks directly at me. She doesn't say anything at all, but she seems surprised. For one moment the sparkle goes out of her eyes and then, in an instant, it's back again.

'Well, you should try to be good all the time and not just when you want something special. I'm sure we can arrange it. Now, Lily, have you decided which cupcakes you want to take back with us?'

'The sparkly ones, please, Dad.'

I roll my eyes and both Katie and Lily start giggling. 'Why am I not surprised?'

In the car on the way home, Lily soon drops off to sleep. The constant chatter from the radio is irritating and I turn it off, letting my thoughts take over. I remember hugging Katie as we cried in Grace's bedroom. Then, at the funeral, I recall Katie putting her arm around Lily and holding her close as she sobbed her heart out. Leonie was there too, but she stayed aloof throughout, seemingly untouched by our loss. Afterwards, Leonie said she was horrified that someone who wasn't family should have 'invited herself along' to the funeral. When I corrected her and said that not only was it very kind of Katie to attend, but that she had been invited, Leonie was scathing.

'She doesn't know us, Adam. She's just someone who sells cakes.'

There was no point in responding, as whatever I had said would have fuelled the fire of Leonie's indignation. What she failed to comprehend was that Katie was the first person to see Grace after she had passed. In my eyes that gave her every right to be there and every right to shed tears. You'd have to be heartless not to be affected by something as meaningful as that.

As darkness descended my mind was waging a battle. On one side there was Leonie, and on the other, Katie.

Every time something popped into my head, I found myself comparing them. Little things, like the way Leonie talks to Lily and the way she often says the wrong thing. Then Katie, always positive and upbeat, treating Lily as if she was an adult, rather than talking down to her.

I remember Grandma saying to me once that everything happens for a reason. Is this my wake-up call? Are my instincts finally telling me that Leonie isn't the right person for me? As the reality of that thought sinks in, my stomach begins to churn. I've been avoiding the issue because I'm feeling ground-down and this a very bitter pill to swallow. But what sort of an example am I setting Lily, who doesn't deserve the upheaval of another break-up? Although, if I'm honest about it, I'm not sure she'll be too unhappy. I think Leonie liked the idea of being a part of a family, but the reality of the situation was something very different. She soon tired of having a third person to consider when it came to our relationship, even though I made it clear from the start that Lily has to be my first priority.

The more I think about what I have to do next, the more depressed I feel. With no one to talk to now Grace is gone, I feel very alone at times. She was my comfort during hard times and also my voice of reason. What do you think I should do, Grandma? My mind sends out the appeal, as if expecting some sort of sign. But my journey home continues in silence, each passing mile reminding me I'm going back to a mess and there is no one to blame but myself.

No One Really Wants To Be Alone

My heart missed a beat when I saw him. There hasn't been a single day since the funeral that I haven't thought about Adam and Lily. I had to resist the temptation to jump in the car and drive up to see how they were doing. Then I would remind myself that Adam knew nothing about Grace's plan and, even so, his life was moving forward in another direction. Watching them leave is tough, a reminder that there is no link between us other than the fact that he's a customer.

'I can't believe you let him go, just like that, without saying anything!' Hazel walks towards me, eyes flashing with indignation. 'Clearly the guy has feelings for you and his lovely grandma said exactly the same thing. You're lonely and alone – hello, wake-up call here.'

I try to walk away, but Hazel follows me into the office.

'Look, even if he did like me, maybe the timing is right for me but it isn't right for him. He's still with Leonie, Lily mentioned her by name. Besides, I think you're reading this all wrong. He's lost his grandmother and his best friend, his confidante. All we've ever done is talk, as friends, and the sort of friends who aren't involved in each other's lives. It's comforting being able to share things with someone when you have no idea if you will ever see them again. They don't meddle in your life, because they aren't a part of it and they don't judge you, because they don't really know you. It's convenient.' It's also very, very sad.

'How can you be so totally clueless when it comes to reading the signals that people give out? If you don't start opening your eyes soon, you're going to end up spending the rest of your life alone. Just because Lily mentioned her, doesn't mean to say it's all hearts and roses.' Her tone softens and I know she's only trying to look out for me. 'I tried so hard to get you to see the truth about your relationship with Steve and now I'm wondering whether I did the right thing. It's hard to stand by and watch my best friend pushing the world away.'

She places her arm around my shoulders and gives me a well-meaning squeeze.

'I want you to be happy, Katie. You deserve that, but it will only happen if you let it.'

Hazel's words hurt, not least because of the fact that I feel a connection to both Adam and Lily, as if it was real. There is a little ache deep inside of me, like a nagging pain, that won't go away whenever I think of him. But I'm the only one who is free as a bird. How could I say anything, even if I found the courage to admit how I feel about him? Once again, I've backed myself into a corner and I have to stop dwelling on things that aren't meant to be. Hazel is right in one way, but very wrong in another. If Adam was truly interested in me he would have said something by now, wouldn't he?

If I saw a relationship expert, I'm sure it would be pointed out that I keep making the same mistakes. I'm afraid to talk about how I feel and act upon those feelings. Happiness always seems to elude me. I let one day follow another, waiting for things to happen rather than grabbing the moment. With Steve, I was hanging in there out of a sense of duty, when all it did was delay the inevitable. Look at us now. Steve is sorting out his life and moving on. Our business relationship is working well now I've seen sense and stopped letting my heart rule my head. I guess he was right all along.

I'm the one who can't seem to move forward and yet I was so sure that Steve would be the one to fall apart. I believed he was fragile, what a fool I am! What makes life hard at the moment is that everyone I know is in a relationship and suddenly I'm the odd one out. Hazel says my problem is that I've forgotten how to have fun. What she doesn't understand is that it's all about confidence and mine has taken a knock lately. Where do I begin, when it comes to making a fresh start? How do you get yourself back into the world of dating? Well, obviously it's all about making better decisions in the first place. I have to accept that just because I want something, doesn't mean to say I'm going to get it. Alternatively, I shouldn't go for the easy option and grab every opportunity that comes along. I knew this wasn't going to be easy, but it's actually a minefield. However, if I don't make some sort of effort, then nothing at all will change and I will remain in limbo.

Maybe I'll join the local gym. It will give me something to do and who knows, if what I hear is true, then it's better than signing on with a dating agency.

It's official. Being single isn't fun. It's all solitary meals and always being the lone female if all of your friends happen to be couples. Walking into places and having to make an effort to talk to total strangers is daunting. I enjoy working out though and I'm seven pounds lighter after just the first couple of weeks. My arms and legs are looking toned and I'm on nodding terms with at least a dozen regulars. Talk usually revolves around the equipment, or the weather, and it's very plain that I'm useless at making small talk. I look around at the other, obviously single, ladies and the reason men talk to them is that they are easy to approach. They seem to slip into conversation mode so effortlessly and I envy them that. The moment a guy starts talking to me, I clam up and it feels awkward. They soon give up, despite my best efforts. I'm not being unfriendly – I'm simply out of practice and a little shy with people I don't know. Another session over and it's a success on the workout front. It's a total disaster in terms of getting to know people, as I haven't spoken to anyone at all during the session. Except for the receptionist, of course, and that was a simple 'good evening'.

Arriving home, my landlord is waiting outside the house. He looks like he's loitering with intent, which is extremely odd, to say the least.

'Anything wrong? You look like you've been waiting a while. Problems?' A horrible thought runs through my mind that maybe there's been a glitch at the bank and my rent hasn't been paid this month. Landlords like prompt payers. Until I can get a mortgage sorted out, and find the perfect property, this is my home.

'I was waiting to see you, actually.'

'You'd better come inside.' I swing open the door and the irony of inviting my landlord into his own house makes me smile.

'What's funny?' Liam asks, quizzically.

'It's weird, that's all. I'm not used to renting and this is your house, after all. Sorry, it's been a long day. What can I do for you?'

I don't want to offer him a coffee or anything because I'm longing to have a shower, pour myself a large glass of wine, and lounge on the sofa with my feet up.

'I wondered if you fancied going for a drink sometime.'
Well, this is a surprise. He's very casual about it, considering
the few times we've spoken to date have been rather short
and to the point. I take a moment, evaluating whether or
not this is a good idea. Am I even remotely interested in
him? I can't decide.

'Ooh, not quite the response I'd hoped for. Tough
decision?' He looks put out.

'I'm thinking,' I muse. 'Okay, I can't see why not.'

'Well, there's no need to sound so excited about it.'
He's amused, but thankfully he doesn't seem to have
taken offence. Why am I playing it so cool? Normally I'd
be nervous and overly-polite. Grace's words, 'everything
happens for a reason', pop into my head. Maybe this is
the new me, the one who thinks with her head first and her
heart second.

'A drink would be nice, thanks.'

'Great, well, shall we say Saturday at seven and I'll pick
you up here?'

It's funny how you don't really notice someone until
something happens to make you stop and look at them
in another light. He's quite cute, rather tall, and very
confident. I could do worse.

'Seven it is,' I reply, sounding extremely laid-back,
indeed. I think Hazel would be proud of me on several
counts.

Maybe someone up there is taking pity on me, showing
me it isn't that hard to get back into the swing of being
single. As I watch him walk back down the path he turns
and gives a little wave. I suppose a part of me is flattered,
but another part of me is wondering whether this is going
to be one complication too far. Well, I'm already living in
his house, so I suppose the least I can do is have a drink

with him. I smile to myself, thinking it's like a scenario from a sitcom.

Liam is a distraction. I admit he's beginning to grow on me a little and he's doing my ego the power of good. Suddenly, all of the small things that need repairing are getting done. He calls in on his way home from work with a few tools. Now the basin tap in the bathroom no longer drips and the window in the bedroom shuts properly. He's handy to have around, that's for sure. He's trying to impress me and yet I must come across as the Ice Queen. The harder he tries, the more I hold him at a distance. It's like a game and it's rather fun. That sounds mean, but I've been straight with him, so I can only assume he has nothing better to do.

Liam's head pops around the door. 'The washing machine isn't leaking any more.'

'About time,' I retort. 'What took you so long?' Lifting my head up from the book I'm reading, I notice his expression is one of disappointment. I was supposed to say how clever he is, being such a multitasker.

'I don't suppose I could get a cup of coffee?' He looks at me, hopefully.

'Well, I guess you've earned yourself one,' I reply, begrudgingly. I wouldn't want him to start feeling at home. He might own the bricks and mortar, but this side of the threshold is my domain.

'Has anyone ever told you that you're a hard lady to impress?'

He follows me into the kitchen and I look back over my shoulder, throwing him a dismissive stare. 'Repeatedly.'

'What was the verdict on Saturday evening?'

'The jury is still out.'

'Oh, I thought it went rather well, for a first date.' He

pretends to look peeved and I can't resist a smirk. I wonder what my problem is and maybe it's because he's a few years younger than me. I'm having a hard time taking him seriously.

As all of these thoughts are running through my head, I fill the kettle and flick the switch into life. Turning around to grab some coffee mugs, Liam is suddenly there in front of me and before I know what's happening, his lips are on mine. I have one mug in each hand and as he backs away I'm left with a look of sheer surprise on my face.

'That was totally pointless,' I remark, not sure how I feel about it.

'Oh, I thought it was rather nice.' He looks a bit crestfallen considering it was unasked for, and unwarranted.

'Wrong girl, wrong time. I thought I'd made it quite plain, Liam.'

He looks at me, jutting out his lower jaw while he considers my remark.

'As surprise kisses go, how did it rate?'

'Don't you ever give up? It's bad form to ask for a rating on a kiss and very ungentlemanly of you, given the circumstances.'

'I can't help it if I find you very attractive, Katie. I don't throw myself at every single woman I meet, honestly. Okay, that was out of order. I feel it was justified though. I want you to know that when you're ready to get back into a relationship, I'm here for you. A guy has to make an impression when he can because you only get one chance.'

Now that's grown-up talk, maybe he isn't such a boy after all.

'Impression made, but your chances are slim to none. However, when it comes to assessing you as a landlord, you are up there at the top of the scale.' I can tell by the expression on his face that he isn't listening to what I'm saying.

He's at that point where he finds me intriguing, new territory as yet undiscovered. I've already walked through the whole thing in my head. The handholding, the passion, and then the long drag as we discover our interests are very different. I don't have the patience to go through all that again, even though that early rush of excitement can be exhilarating. I simply can't see the point and that's down to the fact that we have a little sexual frisson going on, but that's all.

Now if it was Adam standing in front of me ... that would be a very different matter, altogether. But Adam has never chosen to seize the moment and I can only assume that was for a very good reason.

Adam

I'm An Idiot, A Lovesick Idiot

Grace was right when she said everything happens for a reason. Walking around the empty house for the first time was a wake-up call. It made me think about my life and what she would be saying to me now. As soon as I returned home I knew I had to face facts and make some radical changes.

The first was to break the news to Leonie that our relationship wasn't working. I expected tears. Instead, I was met with a caustic stare. She wasn't upset that I was saying we were over, only that I was the one breaking up with her. Afterwards, I sat Lily down to explain what had happened, thinking maybe it would be one more thing to unsettle her. She didn't seem at all concerned either way and I was a little surprised about that. It did serve to remind me how strong kids can be and that they often understand more about what's happening than we think they do.

Since we've been back I haven't stopped thinking about Katie. I know that's wrong, but you can't help being attracted to someone and it's not like she's a married woman. Maybe her love life isn't a done-deal. Many relationships move on when things change. Rightly, or wrongly, I've decided that I have nothing to lose in letting her know how I feel. I still have to work out how I'm going to do that. It's not easy, given the physical distance between us, and the main problem is that I can't simply turn up at the shop and blurt it all out.

So, I'm hatching a plan. Kelly is flying off to Spain with her partner and I have Lily for two whole weeks at the start of the school summer holidays. I've arranged for decorators to paint through Grandma's house. When they're done, contractors are going in to replace all the flooring. I've ordered some new furniture and it will mean a stay at the house to unpack the deliveries as they arrive. I explained to Lily that I've rented Grandma Grace's house to the daughter of the lady next door. She's going to be living there for a year. It will give me time to think about what to do with it after that. That's the excuse I need to be within range of Katie. If I'm going to engineer some time with her, then it has to be in a relaxed manner. I thought that maybe I could ask her advice about getting the house all set up. Men aren't supposed to know about curtains and things, so I'm hoping to use that as an excuse. I realise it's a bit sexist assuming she's the sort of lady who enjoys picking soft furnishings, but I'm riding my hunches here.

There's a lot to arrange to get everything geared up, but I'm fighting for a chance to follow my heart. I've never pursued anyone before. I might be wasting my time, but the other option is to do nothing. Then I'll always find myself wondering what might have happened. Whenever I waver, I simply think about her and then all the 'ifs' and 'buts' disappear. If you want something badly enough, then you have to be prepared to fight for it. Women like Katie don't come along very often.

'You're barking mad, mate. What if she turns you down? You will have exposed your hand and set yourself up for a big fall.' Tom looks at me with a look of sheer horror written all over his face.

'So you don't think it's a good idea?' We're side by side, running on treadmills, and talking isn't exactly easy.

I'm beginning to get cold feet, so I need someone else's perspective on this.

'Can't you make it a bit more ... casual?' His voice booms out and I'm conscious other people might be listening. I hit the cool down button, hoping Tom will do the same, and my machine slows to a fast walk. Tom follows suit.

'It's awkward. I know a little bit about her, but there's no way I can get any more information. I do know she's had quite a few problems with the guy she lives with. He's also her business partner now. It might have cemented their relationship, so there's a chance I could be wasting my time. I have to take that risk.'

Tom swipes his towel over his face. He looks up, shaking his head at me.

'Mate, you have it bad. Has she ever indicated that she even likes you? This isn't a rebound thing, after blowing off Leonie?'

'No, it isn't a rebound thing.' Maybe Tom isn't the one to ask, after all. How can I expect him to understand?

'We've talked, that's all. Oh, and she came and helped out at Lily's party. There was definitely something there, between us, I mean. But you know me; I'm not good at reading signals.'

'Your problem, Adam, is that you're too polite. Women like men who keep 'em on their toes.'

As my treadmill grinds to a halt, I feel totally deflated. How on earth am I going to impress Katie? I don't know her well enough to second-guess how best to tackle laying out my emotions. Fear hits me in the gut like a blow.

'Helpful. Thanks, Tom.' Maybe he has a point, or am I over-thinking this and all I can do is stand in front of her and explain how I feel? If she's not interested and she's happily in love with this Steve guy, it will hurt like hell.

One thing I do know is that this is my one and only chance. If this doesn't work out, then at least I won't have any regrets.

'Aren't you forgetting the bigger issue?' Tom shoots me a worried look.

'Which is …?'

'Well, from what you've told me, she lives, works, and her family are all based in the same area. There's a little problem of one hundred and fifty miles to consider. Is it likely she'll pack her bags, leave her career behind and move up here?'

It feels like I've just walked into a brick wall.

It's been one of the hardest weeks of my life. When Tom reminded me that I'd overlooked the one big flaw in my plan, I was devastated. Why did I think it could ever work? Setting aside the fact that I have no idea how Katie feels about me, Lily's school is here, near her mother. There's no way I could uproot her, even if the opportunity arose. Sharing parental responsibility means that I'm tied to living close to Kelly for the foreseeable future. You can't sit someone down to tell them you have feelings for them and then ask them to let go of everything they have, to move away with you.

Whether I like it or not, I have to accept it's unlikely to work out. Even if by some lucky trick of Fate Katie was prepared to be more than simply friends, how could it work? All I can do is make the trip and at least sort the bit of the plan that will work. Getting Grandma Grace's house ready to rent out is something I don't relish, but has to be done. I'm committed to that now and there's no turning back. The phone rings while I'm feeling the most depressed, and dejected, I've ever been in my whole life. I soon wish

I hadn't answered it, when I hear what the contractor has to say.

'No, the work has to be finished by next Friday, at the latest. If the flooring hasn't arrived yet, then find out what *is* in stock and we'll go with that. I need to be able to start moving furniture in quite quickly. I have two beds being delivered on Thursday. I'm staying there with my young daughter and we're arriving on Friday morning.'

I come off the phone feeling annoyed. Managing contractors from a distance isn't easy and not being able to drop in and check whether or not they're on target is stressful. Now I'm being told that the flooring still hasn't arrived and it's going to take at least three days for their team to lay it.

'Dad, what are we going to do about bedding?' Lily's voice breaks my chain of thought. I have to lift myself out of this miserable funk that has descended over me and keep going.

'Good point.' Yet another thing I haven't thought about yet. It's on my 'to do' list, but I'm running out of time.

'We'll call into a shopping mall on the way there. You need to start thinking about what you want to take for the stay. The first couple of days are going to be like camping, until the rest of the furniture arrives. It will be fun.' I sound more upbeat about it than I'm actually feeling.

'We won't have TV,' Lily says with a pout. I'm not sure she's as excited about this adventure as I'd hoped. I can hardly expect her to be enthralled about a couple of weeks away from her friends.

'I'm taking my laptop and a dongle, so we'll have the Internet. You can pack some of your favourite DVDs, too. It will be an adventure. Besides, it will be great to get Grandma's house looking nice.'

Lily sits for a moment, deep in thought. 'Grandma definitely isn't a ghost?' she asks, innocent eyes appealing to me.

'The house is filled with Grandma's love. That will never change, no matter how much fresh paint we put on the walls. Think about how happy it would have made her to know that her neighbour, Marie, will have her daughter living next door for a while. She will be making lots of new memories there, happy ones.'

Her little face doesn't show any particular emotion, only that she's deep in thought.

'Will their memories wipe out all of Grandma Grace's, and Pop's, memories?'

My heart sinks. If this is going to upset Lily, then maybe I should hand it over to a local management company to oversee the final bits.

'It's not the house that stores the memories, it's in here.' I tap my head, and then my chest. 'Memories live on forever. You don't only think of Grandma Grace when you're in her old house, do you?'

'No, I think of Grandma Grace every single day, Dad.'

'I know, and I'm glad to hear that. I think of her all the time, too, but we have to accept that Grandma's house can't remain empty forever. She wouldn't have wanted that and it's our job to get it ready. It won't be all traipsing round shops and buying stuff for the house, we can take some trips out. If the weather is good we can laze in the garden and read.'

Her little face brightens. The moment of concern has passed.

'Dad, do you still love Mum?' Her words come without a hint of warning and it catches me unawares.

'I'll always love your mother, but I'm not in love with

241

her any more. It happens sometimes, Lily, and it's very sad. You have to understand that Mum is much happier now and so am I. What's important to remember is that we love you more than anything else in the whole wide world and we always will.'

Her eyes are glued to my face, taking in every single word as if she might miss something.

'But you aren't happy, Dad.' Lily sounds upset and I have no idea why this is raising its head now.

'What makes you think that?'

'Leonie didn't make you happy and now you're alone again.' Her voice wavers and my heart sinks even further. How can I explain something as complex as adult feelings?

'The thing is ... it's a bit like having a best friend. No one stays the same forever. We learn new things and it changes us. Can you remember your first best friend? I can, it was Eloise and you were three years old. You used to have play dates together. As you grew up your interests changed and since then you've had two very different best friends. It doesn't make you sad though, does it? A new best friend makes you feel happy and they help you to grow, and change. They share their friends, and their interests, with you and you do the same in return. Sometimes a best friend is forever, and sometimes for only a little while.'

I hope I'm making some sense. If I'd had some notice, I could have come up with a polished answer that would sound more reassuring. On the spur of the moment it's the best I can do.

'Dad, it isn't quite the same thing.' She looks at me, soulfully.

This is a path I don't want to tread just yet and I'm holding my breath, wondering where this is heading.

'It isn't?'

242

'Dad, I heard Grandma say she wanted you to find your soulmate. You won't give up, will you?' Now her lip quivers and she gulps, as if stifling a sob.

'Of course I won't give up. One of these days I'll meet someone really special. One thing I know for sure is that she's going to love you too, just as much as I do!'

I kneel down next to her and pull her into my arms, rocking her gently. I hate the fact that my nine-year-old daughter is worrying about me.

What worries me most of all is that I keep repeating the same mistakes over and over again. What sort of example is that for an impressionable nine-year-old? Guess it's time to man-up, Adam, and stop letting life happen. So, you've fallen for a woman who's in a shaky relationship and it's complicated. There are likely to be problems because of the physical distance between you. I'd say it's time to lay your cards on the table and let her decide. If you don't do this now, you will live to regret it and you know that. You've known it for a little while. Worry about the potential problems if it gets to that stage. You have nothing to lose, but your heart.

In one week I've done a three-hundred-and-sixty-degree turn; I've come full circle and the big plan is back on. I'm going to try to convince Katie that we have a chance. Maybe the problems she's had with Steve are because they aren't the proverbial *match made in heaven*. She could be hanging in there for all the wrong reasons, as I did with Kelly. That would be such a waste. If she tells me to go away, I'll respect her wishes, but I'm going to put forward the most persuasive case possible. If there's even a shadow of doubt in her mind about her current relationship, maybe she'll listen to me. If Katie, too, feels that we have some sort of attraction going on, that would be a perfect place to start.

Katie

Putting Down Roots

Okay, so Liam is beginning to grow on me – bit, by bit. He's like a terrier, he doesn't ever give up and he keeps coming back for more. He has fixed absolutely everything in the house that needed fixing and now he's insisted on building a wooden deck in the garden. It's merely an excuse to spend time around me and he doesn't appear to be at all concerned about his lack of subtlety. He's trying everything, and anything, to grab my attention.

Hazel thinks he's cute and she says I'm mad not taking him seriously. The main problem for me is that, at twenty-four years old, he's five, soon to be six years, younger and that feels significant. Besides, his life experience is very different to my own. I know it's easy to judge people when you hardly know them. After what I've been through, I now look at life from a completely different point of view. There's no rose-tinted overlay. I just need to ensure I don't go too far in the other direction and look at everything in an unnecessarily negative way.

Liam is a fun guy and he doesn't come with any baggage. He hasn't yet had to jump over any of the really testing hurdles life can put in front of you. He quite freely admits that his family has money and his portfolio of properties was a gift for his twenty-first birthday. I'm not implying that he doesn't work hard. He has a business degree and he chose to take a few DIY courses to learn some basic maintenance skills. He's financially clued-up and soon realised that being able to mend a leaking tap, or make good a broken window, would save him time and money in the property game.

The only test he's had to face is that his parents hoped for a consummate businessman. They struggle to understand his love of working with his hands, but they don't interfere. He's one of those people who seem to glide through life avoiding the big highs and lows. I sound jaded and I know that. It is nice to spend time with someone who has a simplistic view of life and I'm trying not to hold his age against him. How can I say this without sounding paranoid, or judgemental? Some things you experience in life change you forever and there's no going back. I can't become this light, bright, carefree, single woman whose past doesn't colour the way she looks at the future. I know that maturity isn't only an age thing. With Liam, I feel that I would have to be the worrier and what I'm looking for is a man who will be my rock. I'm tired of having to be the strong one. I'm drained of energy. What I need is someone who will wrap their arms around me and say, 'I'm here, and everything is going to be all right.'

'What are you worrying about, now?' Hazel's voice makes me jump.

'Oh, I was deep in thought. Daydreaming, that's all.'

'Hmm ... I'm not sure that sounds good – work, or pleasure?' She knows me too well and it's hard to hide anything from Hazel.

'Liam,' I admit, rather reluctantly. Only because I'm not good at telling lies and Hazel would only see through it.

'He's a nice guy,' she replies, with a sigh. 'He's easy-going, good on the eye, plus he's financially secure. His car is amazing.' She adds the last comment to taunt me, knowing that I'm not impressed by things like that.

'Yes, and doesn't that smack of boys' toys? A flashy car isn't number one on my list of prerequisites when it comes to a relationship.'

'You're a tough one to please, Katie. What does a guy have to do to hold your interest? Seriously, I'm not joking around here. I know you've had an awful few years with everything that's happened, but life is better now, isn't it?'

I know she wants me to be happy and I want that too, but it has to feel right.

'Yes, life is calmer and maybe even a little dull at times, if I'm honest. The only time I feel truly content is when I'm here, working. Steve was right when he said I don't have a head for business. Since agreeing to the partnership, and handing the finances over to him, a huge burden has been lifted from my shoulders. I'm grateful to him for not giving up on me.'

Hazel flashes me a look of concern.

'You're not considering going back to him, are you? Because if you are, there's something I need to tell you.' I can't believe there are any more surprises left when it comes to Steve. Is this going to turn out to be another well-meaning lecture, I wonder? Before I can ponder any further, she drops the empty trays she's carrying rather noisily onto the pile already stacked on the pallet.

'When I said he cheated on you, there was a little more to it than just a one-off moment of madness.'

'What do you mean?'

'He was planning to leave you. I know that for a fact and I wish I didn't. At the time there was no way I could tell you because by then he'd been diagnosed and everything changed overnight. I figured out that maybe it put everything into perspective for him and he did love you, after all. Sometimes people make mistakes and, anyway, you wouldn't have listened to me.'

'I don't know what to say, Hazel. Are you sure?' At first I'm numb, then angry. Then I realise I don't care any more. That was then and this is now.

'I'm only telling you now in case Steve tries to get back with you. If you are even a little tempted, you have to know the truth. The cracks were there before he became ill and that's why things fell apart afterwards. You were his crutch, Katie, and I think he became yours, too. Safe isn't the answer for either of you, no matter how hard it is to start again.'

As her words sink in, instead of feeling wounded, something clicks into place in my head. I always thought it was his illness that separated the two Steves I knew. I thought of it as *before*, and *after*, assuming getting sick was the trigger. Now that I know his affair wasn't simply a mad, meaningless moment, it all becomes very clear. He clung to me because I stood by him when someone else wouldn't. What held us together wasn't love, but as Hazel pointed out, a sense of safety for all the wrong reasons. He's dating, off and on, but I know he misses the permanency of a long-term relationship, as I do. Ironically we're both experiencing the same problem. The whole dating thing is stressful. Having to encapsulate your life into a meaningful conversation as someone new tries to get to know you isn't easy. Listening as they lay out their life in return and trying not to judge them, as I do with Liam. All you can do is skate over the surface because it takes time to get to know someone.

'Don't worry.' I exhale sharply, looking at Hazel with determination. 'I understand why you couldn't tell me. Be assured, we're over when it comes to a personal relationship. It's strictly business-only and that works for me because he's the right guy for the job.'

'What about Liam?'

'I don't know. Maybe I've been a little hasty. It's not his fault he's younger than I am.'

Hazel absentmindedly squares up a pile of flattened cake boxes.

'And Adam?'

We exchange meaningful glances and the silence is tense.

'Adam never was an option. Our lives centre around two very different worlds. Maybe our paths crossed because it was meant to be a wake-up call. It could be a sort of reminder to me that you can meet someone and instantly want to get to know them better. Okay, that hasn't happened with anyone else so far, but maybe I should hold onto that thought. If I can feel a spark with Adam, then at least it's hope for the future. What about you?'

Jenny has been back almost a month, after telling Hazel she needed some 'alone' time to think. Being apart for a week was probably hard on them both, and it was obvious to us all that Hazel was scared it was over between them. Although she hasn't actually said very much since Jenny returned, I can tell something special has happened. I'm not sure why she's hesitant to broach the subject and hope it hadn't been because of my own situation.

Hazel sighs, her hands still busily tidying things that don't need tidying.

'We've decided to give it another try.' Her voice is full of angst, but the words delight me.

'I'm thrilled for you,' I can't help but enthuse. 'Hazel, you two were meant to be together and I'm totally convinced of that. No relationship runs without hiccoughs and sometimes I think we are all guilty of becoming a touch complacent. I think you hit the seven-year itch a year late.' I smile, trying to lighten the moment. 'If you can pick things back up after a little breathing space, then I think you'll both be stronger for it.'

'You really believe that? I never stopped loving Jenny.'

I nod and Hazel's face relaxes.

'We talked honestly about our problems and she admitted her body clock is ticking. We're going to look into the options for having a baby.' Hazel glances at me, nervously awaiting my reaction.

'That's great and wonderful you both want the same thing.'

'Thanks, it's a relief that you understand. That means a lot to us both. We have an appointment with an organisation that can set it all up. The deciding factor will be the cost. It isn't cheap and sometimes you have to go through the procedure more than once.'

I can see from her expression that she's serious about this and I'm happy for her.

Life grows a little bit brighter as each day passes. Liam is still being overly-attentive and every time I turn around he seems to be there, like a shadow. He comes into the shop every day to buy a box of cupcakes. Having established that he's a man who prefers savoury over sweet, I have no idea what he does with them. I've been out for a drink with him twice, although I'm now declining his invitations. I told him I'm not looking for a new boyfriend. I'm going to focus on finding my dream property, somewhere I can begin putting down new roots. I'm looking at the outskirts of town, which isn't easy as properties tend to be more expensive because there's less choice. But I'm hoping to be able to buy a two-bed, semi-detached cottage, with a small garden. I've seen a few that were well within my price range, although they all needed more work doing to them than I could manage. Of course, Liam has offered his services and I had to forcefully reject that suggestion.

However, he's been an absolute star finding me properties

to consider and has accompanied me on viewings. Without his expert eye I wouldn't have a clue. One property I thought was near-perfect turned out to have a major subsidence problem. I've told him that I'll pay him for his time, and advice, but he won't hear of it. I think he's hoping he'll continue to grow on me and I'll get used to having him around. That's fine if you're in the market for a dog, but it's hardly the basis for an adult relationship.

Am I happy? Well, yes, I suppose I am happyish. Sweet Occasions is now making a significant profit and if it continues, under Steve's guidance, then I'll be able to pay off my mortgage within the next ten years. He's turned it into a commercial operation and while he isn't at all interested in the product, he knows how to grow a business.

The downside of being on your own, for me, is that you have no safety net. I've decided that I'm not going to panic about that, or risk sacrificing my newly-found freedom. All those hang-ups are now behind me. Not having to worry about Sweet Occasions and the cash flow situation has helped enormously.

Hazel and Jenny took me off to a spa for a pamper weekend as a pre-birthday treat and it was the most fun I've had in years. I came back with skin glowing and a new hairstyle. I felt like I'd just drawn a line, and was stepping over it into a brave new world.

Saturday is the day and it's a landmark birthday. I hit the big three-o, which I'm desperately trying to play down, because – more importantly – I have three properties to view. Hazel is going to cover the afternoon shift and Liam is collecting me at one o'clock. Fingers crossed, one of them will turn out to be my future home and the plan is that he'll take me out on Saturday night to celebrate.

Adam

Making It Happen

Walking in through the front door of Grandma Grace's house, there's an unmistakable chill in the air. Outside it's a gloriously sunny day and I can only hope that Lily doesn't feel uncomfortable and start talking about ghosts again. Obviously the painters have had the windows open for the last few weeks and it has been empty now for over six months. At least the work is finished.

Lily seems reasonably content to wander through the rooms, overcoming any concerns I had about whether it was the right thing to do, or not. I don't know whether it's a good, or a bad thing, that it no longer feels like Grandma's house.

'She's not here any more,' Lily whispers as she turns to face me. 'That must mean she's happy.'

'I'm glad to hear it.' My response is automatic and then I find myself wondering what exactly Lily meant. 'Any more?' I question as an afterthought.

'Yes, Dad. She's not here, and Pop isn't here, either.' She looks at me with wide-eyed innocence, as if I should understand what she's trying to tell me.

'As in ... they were here before, when they were alive?'

'Well, that's obvious! No, I mean when we came for our first visit they were both here. I know you said Grandma wasn't a ghost, but she talked to me. I told you, Dad, she wanted us to go and see Katie. I saw Pop, too.'

I'm rooted to the spot and a small shiver travels up my arms and succeeds in making the hairs on the back of my neck bristle. Maybe we should have stayed in a hotel and this isn't such a good idea after all.

'Here, you saw them here?'

Lily doesn't appear fazed, only irritated that I'm questioning her. She says nothing.

'Where did you see them?' Now I'm worried that Lily isn't taking this quite as well as I'd first thought. A child's imagination is a wonderful thing, but there are times when it can be over-active and I don't want Lily to be fearful of any situation.

'In the sitting room, Dad. Pop was in his chair and Grandma was sitting on the sofa next to the fire. Pop winked at me and Grandma smiled.'

Lily seems more interested in investigating the freshly decorated bedrooms. I follow her around, beginning to feel spooked by the whole thing.

'Were you afraid?'

She stops in her tracks, and spins around. It's nonsense, of course, the whole house had been cleared by then.

'What? Of Pop and Grandma?' Her voice is scandalised.

'No, what was I thinking, of course you weren't. I'm sure they will love it once the furniture arrives and we get something arranged for the windows. We have two weeks to sort it out and I hope that Marie's daughter, and her husband, like it. Grandma would be delighted, as I hear they now have a baby daughter.'

'I thought they lived in Australia?' Lily frowns. I'm surprised she remembers them at all, it's been three years.

'Ashleigh's husband was working there, but now they're back for good. They're going to have Grandma's house for a whole year. Won't that be nice for Marie, having her granddaughter living next door?'

'Grandma would like that, Dad.' Her smile tells me whatever she imagined, or thinks she saw, we're doing the right thing.

'Dad, you mustn't forget the other thing that we need to do.' Lily's voice acquires a serious tone, as if this is going to be a lecture. I wonder what on earth I've forgotten that will need to be added to my long list of things still to be done. 'We have to go and see Katie.'

She stands there, looking directly at me as if needing to labour the point.

'I hadn't forgotten. It's on the list for tomorrow.' I give her a small smile, holding back on a laugh, as I get the distinct feeling she's concerned I will forget.

There's so much to do and emptying the car is going to take a while. I have two double beds to assemble and judging by the stack of boxes in the garage, I'm going to have my work cut out.

It might be my imagination playing up this time, but as the day goes on and the house begins to fill with the trappings of a home, it seems to warm up. I can hear Lily upstairs singing as she unpacks the towels and bedding, and it's a relief. The first half of the plan seems to be working well and I hope that's a good omen for tomorrow.

Katie's Birthday

Adam

Nothing To Lose

The birds' incessant chorus wakes me at dawn and it's almost impossible to get back to sleep. I can hear Lily in the next room snoring away softly as I creep down to make a cup of coffee.

The house feels renewed and even though I keep getting momentary flashbacks from earlier times, I'm feeling a much more positive vibe. What's worrying me now is what on earth am I going to say to Katie? Even if I can succeed in getting her here to give me her opinion, there's going to be that awkward point of no return.

As I wait for the kettle to boil I go through a few scenarios in my head.

'Katie, you need to know that since the first time I saw ...' No, too predictable.

'Katie, do you believe in love at first sight?' She'll probably run a mile.

'Katie, you can tell me to go away, but I need you to know ...' Now I sound like a total creep.

The kettle clicks off, interrupting my flow, and when I begin pouring it into the cup I realise it hasn't finished boiling. In fact, it's only lukewarm. I flick the switch again and return to my train of thought. It flicks off again. This time I pull the plug out of the socket and re-insert it, then flick the switch for the third time. And that's when, out of nowhere, the perfect opener pops into my head.

'Katie, sometimes people's paths cross for a reason and I'm here to let you know how I feel.' Simple, honest and from the heart – perfect!

The kettle begins to steam and it switches off with no problem at all. As the sentence whirls around inside my head, it feels rather foreign; perfect, but foreign. I can't recall the thought process at all, it was suddenly there. Leaning against the kitchen cabinet, I close my eyes and try to tune in to whatever's around me. Can I feel anything? Was that thought really mine, or was it given to me?

I guess I'll never know for sure, but whatever, it works and I can imagine myself saying it. What I can't imagine is what Katie's reaction is going to be.

It's almost twelve-thirty by the time the two sofas and the dining room furniture have all been delivered. Lily and I quickly get ready to head off to Sweet Occasions. It's only a couple of miles away and Lily keeps up a constant chatter, for which I'm grateful. I'm a nervous wreck and it shows. It's almost one o'clock by the time we find a parking space and as we're about to enter the shop we bump into Katie, who is on her way out. She's closely followed by a man I haven't seen before. At first I assume he's a customer, but when Katie recognises us and stops to speak, he loiters nearby. She waves a handful of estate agent's brochures in the air.

'Hey, guys, I didn't know you were paying a visit. I'm off to view some properties. What a shame! How long are you here?' She seems genuinely sorry. The man points to his watch. 'Look, we're running late. Promise you will call in again before you go back, won't you?'

She makes eye contact with me for one brief moment and I can see she's in a quandary. She hesitates, but the man prompts her again. This time saying, 'We're going to be late, Katie.'

'Promise,' she calls, following after him. He walks up to

a very smart Porsche, which is parked directly in front of the shop. 'Take care, guys, see you soon, I hope.'

Lily and I are left staring at the empty parking space; so much for my carefully laid plans.

'Well, that's a shame,' Lily says, a little indignantly. 'Another two minutes and we could have parked there, Dad.'

If I wasn't so deflated, I'd have laughed at her comment.

'What shall we do now, poppet?' I'm still a little shell-shocked. Probably due to the fact that my stomach did one almighty lurch when I first caught sight of Katie. Then it hit the floor when I noticed her companion.

'You're not giving up, are you, Dad? Katie said to come back and that's what we're going to do.'

'Yes, boss.'

We walk off down the High Street like two lost souls, feigning interest in the various shop displays. Even Lily is bored and I'm trying not to lose the plot. Who *was* that guy and what was he doing with Katie? Estate agents don't drive Porsches and although I've never met Steve, I'm certain that wasn't him. The colour starts to drain from my face and I let out an involuntary groan. Fortunately, Lily doesn't catch it. Oh, no, don't say the timing is off yet again. Last time I saw Katie she mentioned something about it being time to move on. If she and Steve did break up and that's Katie's new boyfriend, then I'm sunk and I've probably missed the only opportunity I'm likely to get to tell her how I feel. What I need now is a miracle, really. This guy is a good few years younger than me, looks like he could party with David Beckham and drives the sort of car that impresses most women. I'm going to have one hell of a fight on my hands. But for some very obscure reason, that only serves to spur me on.

* * *

The afternoon seems to drag on forever and even Lily can't quell my nervous energy. We spend most of the time in the garden and in between I try to sort a few things inside the house, but my mind is elsewhere.

When we call in to see Katie on Monday should I ask her straight out whether she is seeing someone new? At least it would put me out of my misery. But what sort of a romantic opener is that? If it goes to plan, I don't want her forever remembering our magic moment, the sentence that changed our future as, 'So, who's the young guy with the Porsche?'

I suggest we pop out for ice cream at six o'clock, much to Lily's amusement. It's a lame excuse to be able to drive past Sweet Occasions, on the off-chance Katie might still be tidying up. No such luck. The shop is in darkness and it's another thirty-nine hours until it's open again. Fancying someone like mad is pure, and utter, agony. Why do they call it love, when torture is a more honest description?

Katie
Is It Bad Timing, Or Is It Fate?

When I awoke this morning, it felt like just another day. Even opening the pile of birthday cards that had been arriving in the post over the last couple of days, my heart wasn't in it. I should, at least, be excited about the viewings and the prospect that today might be the start of moving forward. Instead I just felt alone and lonely, for all of the company that Liam has been. Hazel said I was being miserable refusing to celebrate my thirtieth birthday with a proper bash. I pacified her by saying I would have a joint moving-in and birthday party, thinking that at least then I'd have something worthy of a celebration. Being thirty and starting over is hardly something you want to shout about.

When Liam wrenched me away from Adam, and Lily, my head was still spinning. On Adam's last visit he said they were coming down again soon, but I thought maybe he'd phone beforehand. I guess I was living in the hope that their visit meant something and that the next time he'd want to make sure I was around. But a visit today, of all days – when just the sight of them was a tonic in itself – felt meaningful. I would have cancelled the appointments if I'd known. And why would you have done that, Katie? You can't live on dreams. You've travelled that road and you know it leads to a dead end. But my heart still began to race the moment I found myself face-to-face with him. Goodness knows what my expression was saying. Liam was clearly put out when I didn't say 'hello', and move on. I should have introduced him. Damn it!

My mind was distracted from that point onwards and

Liam had to keep dragging me back down to earth. All three properties were around the same price, but two needed too much work doing to them. The other one had potential and most of the work was simply redecoration. It did need a new kitchen, unless you are into seventies nostalgia. It wasn't classic retro, more shabby retro. But it was a darling little cottage with a manageable garden. Liam couldn't seem to find anything wrong with it.

'Pretty near the mark,' he commented, the moment we were out of range of the estate agent's ears.

On any other day I know I would have been excited, but today all I could think of was Adam, and Lily. What if they go back home tomorrow and this afternoon was the last chance I would have of ever seeing them again? Could I use that as an excuse to give Adam a call if they don't turn up on Monday?

On the drive back to the shop my mind plays out several scenarios. The first is that they don't come back and in a fit of desperation I jump in the car. The next thing I know, I'm knocking on Adam's door. The scene is so vivid I make a strangulated sound, as I imagine Adam standing in front of me. Liam asks if I'm all right.

In the next scenario I'm unlocking the shop on Monday morning. Adam and Lily are there, patiently waiting. As I open the door Adam steps inside, 'Katie, I love you,' he murmurs throatily, taking me in his arms. He kisses me passionately, while Lily stands behind him, smiling.

That scenario sends me into a fit of giggles.

'What's up, birthday girl?' Liam asks, trying hard not to look at me, but to keep his eyes on the road. 'I hope this is a joke you're going to share?'

'Nothing, I'm just ... erm ... thinking through a few scenarios, you know ...'

'Well,' he interjects, 'the first one has dry rot and the last one, with the shared drive, has boundary issues. Okay, the people who live there happen to be friendly with their neighbours. If, for whatever reason, you didn't get on with them, they could make your life hell.'

Liam then explains in detail why shared drives with no proper parking bays are problematic. I switch off and imagine a third scenario. Adam and Lily arrive at the shop to buy some cupcakes. We sit and have a coffee, then they wave goodbye with a, 'have a nice life'.

My stomach feels like a lead weight is lying at the bottom of it. This is crunch time and if they do turn up, it could be the last time I ever see them. It feels all wrong. This can't be the last time. I know I said I was enjoying my freedom, and I was beginning to imagine my cosy little cottage retreat, but I guess I've been fooling myself. When I went through that *I'm looking for a hero* moment, a couple of weeks ago, that was the real me coming out. Except, for *hero*, substitute the name Adam. I want Adam. Oh, damn, I want Adam. I *want* Adam!

Eureka! I need to get back to the shop as quickly as possible and ask Hazel's advice. This can't wait until Monday morning. I would regret it forever if Adam, and Lily, left without saying goodbye. If Grace was right and I'm the one who could make Adam happy, really happy, then maybe sometimes Fate needs a little helping hand. As we pull up outside the shop I feel rather rude, knowing I've missed most of the one-sided conversation during the ride.

'Liam, thank you so much, you've been wonderful. I feel dreadful saying this, but there's no point in pretending. Dinner together this evening isn't a good idea. I've just realised I've been a fool and it's time I followed my heart.'

He leans across, probably hoping for a hug, but I'm out

of the car before he even realises I've opened the door. I sprint into the shop, forcing myself to slow my pace as I cross the threshold in the interests of customer safety.

'Hazel, can you pop into the office, please?' I pant, nodding my head in the direction of the office in case she didn't catch my garbled words. She excuses herself and leaves Marcie serving.

'What on earth's happened?' She follows me inside, shutting the door firmly behind her.

'Adam, did you see him earlier? He hasn't been back in, has he?'

'No, I haven't seen him. Was he here?' She's puzzled by my erratic behaviour and I can't blame her. I gather up the few items lying loose on my desk and scoop them into my handbag.

'Look, I have to go. Adam arrived as I was walking out with Liam. I think he came to say goodbye. I'm going to pop home and calm myself down. Once I think Lily is likely to be in bed, I'm going round to see him. Fingers crossed he's staying at Grace's house and not in a hotel. Hazel, if you were me, what would you say? My mind is a total blank and I'm shaking life a leaf just thinking about it.'

'Gosh, Katie, I don't know … if he sees you like this you'll scare him off. I've never seen you in this sort of state before.'

'Words, Hazel, I need some words.'

She looks totally wordless.

'Okay. Let me think. How about casual – ask him how long he's staying and if he'd like to go out for a drink? It is your birthday – that's a great excuse.'

'Good, but he'd need a baby-sitter for Lily. Think of something else.'

'How about, "I love you and I want to have your babies". I think it's a line from a film. I doubt its one he will have watched.'

I look at her incredulously, as if she's lost her mind.

'Helpful. Not.'

'Look, I don't know what you should say. Don't over-think this, he isn't going to run away the moment he sees you, is he? He'll probably invite you in for coffee. It will be relaxed, so you'll have time to figure it out.'

'You think so?'

'I think so.'

'Okay, I'm gone. Thank you, sorry, here are the keys – I should have asked …'

'Go, you're doing my head in. Ring me … afterwards.'

I run to the car and all the way home I talk to myself, practicing opening lines. Nothing sounds remotely right. This could be the most important moment of my life and yet I have no idea at all what I'm going to say. Grace, if you're listening now, I really, really, need your help! There's only one thing I want for my birthday, well two, actually – Adam and Lily.

Dad, Pull Yourself Together

Dad's been on edge all afternoon and it's driving me mad. He even insisted on taking me out to buy ice cream so he could drive past Sweet Occasions. It was closed and no one was in the shop. Katie looked shocked when she saw us this afternoon and very sad when she couldn't stop to talk.

This evening Dad and I are playing board games. He isn't concentrating and it's getting very boring. I like to win, but I have to keep reminding him it's his turn because he's deep in thought.

'I think I'll go to bed, Dad. Can I read for a while?' Usually he says no, but tonight he nods and I walk over to give him a hug. Not because he said yes, but because he's feeling down and I hate to see him so sad.

'I'll be up in a bit to tuck you in. Guess I'm a little pre-occupied at the moment. I promise I'll be back to normal tomorrow.'

He smiles and I love the little crinkles at the side of his eyes when he gives me his special Dad smile.

As I get ready for bed, Dad puts on one of his favourite bands and I know that listening to music is how he relaxes. Grandma, you need to give Dad a bit of help at the moment, he's not good at this sort of stuff.

I look around to see if she's here, but she's not. I'm sure she can hear me though and I know she'll sort it all out.

When the doorbell chimes I wonder who it can be. Standing on tiptoe to peer out of the window, all I can see is the roof of the porch. I creep along the landing in time to see Dad opening the door and I crouch down, out of sight.

'Hi. You're the last person I was expecting. Not that I was expecting anyone at all, of course, being that we don't know anyone …' Dad suddenly loses the plot and starts mumbling a load of rubbish. As I peer down, he steps back and in walks Katie! I want to yell and jump up and down. Instead, I hug my knees and stay super quiet.

Dad closes the door and they stand there, like statues. They are facing each other, but neither one says anything. I'm holding my breath and about to explode, when they both begin talking at the same time.

'Adam, sometimes people's paths cross …'

'Katie, sometimes people's paths cross …'

And then the most magical thing happens. They stop speaking and start k-i-s-s-i-n-g! Thank you, Grandma, I think I can go to bed, now.

Sometimes People's Paths Cross for a Reason

If people took the time to think back over past events they would clearly see that even though the path meanders, each little step counts for something. Life is a learning experience. If it wasn't for the ups and downs it would be distinctly boring. The good times are much sweeter because of the bad things every single one of us has to battle through.

It's also true that anything, and everything, is possible when it comes to affairs of the heart. But sometimes patience is a virtue and a necessary part of life. We have to wait for all of the little steps to be played out, for good reason.

To see my darling Adam, and wonderful Katie, hugging and kissing like the lovers they are destined to be, was truly wondrous. As the weeks fly by Katie says goodbye to Sweet Occasions for good and moves north to be with Adam, and Lily. It's the start of a new and happy chapter in their lives.

Adam surprised and delighted me, making a tough decision that didn't sit well with his innate sense of right and wrong. He was prepared to stand up and fight for Katie, believing in the love he knew he could offer her. Being Mr Nice Guy is very gentlemanly, of course. If Adam's strong sense of right and wrong had caused him to hesitate, the outcome could have been very different.

Thankfully, there are times in your life when you only

need to take one small step in the right direction for things to begin falling into place. If you miss that all-important step, who knows for sure whether you will be given another chance? Perhaps your Fate will simply be rewritten. Miraculously, Adam found the strength he needed at precisely the right moment in time and I'm so proud of him.

Katie has come to realise that sometimes the dream has to change. Letting go of what she thought she wanted wasn't easy. On this occasion it merely signalled the beginning of an even bigger, and more fulfilling, dream. I think the fact that Katie chose Adam over Sweet Occasions clearly shows the depth of her feelings. Of course, I sensed that from the very start when Adam first mentioned her name. The light in his eyes said more than any words could have conveyed. That instant sense of attraction when he least expected it was something he couldn't explain, but also couldn't ignore. It wouldn't let him go, for a very special reason. Lily can, at last, see that when soulmates find each other, everything suddenly slots very neatly into place. Her tenth birthday party saw them all together, celebrating it as a family unit and it was a heart-warming scene. There really can be a magical 'happily-ever-after' ending to the tale, where love is concerned. One day Lily, too, will find her own Prince Charming and the fairy tale of life will continue.

I learnt something, too: that when your time is coming to an end, you have no choice but to let go and embrace a new beginning. What I can see now, with hindsight, is that those you leave behind are often stronger than you could ever have imagined. All it required was a little nudge in the right direction and I'm glad I was here to do that. Where affairs of the heart are concerned, when love rears its head, it brings with it an inner strength. There's a burning desire to grab whatever happiness you can.

My job is done and I can now relax. Jack smiles at me and gives a nod of approval. 'You were there for him when it counted, my dear. And I bet you have no intention of missing their wedding day.'

Katie

Until Death Do Us Part

As I stare at my reflection in the mirror the face looking back at me is almost unrecognisable, as if this is a stranger I'm seeing for the first time. I'm not talking about the beautiful, beaded dress that fits like a glove and makes me feel like something out of a bridal magazine. Yes, it's the fairy tale come true, but it's the change in me that is almost unbelievable.

Life had become heavy, onerous and each day I battled to retain hold of what felt like a fast-disappearing dream. I never once stopped to question whether I was doing the right thing. When I finally let go and realised that my heart was trying to tell me something, it was as if someone had lifted a heavy load from my shoulders. Things could be different and life is too short to waste even one precious moment of it. When you truly love someone and they return that love in equal measure, you can face the future without fear. Feeling that for the very first time was empowering and I know Adam felt it too, the moment he slipped that engagement ring on my finger. Now I'm ready to say my vows and Adam will be mine until death do us part.

'I haven't seen Lily for a while, I think she wandered outside with Emily. I'm just going to check on them.' I stand on tiptoe to give Adam a quick kiss on the mouth, but he pulls me in closer and I almost lose my balance as the seconds race by. Pulling away from him, he laughs.

'Don't be long, Mrs Harper. I'm missing you already.'

Our eyes meet, and for one second time stands still and

everything else fades into the background. There is only 'us' and the look in his eyes is a joy to behold.

'I just want to make sure she's happy and not feeling left out, or missing her mother.'

'I know and that's one of the many reasons why I love you so much.' He reaches out and touches my cheek, softly brushing it with his fingers. I walk away feeling his eyes on me and his love all around me.

As I head towards the French doors leading out into the hotel grounds, I pass a sea of smiling faces. Our wedding party isn't huge, but every single person here has a meaningful place in our lives. The fact that Kelly declined her invitation was actually rather a relief in one way, but I was disappointed on Lily's behalf. Going forward Kelly will be a part of our new life and it's going to be important that we can all get on.

I can hear Lily's voice even before she appears in my line of vision, and as soon as we have eye contact she runs towards me.

'Have you seen the maze?' she asks, slightly out of breath from all the running around.

'No. Would you like to show me?'

'This way, Katie, it's awesome!'

As I gently lift the fishtail tulle so I can follow Lily along the gravel path, it brings joy to my heart to see her skipping along without a care in the world. More than anything I want her to feel that today she's simply gaining another person who will love and care for her, and not to feel that I've come between her mum and dad. Surely it's only natural that any child coming from a split family would secretly long for their parents to reunite at some point in the future? When one of them marries someone else, no matter how accepting everyone involved is at the time, it must be tough to see that dream snatched away.

She stops, turns and smiles at me.

'Isn't it magical?' Her voice is full of enchantment as she spins around and for the first time I take in our surroundings. The tall hedging is quite dense and having followed her blindly, my head whirling with thoughts, I have to agree. The air is still and all I can hear is the sound of birdsong. Ahead of us, the narrow gravel path extends about another thirty or forty feet, before taking a sharp turn to the right. I glance up at the blue sky above and when I look down again Lily has disappeared, but I can hear her tinkling laughter. This time I grab the flared tulle skirt around my ankles, gathering it up so that I can run without tripping.

'I'm coming,' I shout, and I run as fast as I can to catch up with her.

The twists and turns seem to go on forever, until quite suddenly I'm there in the middle of the maze and find Lily sitting on a bench casually swinging her legs.

Now I'm the one who is out of breath and I drop the tulle, run my hands down over the form-fitting skirt and settle myself down next to her.

'Are you having fun?' I turn to face her, scanning that perfect heart-shaped face for any sign of hesitation.

'I love it here and you look beautiful, Katie. I've never seen Dad so happy.'

As she speaks she fusses with the hem of her dress, which is a knee-length, A-line style in lavender taffeta, with a beaded sash. She chose it herself and she looks like a little princess in it. As the seconds pass it's nice to just sit quietly together, as if we're sharing a secret moment, made even more special by the tranquillity of the setting.

'It's been a good day, hasn't it?' Lily's voice breaks the silence and for some reason her words bring a tear to my eye. I swallow hard, but before I can reply she continues.

'I didn't know spirits could go *anywhere*. I thought maybe they were stuck, you know, somewhere they'd been. Like Grandma would only ever be in her house.'

I try to keep a composed look on my face as I search for something to say. I knew that even if she accepted her mother not being here, that she would miss Grace's presence.

'Our loved ones are always with us in here, Lily.' I place my hand over my heart and give her an encouraging smile.

'Oh, I know that because Dad says the same thing. I just didn't think Grandma Grace would be here, or my real grandma.'

'Your real grandma?' What does she mean?

'You know, the one I never met. Dad's mum.'

Despite the warmth of this wonderful summer's day a chill runs up and down my arms, as if I've been blasted by a sudden waft of cold air.

'Have you seen her before?' Oh, I wish I hadn't said the first thing that came into my head. I'm not even sure I should be encouraging this line of conversation. Maybe it would be better if we just headed back to the wedding party. I'll mention it to Adam later, just in case he feels it's something he should talk through with Lily.

However, Lily seems totally unconcerned and definitely isn't upset in any way. She looks at me with a lovely smile and pure happiness reflected on her face.

'It's all because of you, Katie. They're all here today because they are so happy.'

All? 'Well, I'm glad of that, Lily. I wouldn't want you to feel sad about anything today.' Actually, I think it's rather wonderful that Lily isn't focusing on the fact that some of the people she loves can't be here today. The imagination of a child can be so wonderfully comforting. Love is a strong emotion that never dies and it never goes away. How can anyone believe that life is only about the physical? Haven't we all felt it at some time, or other? That moment when you simply know you aren't alone, even though it appears you are.

'And Grandma Grace is wearing a hat. It's rather large and very pink. Pop is wearing his best bow tie, but only because Grandma made him.'

I laugh and the sound of my voice echoes around the little space contained within the boundary of the tall, neatly clipped hedges. That's some imagination.

'My other grandma told me that I'm a lucky girl to have two mums who love me so much. I've never spoken to her before, so it really has been a perfect day.'

I close my eyes for one moment, hoping to sense what Lily can see. One moment everything is as it was and then, without warning, it's almost like being caught up in a whirlwind. I may not be able to see with her eyes, but I can feel it. My head is full of shooting stars of light and my body reacts to an embrace as if I've been wrapped in a blanket of love. A few seconds pass before I can find my voice again.

'I'm truly honoured you decided to share your wonderful experience with me. It makes this day even more special. You know that I'll always be here for you and we can talk about anything. That's what friends are for.' Lily nods and reaches across to put her little hand in mine. I hope that one day, soon, she'll think of me as so much more than just a friend.

Her beaming smile confirms what can't be put into

words and I send out a silent 'thank you' to Grace, Jack and Elizabeth. The fact that they are here today to support not only Lily, but Adam and me, means so much.

'I'll look after them both,' I make a silent promise with all of the solemnity with which I repeated my wedding vows to Adam, earlier this afternoon. The air is still and there isn't a sound to break the spell of this magical moment with my step-daughter.

For the first time I can see that the plan was in place from the very first moment Adam and I gazed into each other's eyes; the only one who knew that, though, was Grace – until today.

Thank you

I just love a happy ending and, dear reader, I hope you do too! In my heart I truly believe that we all grow up in the hope and expectation that we will find 'the one'. Our soulmate. The person who makes us complete and who comes to instinctively know and understand what lies within our heart, and in those dark recesses of our mind. The things we choose not to show the world at large, but can only share with that special person.

And that's why I write; inspired by real relationships and the way in which people survive life's twists and turns to reach their goal. Love is a truly wonderful thing and I believe that it makes the world a better place for us all.

As a writer I consider it a blessing to spend my days wrapped up in storylines with characters who feel very real to me. When I finished writing A Little Sugar, A Lot of Love I felt sad to say goodbye to Katie, Adam and Lily. I cried when I wrote the final scene with Grace. And that's the joy of what I do. But then comes that nerve-wracking moment when the book is out there and the reviews start coming in. I find myself holding my breath, nervously awaiting the reaction of the wonderful readers who choose my book to escape with for a while.

When a reader takes the time to post a review, having enjoyed the journey the story has taken them on, it fills my heart with a joy that is very unique. I feel humbled, ecstatic and fulfilled. Writing is my guilty pleasure and I'm addicted. So when someone is kind enough to help spread the word in any way, or choose another of my books to curl up with, it means so much to me. It's what keeps me writing and reader power is very, very real.

Reviews on Amazon, Goodreads and retailer websites, and word of mouth recommendations, have a snowball effect, so never feel you are just one small voice because that isn't the case. Yours is a voice I'd love to hear and I can always be contacted via my website. I want to write the books that YOU want to read!

I sincerely hope that you enjoyed your time with Katie, Adam, Lily and Grace, as much as I enjoyed writing their story. Life is always full of surprises and that's what keeps hope alive!

Wishing you all peace, love and happiness,

Linn B Halton

x

About the Author

Bristol-born Linn B. Halton lives in the small
village of Lydbrook, which nestles on the
edge of the Forest of Dean, in the UK.

She's a hopeless romantic, self-confessed chocaholic, and
lover of coffee. For Linn, life is about family, friends, and
writing. Oh, and the occasional glass of White Grenache …

Linn's novels have been short-listed in the UK's Festival of
Romance and the eFestival of Words Book Awards. Linn
won the 2013 UK Festival of Romance: Innovation in
Romantic Fiction award. Linn has published seven novels;
A Little Sugar, A Lot of Love is her debut with Choc Lit.

For more information follow Linn on:
Twitter: twitter.com/LinnBHalton
Facebook: www.facebook.com/linnbhaltonauthor
Blog/Website: www.linnbhalton.co.uk

More from Choc Lit

If you enjoyed Linn's story, you'll enjoy the
rest of our selection. Here's a sample:

The Wedding Proposal
Sue Moorcroft

**Can a runaway bride
stop running?**

Elle Jamieson is an unusually
private person, in relationships
as well as at work – and for
good reason. But when she's
made redundant, with no ties
to hold her, Elle heads off to a
new life in sunny Malta.

Lucas Rose hates secrets – he
prides himself on his ability to lay his cards on the table and
he expects nothing less from others. He's furious when his
summer working as a divemaster is interrupted by the arrival
of Elle, his ex, all thanks to his Uncle Simon's misguided
attempts at matchmaking.

Forced to live in close proximity, it's hard to ignore what
they had shared before Lucas's wedding proposal ended
everything they had. But then an unexpected phone call from
England allows Lucas a rare glimpse of the true Elle. Can he
deal with Elle's hidden past when it finally comes to light?

Visit www.choc-lit.com for more
details, or simply scan barcode using
your mobile phone QR reader.

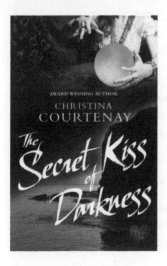

The Secret Kiss of Darkness

Christina Courtenay

Book 2 in the Shadows from the Past Series

Must forbidden love end in heartbreak?

Kayla Sinclair knows she's in big trouble when she almost bankrupts herself to buy a life-size portrait of a mysterious eighteenth century man at an auction.

Jago Kerswell, inn-keeper and smuggler, knows there is danger in those stolen moments with Lady Eliza Marcombe, but he'll take any risk to be with her.

Over two centuries separate Kayla and Jago, but, when Kayla's jealous fiancé presents her with an ultimatum, and Jago and Eliza's affair is tragically discovered, their lives become inextricably linked thanks to a gypsy's spell.

Kayla finds herself on a quest that could heal the past, but what she cannot foresee is the danger in her own future.

Will Kayla find heartache or happiness?

Forbidden love, smugglers and romance!

Introducing Choc Lit

We're an independent publisher creating
a delicious selection of fiction.
Where heroes are like chocolate – irresistible!
Quality stories with a romance at the heart.

See our selection here:
www.choc-lit.com

We'd love to hear how you enjoyed *A Little Sugar, A Lot
of Love*. Please leave a review where you purchased the
novel or visit: **www.choc-lit.com** and give your feedback.

Choc Lit novels are selected by genuine readers like yourself.
We only publish stories our Choc Lit Tasting Panel want to
see in print. Our reviews and awards speak for themselves.

Could you be a Star Selector and join our Tasting Panel?
Would you like to play a role in choosing which novels we
decide to publish? Do you enjoy reading romance novels?
Then you could be perfect for our Choc Lit Tasting Panel.

Visit here for more details …
www.choc-lit.com/join-the-choc-lit-tasting-panel

Keep in touch:
Sign up for our monthly newsletter Choc Lit Spread for
all the latest news and offers: www.spread.choc-lit.com.
Follow us on Twitter: @ChocLituk and Facebook: Choc Lit.

Or simply scan barcode using your mobile phone QR reader:

Choc Lit   *Twitter*   *Facebook*
Spread